ROMANCING THE BOSS

# ONCE
# UPON
## A One-Night Stand

Z.L. ARKADIE WRITING AS
## ZOEY LOCKE

ISBN: 978-1-952101-92-2

# CONTENTS

# ONE
# XENA ST. JAMES

I can't believe what just happened.

That's why I'm pacing in front of the stacked washer/dryer unit in my cousin Lilly's apartment. I'm like a pinball bouncing between two pegs, mortified by what came out of my mouth. I shouldn't have said it, even if it was true. Not every thought or emotion a girl experiences needs to be expressed verbally.

I exhale heavily, expelling the air from deep within my throat. My head feels like it wants to burst as I picture myself blurting out to our unexpected dinner guest that his mere presence has made me wet down there. Those were the words that came out of my typically thoughtful and wise mouth. Sure, I can be a little cynical sometimes. But crass? Never.

"Ugh..." I groan, the weight of my embarrassment still lingering.

I know why I feel less inhibited this evening. Today was a tough day at work, and to unwind, I brought two bottles of red wine and rum to my cousin Lilly's apartment in Chelsea. I mixed the drinks in a glass pitcher and indulged in a few too many. Then, Mr. Gorgeous Billionaire crashed our dinner, which was originally meant to be Lilly and me venting about our exes, our jobs, and, before the night was over, my mom. Our unexpected guest had no clue that my tongue was looser than usual. He must think I'm a promiscuous fool.

All of a sudden, a realization hits me, and I come to a halt. I would, though. I would sleep with him in a New York minute. Our unexpected guest's name is Lynx Grove—yes, the Lynx Grove from that prominent family of tech billionaires. When he crossed the threshold, carrying Lilly's grocery bag, I couldn't help but notice how incredibly attractive he was in person. No man's bone structure should be so perfect. And his lips... They're like succulent rose petals. I still have the urge to kiss them.

I take a deep breath, attempting to regain control over my long-burning arousal towards the man in Lilly's kitchen, who is now peeling and deveining shrimp—an unexpectedly mediocre task for someone of his stature. The worst part of my impulsive remark is that I wasn't lying about my panties. While we were preparing dinner, Lynx and I had been maneuvering around each other, reaching for ingredients and rinsing utensils. Despite Lilly's spacious kitchen, it still feels too confined to accommodate a man of Lynx's height and athletic build. He's like a statue sculpted by Michelangelo himself. His arm even brushed against mine—twice! It was firm, akin to granite. And those navy blue track pants he's wearing, made of a generous satiny material, accentuate his lean muscular legs and enticing bubble butt. Oh, and the way his tan T-shirt clings to the hard contours of his chest is undeniably sexy. His tapered waist is the proverbial icing on the cake. Or perhaps the icing is his tantalizing cologne, a blend of citrus, sandalwood, and vanilla, that makes me yearn to devour him. Any red-blooded woman would react to him the way I did—it's simply unavoidable. Lynx Grove is objectively a perfect ten out of ten. Therefore, it was virtually impossible for my panties to emerge unscathed from his presence.

Lilly only discovered Lynx's true identity recently. But before we knew his name, whenever she gushed about him, we referred to him as Mr. Eleventh Floor since Lilly only encountered him whenever he entered the elevator from the eleventh floor. Now, they're friends, and she said something about him recently that might help resolve my lust.

"Lynx Grove is in love with someone," I whisper and then pinch my nostrils as I groan with dread.

But my next thought makes me chuckle. *I bet he's awful in bed.* He's probably never had to work hard to please anyone, let alone the woman he's having sex with.

I look down at my crotch. "So get it together Girlie. He won't be able to satisfy you." My ex-boyfriend's face comes to mind. "Haven't you had enough bad sex?"

Suddenly, a man's voice booms from the front of the apartment, capturing my attention. It's not Lynx. My ears perk up as I strain to identify the speaker. "Oh, really?" The words are tinged with surprise and disbelief.

"Don't get your panties in a bunch Orion. We're just having dinner!" That was Lynx.

I gasp, my fingers instinctively slapping against my lips. Orion!

My insides shout, "SOS!" Lilly's ex-boyfriend and boss, Mr. Poisonous Apple, has made a surprise appearance. I drop my folded T-shirt and race to the living room. Lynx can stay, but Orion has to go.

I call Orion's name and rush to remind Lilly that she's better off without that selfish prick. Life feels like it's happening in slow motion as the front door closes behind her. And now they're both in the hallway. I shake my head as if I've just been slapped.

"So…" Lynx says.

I go rigid, hating how his voice makes my insides flutter. I steady my breathing and tell myself to smile, look unfazed by his gloriousness, and hope Lilly gets back in here sooner rather than later.

Finally, I face him. I can't stop my eyebrows from floating high. *Damn it. He's still too gorgeous for his own good.*

Lynx shows me his palms and wiggles his manly fingers. "What next?"

It takes a moment to figure out what he's referring to. "Oh. Dinner. Right." I check nervously over my shoulder. *What is taking her so long?*

I didn't think his smile could get yummier until now. "Yeah, dinner."

"Um…" I say, stalling. "I don't know. It's Lilly's recipe, so…" I check over my shoulder again. "We should wait until she's back."

We stand in silence, looking at each other. I'm mesmerized by watching his slow sideways smile blossom. *Oh my, that was magnificent.*

"All cleaned up?" he asks.

I frown, confused. "What?"

"You went to…." His raised eyebrows finish the sentence.

I go completely still, unable to speak or close my mouth. This is like a bad dream. However, it's not a dream. It's real life, and by the looks of it, I'm more embarrassed about the admission I made earlier than he is.

Finally, I cough to clear my throat. "Um… That was…" I shake my head. How do I explain that I hadn't changed my panties, and they're still slightly damp, well, more than slightly, but I shouldn't have voiced my predicament?

Lynx doesn't take his eyes off me. One of his

eyebrows quirks up curiously. He's not going to let this drop.

I glance nervously over my other shoulder. *Where the hell is Lilly?*

"Excuse me," I say. I might pass out at any moment as I hightail it to the front door, open and... I gasp.

She's gone, and so is Orion.

---

## 5 Minutes Later

Lynx has washed his hands, and now he's watching me with an unceasing lopsided grin as I make my third call to Lilly. At least she hasn't turned her cell phone off.

I turn my back on Lynx. How could she do this to me? Lilly isn't generally this selfish. To leave me alone with her guest—that's not like her at all. She's changed since her trip to Vegas with Orion. I tried to warn her about going. I really did. But she gobbled that poisonous apple named Orion Lord to the core, and since then, she's been unrecognizable.

"What's that sound?" Lynx asks.

I whip around, ears open, but we keep our

attention pasted on each other. Then Lynx looks away, and I follow his line of sight.

"Oh no," I painfully whisper. I raise a finger. "I'll be right back."

I rush to Lilly's bedroom. Everything's in place —her perfectly made bed and dusted nightstands. Lilly will never leave things messy. My attention shifts to the sitting bench she somehow managed to make fit with room to spare. And then I slap a hand on my chest when I see her cellphone on the console against the wall.

"Damn it," I whisper. She is gone, and I have no means of contacting her.

I peer toward the living room. I can't be left alone with Sexy Mr. Eleventh Floor. He's Lilly's friend, not mine. Plus, something about this guy is affecting me differently than usual. I'm not boy-crazy, and I come across extraordinarily good-looking men every day. Maybe it's his eyes—how he looks at me, even when glancing casually. I feel as if he can see deep inside me. That's crazy, though. That has to be all in my head.

I force my rationality to take the wheel. I'll force myself to see Lynx as if he's another gorgeous man who showed up for a casting call. Unfortunately, Lynx Grove didn't get the part. Firstly, he's in love with another woman. Secondly, he had a brief connection with my cousin Lilly, and she and I never pass each other our sloppy seconds. So now I'll never have to see him again.

I straighten my posture and keep walking until Lynx and I are standing not that far from each other. It's time to say something and come hell or high water, I'm determined to sound like someone who has her shit together.

"Sorry, Lynx, but we're canceling dinner tonight." I must look like Creepy-Stepford-Wife Barbie to him. There's a mirror on the wall to my right. I want to check my expression to correct it, but I can't because I don't want to appear too practiced.

I wonder what he's thinking as he stares into my eyes. I feel like I'm breathing him in as his gaze dips down my body and quickly returns to my face. Something just changed with him. It happened so fast that I would've missed it if I had blinked. Lynx Grove has just checked me out again. Suddenly I'm aware I'm wearing athletic stretch pants and a V-neck Nike T-shirt. I made myself comfortable the moment I arrived at Lilly's. I look like I'm either going to bed or to the gym. I wish I had kept on the little black tank dress I wore to work today. I think if he saw me in that, he might've…

I don't know what he might've done. Maybe I'm wishful thinking.

"I understand." His voice is tighter.

A fiery sensation spreads through my core as an unidentified energy weaves through us, binding us together. The seconds won't stop ticking by as his eyes roam my entire being. My hair, my face, my breasts. They dip lower and lower, and…

Lynx's cell phone rings in his pocket, and his eyes stop undressing me as he takes his device out and squints at the screen. "I have to answer this." He laps me up with another penetrating gaze as his cellphone keeps chiming. "It was nice meeting you, Xena."

I swallow to moisten my dry throat. Is this actually happening? Is Lynx Grove attracted to me? Or am I seeing what I want to see? "Nice meeting you too." I'm happy those words came out clearly.

Lynx's right eye narrows slightly. It's like he wants to say something else but decides against it. My insides feel like they're dissolving into flittering butterflies.

It's like he has to tear his eyes away from me as he puts his phone to his ear. "Hello, Leo?"

My feet are glued to the carpet. My heart flutters like butterfly wings, and I can't take my eyes off him until he tosses me one last lopsided grin before he's gone for good.

---

## 30 Minutes Later

As I clean the kitchen, I sing Sam Smith's, *Too Good At Goodbyes*, loud and passionately. Objectively, I have a great voice. I inherited it from my father, jazz musician and singer Hollis St. James. I have no idea why that song is stuck in my head. I also have no idea why I feel so melancholy. But I'm sure Lynx Grove has inspired my mood. My voice is at its best when I'm feeling deeply emotional. It's a strange phenomenon.

My head floats back, and I focus on the ceiling. "That's it," I whisper—no more rum punch for me. I blame the heightened response I had for Lynx Grove on the booze. The sooner I sleep this night off, the better.

Finally, the counters have been cleaned, dishes washed, the shrimp are in a plastic bag and put in the freezer, and the chopped green onions and garlic are in the fridge. Instead of ordering an Uber for a ride to my depressing apartment, I strip out of my clothes and rifle through Lilly's closet until I find her fluffy white robe. The soft fibers feel rejuvenating against my skin. I plan to sleep in it tonight.

The doorbell rings, and I tense up. A deep sense of relief surges through me. It must be Lilly. She left earlier without shoes on her feet. I'm sure she didn't have her keys either. I run-walk out of the bedroom, ready to give my cousin a piece of my mind. How dare she leave me with her guest, especially after I said what I said about my panties. I needed her to take the edge off and help foster enough rational conversation between him and me to make him forget about my momentary lapse of judgment.

I swing the door open with fire in my eyes and a lashing on the tip of my tongue.

But it's not Lilly standing in front of me. A tall, strapping figure impedes the light flowing in from the hallway. My eyes expand beyond a comfortable limit, and I'm infused with shock. "Hey," I barely say past my tight throat.

"Hey," Lynx Grove replies. His voice sounds just as tight as mine had.

I'm waiting for him to say more as his Adam's apple bobs when he swallows hard.

"Did you forget something?" I ask breathlessly.

Finally, Lynx puts his arm against the door frame and leans forward, coming closer. "I was wondering," he says and then clears his throat. "What you said earlier about your panties." His eyebrows raise suggestively.

My breath catches in my throat as our eye contact deepens. "Sorry about that," I'm finally able to say.

"Don't be."

"Okay," I reply unthinkingly.

"I thought we, you know...." Lynx moistens his sensual lower lip. "We could take care of your little problem properly."

*Holy shit.* What is happening? My body feels jerky as I look over my shoulder, into the dim living room, and then back at Lynx to ensure this is happening. This moment *is* real. I'm not dreaming it. Lynx Grove has returned to have sex with me, which also validates all those intense feelings of sexual attraction I had for him earlier. I wasn't alone. He felt them too.

"My little problem?" I say as we gaze into each other's eyes.

He's so close that I feel his minty breath spread across my face. "Yes."

# TWO
## XENA ST. JAMES

Lynx holds my hand, guiding me as dizzying energy envelopes us. That same sensation is trapped inside me. My feet feel like they're walking on air as I shift my gaze from left to right, letting the walls and the duskiness of the unlit hallway ground me. This is not some bizarre dream where my fantasy comes true. This is real life.

The object of my desire glances at me as if he's reminding himself that I'm still with him. I'm acutely aware of how his piercing eyes are glazed with need. His damp palm squeezes tighter as he draws me into Lilly's bedroom. It's a great choice. Her bed is bigger than the one in the shoebox-sized guest room. I'll change the sheets when we're done,

I determine as we clear the threshold, entering the point of no return.

We arrive at the edge of the bed. Desire bursts out of my pores as Lynx draws me against his solid body. I rest my hands on his powerful shoulders. It's as if his insides are made of granite.

My inhale shivers when after sliding down the sides of my body, his strong hands grip my ass, claiming me, pressing me against his massive erection. Lynx's touch is like fire, and our prolonged staring is intoxicating.

"I'm not looking for a relationship," he whispers as if the declaration escaped him without permission.

My brain scrambles to process what he said and why he might have said it at a moment like this. I've never been with a man who proclaimed that he didn't want a relationship before the sex even began. It feels like a power move, a head game. Lynx Grove is letting me know upfront that I'm just a bang. And if I am just a bang, which is not my thing, then why haven't I stepped out of his clutches yet? Instead, I let myself be drawn deeper into his sexy, hooded gaze. He's so horny for me, and I'm trying to work out if that's enough to let this encounter advance to the next step.

His mouth is open in a strange way. As his breath crashes into mine, I feel as if he wants to kiss me but won't.

*But still…*

I drink in his enticingly swollen lips and chiseled jawline. I consider the unseen benefits of doing it with a man like him. He's a billionaire and arguably the most coveted bachelor in New York City. I'm standing on top of a once-in-a-lifetime opportunity here. I shouldn't hesitate to take it.

"Is it because you're in love with someone else?" I ask, and that question alone begins to subdue my lust. He might be the fuck of the century, but nothing makes a woman feel less desirable than knowing she's option two.

Lynx's thick and neat eyebrows pull together. "In love?"

"My cousin said you were in love with someone."

His frown intensifies. "I'm not in love with anyone, Xena."

Lilly is not the sort of person who makes up shit. Also, she doesn't get confused very easily either. "No. You told Lilly that you were in love with someone else, and that's why…." I can't believe I'm about to say what comes next. It finally dawns on me that I have two profound reasons to put a stop to what is about to occur. "You couldn't be with her."

"Umm..." Lynx moans as he squeezes the round of my ass. His swallowing is audible. "As I said, I'm not in love with anyone," Lynx professes as he peels my robe down my shoulders with one eager but controlled hand. My breasts are on full display, and his appraising eyes make my impatient nipples tighten.

I have a reply to his claim, but a small part of me doesn't want to make waves with him because I've mostly chosen to go through with this. But still... I must know.

"Then you lied to Lilly," I whisper past the frog in my throat.

"Maybe." He sounds distracted as his gaze dances lasciviously around the acreage of my breasts. "They're better than I imagined."

*He's imagined my breasts?*

I hear two very strong and contradicting voices in my head. One says go forward and let this happen, and the other tells me to stop, think, and send him back to the eleventh floor.

"I don't know about this," I whisper, dropping my head.

"Hey…" Lynx gently places a finger under my chin, and together we lift my head. "Are you saying you don't want this?"

*Say yes.* "I'm not saying that. It's just… I'm not sure this is the right thing to do because maybe you're in love with another woman, or even worse, you're in love with…."

"Xena." He leans back to ensure steady eye contact. "I'm not in love with anyone. And as far as Delilah, I may have embellished a bit. It was easier that way."

Easier for who or what? I want to ask.

"May I?" he asks before I'm able to ask the question that's stuck in my brain.

I know what he's asking to do because of how he's gawking at my breasts. My head feels floaty as I nod, and then I become an unmovable mass. My breaths hitch in my throat when warm wetness and tingling sensations soak my left breast.

I murmur incoherently, meshing "fuck" with "oh my G…," the G stays trapped in my throat as my eyes flutter closed and my head floats back. An erotic medley of tongue, lips, and just enough teeth titillating the most sensitive spot of my nipple make my body shiver. The sensation feels so sensual. He knows what he's doing. I admit to being wrong about him earlier. Not only is he unfairly too good-looking, but he knows his way around a woman's tits.

"You're so soft..."" The suction of his mouth taking me in again feels so divine. "Like air," he breathes.

I've lost my head and all reason as Lynx finishes getting me out of Lilly's robe, and it bunches around my feet.

"Are you still wet for me," he whispers thickly.

I'm wetter for him, but I'll never tell. However, my secret is ruined when he slides his fingers up my slit. My exhale quivers as his fingers dive in and out of my moisture.

"Oh my G..." I cry out, experiencing pure pleasure when he applies pressure against my hot spot.

He's circling and circling, and I'm getting too close. I cling to his wrist to stop him.

"Wait," I say throatily. My legs tremble, aware that it hadn't taken Lynx long to get the orgasm maker churning. *Shit.*

His swallowing is audible. "What is it?" he whispers huskily.

I shake my head briskly. "I don't know. I just..."

Never gotten this far with someone who told me they don't want a relationship."

He has the best eyebrows I've ever seen on a man. Maybe that's why I always notice them when they rise, pull, or drop. This time they lower, hovering closely over his hypnotic eyes. "Do you want a relationship?"

It's hard to answer that question when his fingers are still applying pressure to my clit, and my first orgasm of the night is on the horizon.

"Um, no." I close my eyes as I shake my head. "I mean, yes. Everybody wants to be loved. But not tonight. I mean, not by you."

His gorgeous eyebrows raise. "Not by me?" I'm not sure if he feels slighted by what I just said or amused.

"You don't want a relationship, so I don't want to fall in love with you," I explain to be more precise.

"It's not personal, Xena. I'm a busy man."

My jaw remains locked even though I want to tell him that I think his excuse is shitty. Hell, I'm a busy woman. And this is New York City, every woman in this city is busy! But we all want to fall in love. Lynx Grove obviously has severe commitment issues, but do I care?

I focus on his sexily swollen lips. No... I don't care. But there's something else that's holding me back. Why doesn't he kiss me already? I think it's deliberate. To test my theory that he is not a kisser and that his intimacy issues run deeper than they already appear, I raise my mouth to his. As I thought, Lynx backs away.

"You don't kiss?" I sound like I'm accusing him of treason.

Lynx's grin is barely perceptible. "I do kiss. Let me show you how."

He is wholly consumed as he takes his fingers out of me and trails them down the round of my hip while flattening the palm of his other hand against my belly to guide my bottom onto the mattress. I'm unable to stop this as he separates my thighs. Then, he's on his knees between my knees. His strong arms hug my bent legs. My pussy throbs as his large hand presses me down onto the mattress. Then, the most sensual sensation of warmth and wetness engulfs my clit.

"Oooh," my voice trembles as I whimper. My head thrashes against the mattress as my orgasmic pussy wriggles against Lynx's mouth.

He moans in delight, and my eyes open wide as I feel fullness in my rear. Ooh... His finger plugs my ass, and it feels so… "Oh, Lynx," I repeat, short-winded while clawing and grasping at the bedsheets.

I've lost my willpower to resist this man. Lynx is showing me the benefits of doing this solely for fun. I feel like I'm having an out-of-body experience hearing myself moan his name and watching myself squirm as relentless pleasure expands where Lynx's mouth stimulates. And his deep moaning exposes how much he likes what he's doing. I wish I could lift my head and watch him. But I'm not in control of myself, especially when, like the constant beat of a drum, my core pulses with orgasm, making me cry out uninhibited.

"I love how you taste," Lynx whispers in a voice thickened by desire as he springs to his feet.

I can't move a muscle as my body still shivers, and I'm hopped up on dopamine which makes me dizzy. But I observe how his cock pushes against his track pants. I've made my decision. I'm going to let him put it in me. So I don't object or stall when he takes a shiny square packet out of his pocket, rips it open, and slides a condom over his enormous cock. It's so big, so broad, so ready. My wide eyes flit up to his face and stick. We can't look away from each other.

I wonder what he's thinking as he stands in the middle of my separated knees, watching me with his cock out and wrapped but his shirt and pants still on.

"You are very wet, Xena," he says in a tight whisper.

I swallow the extra moisture that pours into my mouth. "I know," he gets me to admit.

"I want you too much."

I can see that, and it still shocks me. "Why?" The question breaks past my lips without much thought.

"Because you're sexy. Very, sexy."

I search his face for evidence that he's lying. I can't find any.

He cocks an eyebrow. "You don't believe me?"

I don't believe him, but saying that is not what's at the forefront of my mind. "Why don't you kiss on the lips?" That bothers me so much.

I watch his amazing eyebrows bounce as if he's processing my question like his brain's a computer. "I don't spoon either." Lynx's intense eyes smolder at the slit between my legs. "But I fuck. And I'm good at it. You won't miss any of that shit when I'm done with you."

I swallow to moisten my dry throat. I'm only

now able to perceive that I'm nodding, agreeing not to miss any of that "mundane" shit like kissing or spooning just to be screwed by a sex god.

My breathing is deep and shuddering as I watch him push his pants down his long, powerful legs and then step out of them. My heart batters my breastbone as he takes his shirt by the collar and snatches it over his head like it's an insignificant piece of cloth. Lynx is all six-pack, hilly chest, and smooth, glowing skin. If demigods existed, this man would be one.

I feel myself dripping with need as he moves over me like a sultry shadow, splitting my thighs further apart to accommodate his perfectly lean and muscular body. And then…

"Ha," I inhale sharply as he moves deep inside me, and I wrap my arms around his hard body.

"Shit," he mutters. "You feel so good."

My ear is against his throat, and I'm extra turned on by listening to him swallow and moan as he shifts in and out of me.

He feels so damn good too. He doesn't hump like a jackrabbit. That was how my ex did it. Lynx's strokes are steady and indulgent. Every thrust brings into existence a consuming sensation. My eyes grow wide because I feel it. There's something about the way he's stroking me, the angle at which he's doing it that's…

"Ooh," I coo because I can hardly believe he's bringing me closer to the brink of an actual orgasm by doing it this way.

Our breaths collide as his parted lips hover over mine. I want to kiss him so badly, and I think he wants to kiss me. But I dare not test my theory. I don't want him to stop whatever he's doing. I want to feel it. I need to feel it. It would prove that he's indeed the lay of a lifetime. And then it happens.

My mouth opens wide, and I'm choking on my breath as pure pleasure rips through me. The sensation is so potent I'm forced to squeeze my eyes shut to bear the streaks that have the power of lightning.

"Oh, shit," Lynx says under his breath, and then my lower lip is in his mouth. He's not exactly kissing me, but he's close.

I am on cloud nine as his soft tongue and lips, with the right amount of suction, make me tighten my pussy around his cock and whimper.

Suddenly, Lynx stops pumping and holds very still. My lip is out of his mouth, and he's shaking his head as though I'm being a naughty girl.

"What?" I ask and try to raise my hips to get

him started again. His lower half pins me to the mattress.

"Release my cock," he commands breathlessly.

It takes a moment to figure out what he's talking about. The tight look on his face reveals that he's trying not to come. Then it dawns on me... Lynx is a control freak. He likes calling the shots, literally. I want to experience the second massive vaginal orgasm he's working on gifting me, but I want to take him down a peg or two even more, which is not like me at all. I don't even know what this is I'm feeling, this defiance that's fueling me, but I Kegel him tighter.

I'm risking him shifting to his feet, leaving me wanting but instead he watches me like he's experiencing bliss. Gosh, he's so handsome. I want to touch his skin and kiss his cheek. But for some reason, I feel as if I can't touch him, only experience him. Finally, Lynx releases a deep breath as he shifts deeper inside me. I Kegel his cock tighter, and he holds firm.

"What are you doing?" He whispers.

"Nothing," I say. I can't believe I'm doing this. It's him. It's the power he has over me. This is my way of fighting back, I think.

He raises an eyebrow. "I asked you to let go of my cock, Xena."

A naughty smirk possesses my lips. "Do you want to stop?"

Lynx slopes his gorgeous head slightly to one side, and my eyes dare him to win this standoff of ours by giving up and leaving me wanting. This risk I'm taking just might backfire. And then what? I'll have to use my fingers to get myself off when he's gone for good. I doubt he'll stay after he comes. He doesn't kiss or spoon. What's the use of sticking around if he can't be intimate?

The seconds of stillness pass. What will he do? What will I do? I don't release my squeeze on his cock though. *Is this crazy of me?*

Then, suddenly, like a snake slithering out of the bush to strike its prey, Lynx's cock impales me deeper. I hold on tight as he thrusts me hard and fast. Then, my upper lip is in his mouth, and he's sucking and thrusting. His arousal is like molten fire. His hands slide between my back and the mattress, and he rolls me on top of him to grasp two handfuls of my ass and then he shifts me against his cock harder and harder and harder, stroking me. Jerking back and forth, I can't hold onto my squeezing. But it doesn't matter that I've let go because Lynx's mouth consumes one of my bouncing tits as he pumps into me hard and fast until…

"Ooooh…." The guttural moan he makes originates deep in his throat as his voice and body quake when he comes.

---

### Three Minutes Later

I expected Lynx to roll me from on top of him, slap me on the thigh, and thank me for the shag before springing to his feet, dressing, and then waving goodbye. But he hasn't done that. We're lying alongside each other on the bed, staring at the ceiling. I must say, I hated that I sacrificed my second big orgasm to take control away from the man in charge. That was not smart of me.

"What was that?" he asks.

His tone lets me know what he's talking about.

I turn to face him. "Do you mean what I did to your cock?"

"Yes."

"I don't know," I admit. "I think I was peeved because you said you didn't kiss, and you don't spoon. And on top of all that, you aren't looking to be in a relationship. I guess it was my way of not feeling like a whore." That was actually the truth.

Lynx is frowning thoughtfully. "Whores don't receive pleasure, they give pleasure. And I was pleasuring you." He licks his lips like he can taste the final claim he just made.

My mouth is caught open. I would love to come up with a punchy objection. But nothing he said was incorrect. From the moment he planted his face between my thighs, he's been more concerned with my pleasure than his.

Suddenly, Lynx is lying on his side, and two of his elegant fingers slide across my lower lips. "Although, I've never been so tempted to just…." He grunts his desire.

I narrow my eyes at him as his finger continues gliding gently across my lower lip. He seems very comfortable and okay with himself just the way he is. "I thought you were a nice, well-adjusted guy," I remark.

A laugh escapes him as he removes his finger from my mouth. "I am well-adjusted."

"Bullshit."

"What about you?"

"What about me?" I ask, preparing to defend the obvious gaslighting that is to follow.

"I was about to make you come, hard, and you"
—he wets his delectably swollen bottom lip that
makes me want to maul his mouth—"sabotaged
me." He's smiling. At least he finds what I had done
amusing. "You turned sex into a power struggle,
Xena. I knew there was something about you."

"What in the hell does that mean?" I ask, mildly
insulted.

His narrowed eyes burn with acute desire. "It
means I had fun."

"I probably should've…." I close my mouth to
study Lynx's body language. The way he's lying
comfortably beside me with his dick out and
physique the picture of perfection, it feels as if this,
what's happening between us, is only natural and
shouldn't come with restrictions. But it does, and
that bothers me to no end.

"You probably should've what?" He asks, seem-
ingly losing patience.

I don't want to say that I probably should've
stopped all of this before it started. However, I don't
think I had the willpower to do it.

Instead, I think of something else to say. "Why
did you tell my cousin you were in love with
someone else if you're not? You can tell me the
truth now since you've already banged me."

Lynx laughs as he reaches out to slide his index finger up and down the tip of my right nipple. What he's doing is so distracting. I can stand at least a dozen more orgasms before he walks out the front door. I mean, I actually doubt we'll cross paths again. And if we do run into each other, at least this is out of our systems, I hope.

"I've already told you the truth," he says.

"Lilly said the two of you shared sparks."

"Maybe," he says with a passive shrug. "You have beautiful breasts, Xena. I can suck on them all night long."

"And what about now?" I ask, ignoring his sexualizing compliment.

He moves toward me. "I can suck on them now."

I nudge him back with a laugh. "No. Are you still attracted to Lilly?"

He's increasing the stimulation on my nipple and I press my thighs together to stop the tingling in my vag. It doesn't work.

"Could you stop and focus?" I sigh.

With a slow, sideways, naughty smile, Lynx retracts his hand.

He sighs as if he's ready to comply. "I could've

been into Lilly until I saw her with Orion. But I didn't want her this way."

"What way?"

He pinches the tip of my nipple. "Like this. I could've done without this from her. But I couldn't resist you."

I roll my eyes, even though I picture that wired look on his face when he knocked on my door earlier. Pure lust glistened in his eyes.

"That sounds like a bad pickup line," I say.

Lynx laughs. "It's true." He extends an arm that hooks me around the waist and pulls me under him. Lynx handles me with such ease. He's either very strong or I'm as light as a twig, which I am not. There's no more to say when my right breast is deep in his mouth. There's definitely no more grilling him when his fingers are shifting in and out of my wetness, readying me for our next round of sex with no real kissing.

# THREE
## XENA ST. JAMES

Saturday, Mid-morning

I'm daydreaming again. I've been doing that a lot since waking up Thursday morning after my night with Lynx Grove. I've been haunted by scenes from our lovemaking, which slowly fade into a long-forgotten past as the days go by. However, while I'm still able to remember, sometimes I try to figure out the meaning of things that were said, but mostly I fantasize about the sex. *It was so… Mindblowing.*

I'm at *Limbo,* a restaurant in Hell's Kitchen. The dining room is packed and brimming with spirited conversation. I only secured a table without waiting in a long line because I'm Jojo O'Leary's daughter. People in this town love my mom. On camera and when her fans are looking Jojo is charming, personable, and could sell ice water in the Arctic. In real life and to those who know and love her, she's a hard-ass and knows precisely what must be done to make herself a celebrity for the Home Shopping Emporium show she hosts.

With an annoyed sigh, I check the time on my cellphone again. I'm alone at a table for three. My friend Carol called to cancel as soon as I was seated. She has a family emergency and has to fly back to New Mexico to deal with it. And Lilly, who hasn't arrived yet, is thirty minutes late. That's not like her at all. She's a stickler for being punctual. I've gone ahead and ordered my usual western omelet with truffle home fries. The only thing that's keeping me from fuming is remembering Wednesday night.

After round three of mind-blowing sex sessions, Lynx lay with me for at least half an hour. I got the feeling he felt obligated to stay and pretend as if he were interested in more than a lay. I'm embarrassed to admit that I played along. Having him near for as long as he would allow it felt intoxicating. But he got really personal with me. Too personal, I think—too intimate for someone who fucks them and then leaves them.

With his fingers interwoven behind his head,

Lynx sunk deeper into the pillow and mattress. "What's your story, Xena?" he had asked.

"My story?" I replied, having orgasmed so intensely throughout the night that my limbs felt like jelly.

"Brothers? Sisters?"

Oh, I thought, that story. "An older brother and younger sister. One by my dad's first wife and the other by his third wife. Jojo's in the middle."

"Jojo is your mother's name?"

"Yep. Jojo O'Leary," I said, knowing the name would ring a bell.

He snapped his fingers. "That's why you look familiar to me. The sexy pricetag lady is your mother!"

A snicker escaped me. "Sexy?"

"Yes. She's very sexy. Never doubt that's who you get it from."

I rolled my eyes. It was odd hearing the man I just had sex with say my mom was sexy. Granted, I've heard it before. My mom has that come-hither thing going for her. However, since Lynx made it very clear that he had no interest in getting close to me, there was no need to issue a Jojo O'Leary warning. I tell all guys who are interested in me to don't let Jojo's petal-soft good looks and feminine physique fool them. Jojo is a ravenous shark, and if you get too close and you're too weak, she won't even chew before she swallows you whole and then excretes you out. Yep. That's how she'll do it, quickly and efficiently.

"I watch her show just for kicks too," Lynx revealed. "She's a character."

I grunted with a perfunctory roll of my eyes. "I'll tell her that the guy I screwed on Wednesday night is a fan."

Lynx pointed at me. "You do that."

We grinned at each other for far too long. We did that a lot that night; even while making love, we fell into long spells where we couldn't look away from each other. Then we talked about how hard it was for him to bring a major league baseball team to Connecticut. His father tried to discourage him and said he'd never be able to get it done. That added fuel to Lynx's fire. The more I listened to Lynx talk about securing the votes needed to open the franchise, the more impressive he appeared. He was becoming more like a real person and less like the sex robot who unexpectedly popped in for dinner.

Suddenly, a surge of frantic energy slams into me. "Sorry," Lilly says, bringing my memories of

Lynx to an abrupt end as she drops down in the chair across from me. I can feel the cold air and that slightly pungent odor that gets all over you in this city coming off of her.

I shake my head, trying not to look like I want to strangle her pretty little neck. "You're late."

She pushes her palms at me, gesturing me to back off. "And I've already eaten. I came here because we have to talk, of course."

"You've eaten? Why would you eat before making plans to eat with me?" Why are tears bombarding my eye sockets? I'm whining because I feel the loss of someone I used to see every day and especially for Saturday brunch.

"I'm sorry. Orion has a chef, and we've gone vegan-ish vegetarian."

My face squeezes into a tight frown. "That was fast. Now you're vegan-ish together? I guess that means you're back together. And why haven't you been answering my calls?"

Lilly pins me with a look that tells me she has so much to say and doesn't know where to start. I hate this feeling that I can't shake. She's close enough that I can reach out and touch her, but she's actually existing in an alternate universe.

"That's why I'm here," she finally says. "And yes, Orion and I are back together."

I shake my head in disappointment. "I can't believe you."

"I also live with him."

My eyes expand double their size. "You're gorging on his poisonous apple Lilly."

She frowns mockingly. "I thought he was the poisonous apple."

"You know what I mean," I snap.

"No, I don't." She expels an exasperated breath through her nose. "You know what? I probably should've never taken my work problems with him to you because you blow things out of proportion." She slaps herself on the chest. "I was pissed off at Orion…."

"Yes. You were," I say, happily cutting her off. There's no way in the world I will let her forget her despicable boss's despicableness. "Remember the bottled water episode?"

Lilly exhales audibly as she rolls her eyes.

I slam one finger on top of another, ready to count the list of Orion's infractions. "Having you call his hookups to break booty calls?"

She folds her arms across her chest, showing me she's standing her ground too.

"And don't forget how he made you buy flowers for women right before he broke up with them. Oh, and he never ever showed up for work on time. Dropping the ball and making you do his job."

"I never had to do his job," she finally says. "I thought I was doing his job, but he was working on something much bigger than what we were doing."

I shake my head at this insanity she's spewing. "Wow, that's some spin you're putting on the past. And is he truly over his sister-in-law? Because remember how he made you stalk her and his brother, and that was before he made you his date for their wedding."

Unfolding her arms, Lilly thrusts herself forward, leaning across the table as she clutches the edge, attaching her fingernails to the wood. "Are you finished?"

I raise my eyebrows obstinately. "Not really."

We glare at each other until we turn to the people at the table beside us who are watching us in suspense. Maybe they're waiting for one of us to jump to her feet and storm out of the restaurant. That's not how Lilly and I quarrel. Our mothers, who are sisters, taught us how to stay and battle until we've reached a resolution we both can agree on.

However, realizing we're causing a scene, we both sigh at the same time and retreat deeper into our seats.

I stop shaking my head. "I still think you're making a big mistake."

"You can't judge a person unless you know them thoroughly. And you only know Orion from my complaining about him. Well, trust me when I say I have grown to know the full story of Orion Lord. And I love that book. And I want you to be happy for me." Her tone and glassy eyes plead for my blessing.

I stop myself from rolling my eyes as I battle giving in. "Ugh." I scratch the side of my neck anxiously. I really want to give her what she wants. But all I can picture is Orion's sly grin. Even if she's right. I only know him through her complaining about how awful he was. Although, there were many occasions when he would call her while we were enjoying a girl's night out. Lilly would have to leave and complete some stupid task that he could totally do himself if he weren't such a pampered prick. Granted, I've only met Orion a handful of times, and he's always been cordial and a little flirta- tious in that desperate see-me-please kind of way. But also, Lilly has always known how much of an asshole my ex was, and she has never spoken harshly about him. That's her way. Maybe the time has come when I have to extend the same grace to her and not say another negative word about the man she loves, at least not until he messes up.

But my heart hurts so much, and suddenly I know why. Look at her; she's glowing from the inside out. I think she's outgrown me. She's no longer just mine, and I'm no longer just hers. I have to share her with Orion Lord of all people.

"Give him a chance," she urges. "Give us a chance. Watch us, and if he treats me like crap, I'll let you take the first shot at him."

I snicker, knowing that will never be necessary. If Lilly loves him, then he's sure as hell earned her affection. However, I picture myself punching Orion in the face anyway. But then, to my utter surprise, Orion's face is replaced by Lynx's, and a weird feeling surges through me. *Shit.*

"You know you left me alone with your dinner guest the other night," I say, now that I'm thinking about him.

Lily's eyes bulge as she rubs her palms together. "Ooh. How did it go?"

I pause, wondering if she's run into Lynx in the elevator, and they talked about how he and I spent half the night screwing. Usually, I'm quick to tell Lilly everything about my sex life, the highs and lows of each encounter, but for some reason, I don't want to divulge any of what happened between Lynx and me. However, I do want to clear up a few things he claimed.

"You said he's in love with someone. He said he isn't," I say.

Lilly looks at me incredulously. "Really?"

"Was he lying to me?" Gosh, I sound so vulnerable.

"He told me he was in love with a friend."

I pick up my fork and tap it on the edge of my plate, and when I see that Lilly is watching what I'm doing, I stop.

"Did something happen between you two?" she asks.

I shake my head. Although I'm not saying no, I'm pondering the shit Lynx told me on Wednesday night. "You know he's no goody-two-shoes."

She tapers an eye. "Why would you say that?"

My memory captures the last thing that happened between Lynx and me before our time ended. It was like thirty minutes on the dot when he sprung out of bed and put on his clothes. I escorted him through the living room, and on the way, he told me how much fun he had. *Fun? I was merely fun to him.*

"I'm glad you had *fun*," I said, wearing a painted-on smile. I opened the door for him, and suddenly, all the mushy feelings from the sex and intimate details of our lives that we shared with each other had vanished into thin air. I couldn't wait to kick his emotionally stunted ass out and thank my lucky stars I hadn't fallen in love with that guy.

But then, Lynx stood motionless, allowing his gaze to dance around my face until he stopped at my mouth.

"I just want to...." He lightly pinched my chin between his thumb and forefinger and steadily lowered his mouth to mine.

We never broke eye contact as his sensual lips folded themselves between mine. It was as if he was trying out kissing for the very first time as his tongue gently swept across mine before drawing me completely into his mouth for more. I swear I had engaged in the most sensual kiss of my life. Our kissing was delicate and erotic, and I felt like I was floating on air until Lynx broke lip contact by pressing his forehead against mine.

He exhaled through his nose. "Shit. What are

you doing to me?" he whispered. I don't think he meant to say that out loud.

When he lifted his forehead off mine, he delicately pinched the tip of my nipple and breathlessly said, "Thank you very much."

We engaged in one last bout of prolonged staring. Then, Lynx turned his back on me and walked away. I watched for as long as I could, admiring his flawless physique.

I lick my lips, remembering his mouth on mine and our tongues entwined. "It's just," I say to Lilly, shrugging nonchalantly. "He said he doesn't do relationships. Nor does he kiss," I say as an afterthought. Nor spoon, I want to add, but I can't because Lilly is too bright. She'll figure out that you must get to "point fucking" before you arrive at "point spooning." So we must've had sex if I'm talking about spooning.

"So let me get this right," she says. "You and Lynx discussed kissing and relationships and his being in love with an old friend?"

I shrug nonchalantly.

She angles her head, watching me curiously. "And it never turned romantic between you two?"

"Ha," I scoff at the word romantic. "No." That's the truth. What happened to Lynx and me wasn't even close to being romantic. Because romances have happy endings where the characters live happily ever after, and that is not us.

"But something happened," Lilly claims. She points at my face. "Your eyes are glassy, and that means something occurred between you two. But..." She picks up my fork and digs into my truffle home fries. "I'm not going to push." She feeds herself a heaping serving.

"Should we order you some of this," I say, watching her shovel my food into her mouth like she hadn't eaten breakfast at all this morning.

Lilly waves me off and shakes her head no as she finishes swallowing. "I can't stay much longer. Orion and I are flying to his family's private island in the Bahamas for the weekend. We would stay for a week, but I have rehearsals on Monday." She's beaming again, all lit up about having nonstop sex with Orion on a private island. I mean... Look at her. They've obviously been screwing like rabbits.

"Right," I say in a deadpan voice.

"I wanted to tell you, though." She twists in her chair to dig something out of her coat pocket. It's like I'm watching her in slow motion as she pinches a diamond ring between two fingers, slides it on her ring finger, and then announces, "Orion and I are already married."

I slap my hands over my mouth to conceal a loud gasp.

---

## Saturday Night

I can hardly remember how the rest of the day had passed. I was shocked as I half-heartedly listened to Lilly tell this long story about the trip she took to Vegas with Orion, a ring, security cameras, and being too drunk and high to remember their marriage ceremony. Apparently, one of Orion's friends had the waitress put a party drug in their cocktails. I felt like I was sitting across from a stranger, not my sensible, sometimes equally cynical cousin Lilly. I even mentioned the hell of a hard time I had at the job on Thursday and Friday with Greg pestering me. And how he's hellbent on making me pay for breaking up with him.

"Then get a new job, Zeen. Maybe the time has come for you to pursue a musical career anyway. Do what you love. I've done it, and look where it's landed me," she said instead of joining me in verbally assassinating my ex.

"I can't. My rent is too high, and I don't want to run through my savings," I said as if she should know that already.

Lilly then offered to give me money since her new husband provides her with a monthly stipend of half of what I make in a year. I thought I heard her wrong, so I asked her to repeat the number three times. I wanted to make a smart-ass comment about how he owes her triple that amount for all the hell he put her through. But I was done feeling salty about her new husband, I guess. I've never seen her happier, and I love seeing her happy. However, I would rather gouge my eyes out than take a dime from Orion Lord, especially while the jury is still out on him.

I now stare at my water-stained ceiling. My uptown apartment sucks. The pipes knock all day long. Tonight I have heat but tomorrow, who knows? And I can never get rid of the lingering scent of trash since my only window is over the dumpster in the alley. But there's a lot more wrong with this dastardly place than that. The water runs brown out of the faucets for the first two minutes. I'm without hot water on most days of the week and every morning. I can hear my neighbors upstairs fucking when I'm in the bedroom. When I move to the living room, less than ten feet away, I can hear Jess, the neighbor next door, who's taken sex in the city to brand new heights, sexing all the one-night stands she brings home.

The sound of a creaking bed starts up. Then there's a woman moaning. A man is grunting. But I don't want to get up to escape their carnal sounds. The only comfortable place in my apartment is my bed. I paid six thousand dollars for the mattress and a thousand for the pillows. I don't feel like moving to my hard sofa.

I groan as the couple turns up the volume and intensity of their lovemaking. Unfortunately, the guy has the lasting power of the Energizer Bunny. I smash one of my pillows around my ears, which helps a little.

*Lynx…*

*Lilly and Orion…*

*My job…*

*My apartment.*

Tears burn the backs of my eyes as I come to a pitiful conclusion, "My life sucks."

# FOUR
## LYNX GROVE

Saturday Evening

Leo, my father, alone at the office on a Saturday evening doesn't surprise me. He would work twenty-four hours straight, seven days a week if it were humanly possible. I may have inherited my workaholic habit from him. I should do something about it. Work less. Travel more—that kind of shit.

The elevator doors open to a private lobby with glass walls showcasing expensive Theo Norman paintings. I stop to view each piece which is lit by mood-effecting light. I know they're Theo Norman because I've heard a lot about how happy my dad is with his new collection. I hadn't been able to listen to him gush myself because we hadn't spoken since

Treasure's wedding. However, I'm startled by the gory themes depicted on the canvases. Leo has never been a pleasant guy. But I could've sworn red paint splattered to depict blood, sliced flesh, and dying flowers were out of his wheelhouse.

I once saw a high school photo of my father, and he was just as I thought he would be—dressed in all black, anemic skin, eyes so pale they appear colorless and expressionless. I asked him if he had considered himself goth back then, and he said, "What the hell is that?"

Of course, he wasn't a goth. Leo was nothing. My dad doesn't follow trends. He's not the kind of person who needs to define himself or be liked. And when he saw those traits he despised in me, he did everything he could to wring them out of me. I'm not sure if his methods worked, but sometimes, I feel that I'm awfully screwed up.

*So this is Theo Norman.*

Suddenly, experiencing a rawness I didn't feel before stopping to figure out this Norman bro, I turn toward my father's office. The double doors are open wide, inviting me in. The light is warm and dimmed, and classical music ripples lightly in the background.

"Here goes nothing," I whisper, scratching the

back of my ear. Suddenly it itches, and so do the soles of my feet. I want to stop to collect myself before walking into what is sure to be a battle zone, a war of wills, but I keep going.

After one quick release of a breath I'd been holding, I enter my father's domain. Leo isn't sitting in his executive chair, which is unlike him, at least when he's meeting me. He likes the visual of him sitting while I stand as if approaching his throne. Instead, he's standing in front of a black-and-white drawing of my beautiful mother. In the rendering, Londyn Grove wears a flowing dress as she poses in a tight hallway under a circular ceiling. My mother, who doesn't look much younger than she does now, gazes mysteriously at the viewer. I've never seen that photo, and since she used to be a fashion model, I've viewed many pictures of her.

Also, oddly, Leo is wearing jeans and a black sweatshirt. He never shows up to the office without being dressed in a suit, even on weekends, even if alone. The Theo Norman paintings, the casual attire, and my father not sitting in his chair worries me.

I clear my throat to announce my arrival and say, "Hello, Father." I'll keep it formal until he shows me I can let my guard down.

"I took this photo of your mom," he says, keeping his eyes on the portrait. "I paid an artist friend to redraw it."

He's chill, and that's a green light to walk over and stand beside him. "I've never seen this one."

Leo tilts his head in the opposite direction as if getting a better look at the woman he married thirty-five years ago. "No, you haven't. It's part of my private collection. I recently had this one drawn. It's charcoal. Impressive, isn't it?"

"It is."

"I took this photo a week after I met Londyn in London." He chuckles at his intended pun.

He pauses, and right on cue, I snort a chuckle. My father likes saying that. I zero in on the woman who I love with everything within me. She still has that unsure glint in her eyes. In this family, my parents are the underdogs, constantly playing second fiddle to Max's parents, Xander and Heartly. Instead of being CEO of Grove Industrial Tech, if my father truly had a choice, he probably would've spent his life doing something else. But what happened to my dad occurs when a visionary creates an empire, and his unprecedented success becomes his offspring's burden.

Leo finally turns to me, and I see his face full-on

for the first time in a long time. He's thinner, and his pale eyes are watery. Shit, he's holding back tears. Now I'm more worried.

"What's going on Dad? What's this all about?"

His gaze travels around my face as the skin between his eyes puckers. "I was pretty good with a camera back then." My father clenches my shoulders and squeezes. I tense up because Leo's not a touchy kind of guy. "Let's talk," he says.

---

### Sunday Morning, GIT Stadium

All seats are empty. Access to anyone except Max and me has been revoked. My cousin Max and I always bat in private. And there isn't a much better feeling than the bright stadium lights, the smell of fresh-cut grass, and the steady sound of Max's bat cracking against the ball. He's batting a nearly perfect average against the pitching machine set to speedballs at full throttle. He's been a gifted hitter since we were kids. He knows a lot more about baseball than I do, and I'm the one who owns a team. There's irony in that. But I can forget about recruiting him as a player or co-owner. Max would instead bathe in hydrochloric acid than be involved with professional sports. Not only is Max with the family business one hundred percent, he's everything our family stands for: Grove loyalty above all.

*Tap...* He hits one into the stands, narrowly avoiding a foul ball.

*Tap.* The ball strikes the wall and springs into centerfield.

*Tap.* That was another perfect home run.

"Whoa," I yell, standing on the grass at a safe distance. Max is in rare form today. He hadn't struck out once.

Max raises his bat, prepared to hit another bomb, and then calls, "Pause!"

I smash the off button on the remote control that I'm squeezing to stop the machine, and he tosses the bat like a real major-league baseball player.

There's a reason why we're batting in Stamford, Connecticut on a Sunday morning. We usually do this workout on Tuesday nights. However, we've come here to discuss yesterday's meeting with my father.

Walking toward me, chest rising and falling as he evens his breaths, Max pins me with a one-eyed glare.

"What do you think about what Leo said?" he asks, stopping before me. He's barely breathing heavily. Most of my players would still be struggling after hitting for half an hour, 4 seconds between pitches speeding toward them at 95 miles per hour while knocking most of them out of the park. But Max, who has one arm extended across his chest as he presses it tighter against his body with his other hand, is already close to recovering. Treasure jokes that he's a robot his parents, Xander and Heartly, made to pass as an actual human. If anybody could build themselves a super-son who toes the family line, it's the two of them because they're both brilliant.

"It's a big ask," I say. "He's finally offering me his seat, but there are a lot of stipulations attached to it."

"So what?" Max shrugs like it's no big deal.

I yank my head back. His nonchalance has to be a power move. I have no doubt where he stands —it's why we are here. Max could be a world-class poker player because he rarely shows emotion, and when he does have reactions, they can be hard to identify or just downright inappropriate. For instance, he grimaced throughout his sister and my sister's weddings because he didn't want them to

marry Lord brothers even though our family benefits financially from their unions. Max didn't like the
deal put into place, which could've ended a long-
standing feud if he knew how to let it go. He
thought the Lords had more to gain than us. I see it
differently, although I never argued the case with
him. The guy just hates the Lords, period.

"He wants me to get married and have a son."
The add-on to his request intensifies my frown. "He
said if Treasure has a son, then he'd be a Lord, but
if I breed for the need, my son will be a Grove. And
all I could ask myself was, what century do we live
in, what country do we live in, and what the fuck?"

"He's got a point."

"Then why don't you breed for the need?"

Max shrugs passively. "In the future, sure. But in
the present, how do you feel about taking Leo's seat
as co-CEO of GIT alongside me?" His eyes shine
as he grins. I bet Max has been jerking off to the
possibility of shedding my less hostile father.

I'm not done complaining though. "I'll have to
sell my team because of capital equity issues? I built
this team from nothing." Step by step, I turn in a
circle to get a complete picture of the stadium I
erected from the ground up. Admittedly, co-CEO
of Grove Industrial Tech is a sexy offer, and to run

the whole shebang alongside my cousin, who's more like a brother, would be fun. But still, it's not like they're asking me to give up my private chef or something.

"Lynx, you have a good thing going here. And it's been a good run."

"Ha," I scoff and stop to face him again.

"You franchised a new ball team," he continues. "And captained them to the playoffs twice, barely missing this year. You have six all-star players. I commend you for that. Especially when you campaigned like hell to bring a team to this city." He flips his thumb up like he does when he's getting ready to count up. "You fill your seats. You're operating in the black. Top athletes want to play for you. And your front office is arguably the best in the league."

I'm surprised he's acknowledging all of that. He usually stays mute on subjects of the Rambler's success because he doesn't like that I don't work for the family, just as much as Leo hates it. "You just listed why I should cling to my crowning glory."

During a long pause, Max eyes me sagely. "I need your superior business acumen," he finally proclaims. "*We* need it."

My hand flies up abruptly to rub the back of

my ear. My mother's younger voice tells me to "Stop that and use your words, Lynx. Say what you're thinking."

"I don't know if I can give up my team," I say.

"You can't run them both. And I have one word for you."

I know what he's going to say before he says it. Because that one word is the bloody bone, and I'm the sort of dog whose mouth waters at the sight of it.

"TRANSPOT," we say at the same time.

"Listen." Max checks across both shoulders as if there's someone around to hear what he tells me. "I've never begged you for anything. But I've been alone at GIT since we've had to share half the rights of TRANSPOT with the Lords. And the families have agreed to merge GIT with LTI. I was the only no vote, even your vote went against me. Treasure has Achilles' back no matter what. She's been using your proxy to vote his agenda one hundred percent of the time."

I yank my head in surprise. "What?"

"Yes. She has. And your father cannot push her to give us what we fucking need," he says, thumbing at himself, which reveals the truth of the matter. Treasure is not giving him what he wants. They have childhood discord between them. Treasure loves Max but is prone to push back against him because she's never liked his controlling ways. And Max, who's an expert at persuading anybody to get what he wants, has never been unable to convince Treasure to see things his way. And neither one of them knows how to stop butting heads with the other.

"I see," I say.

Max sinks his hand on my shoulder and ensures I'm looking him in the eyes. "I'm begging you, Lynx. I need you. I need you, brother."

He says the government is releasing TRANSPOT back to the company in late October. Once that happens, the technology will be cleared for product development and distribution. TRANSPOT is more than software. It's the capture and harnessing of a brand new element once unknown to humankind. The simple way to explain the technology is that the novel light source can solidify most molecules that float through the earth's atmosphere. Once the solids are made, programming Earth's solar light reacts with the new light source creating a mirroring effect, which operates like a 3D printer. Any animate or inanimate object can be copied, felt, and experienced in real-time with no activity lag. No invention parallels what GIT has done in collaboration with LTI, Lord Technical Innovations. No human being has ever extracted energy beyond our solar system to create objects that can enhance our daily existence. The new light source has also been found to be repelled by the human body. It doesn't penetrate the epidermis, and that means the technology doesn't present any danger to our health.

"We're going to market. It's happening, Lynx. Once we patent the technology, getting you in as CEO will be exponentially harder, if not impossible. Even if you are family. The Lords have had their way with us. Come December first. They'll have a say-so in who we appoint as CEO of our company."

"And we'll have say-so with who they appoint too, right?"

"Yes, but they're already with Hercules and Achilles. Leo is ready to retire. The Lords will put Paisley in his seat, and she's…."

"Married to Hercules."

My finger shoots up as I'm ready to state a counterpoint that's already dying as I think about it. "But doesn't she own…"

"Not anymore. She sold her stake in LTI back to the Lords."

"Right," I mutter.

We stare at each other, allowing that truth to settle in. Max is correct. If he keeps up the tension between the Groves and Lords, then his sister will never be his ally.

I nod encouragingly. "I'll strongly consider the offer."

His eyebrows furrow. "Are you for real? You jump at this opportunity right here, right now. We draw up the paperwork Monday, and you have that fucking team sold by Friday."

"It's not that easy, Max. I have a stipulation in my contract with Rich."

"Then find out how to get around it," he roars.

I don't flinch. Max isn't scary to me. Also, he knows I'm not easily pressured into making rash decisions. I could keep going back and forth with him, but I know when to end this. Truthfully, I'm not over how much it killed me when Leo wanted to onboard me as a business analyst after I graduated from London Business School. When Max finished at the same school, he took his seat as CEO. He's never been anything but in charge. Leo saw me as less worthy until I proved I could make magic alone.

But now he wants to give me what I always deserved? Fuck him. Fuck them. Max could've fought for me back then, but he didn't. So fuck him twice. He can wait until I decide what's best for me.

I contain my anger though. I've always been good at that.

"You said I have until December first."

"The end of November," he retorts.

"Then give me until then."

Max throws his arms up in defiance. "So sell this fucking team and join the unsinkable warship, Lynx. Or... Better yet, strip the Ramblers for parts. You'll get a lot of cash for your top players, and then what is Rich going to do with a losing team?"

I peer at him through narrowed eyes. "I'm not doing that. These are my guys. I'm not doing that."

Max nods as if he agrees with my stance, which I appreciate.

"How's it going with Penelope?" The question comes out of the blue.

I'm about to ask why in the hell he's asking about her, but my dad said something interesting yesterday. "You know Leo mentioned her as a possible candidate to breed with. I didn't even know he knew about us."

Max cuts a small smile which is something he

rarely does. "I might've mentioned it to him."

I throw my hands up rebelliously. "But why?"

"I had to help him along in making his final decision. Getting him to believe you're ready to take his seat and give him heirs helped him see the light. But who cares if you have kids once the deal is done."

My entire being repels everything Max just said. What in the hell is wrong with him? Sometimes he acts like he doesn't have a soul, but I know he does.

Penelope is a woman I fuck now and then. Also, her father, Richard Chastain, owns the other fifteen percent of my team. I had to bring him in as a co-owner before my franchise could be approved because the organization wasn't comfortable with a person my age holding a team without experience on my side. Penelope's father, who I call Rich, is my token of expertise, being that his business is buying stakes in professional sports teams and then selling to make a large profit. Our agreement is I run my club, and he collects his returns. But he insisted I hire his daughter in an important position, so I made her Director of Communication and Outreach. To my surprise, Penelope has been killing it in that role.

But getting serious about Penelope is like

committing emotional masochism. She and I play fuck games, literally. If my father knew the nature of our relationship, he would not approve of her as the mother of his imaginary heirs. But I see now how she's been worming her way into my family for months. I know of two charity projects she partnered with my mother on. In one of them, Penelope and I are running mates in the *Paws for Claws Couples 5k Run* that's to take place next year in March. But my parents have only known us to be work colleagues, at least that's what I thought.

"So…" I say, nodding at the pitching machine. I need to change the subject. "Is worrying about onboarding me the only reason you've been murdering those balls?"

Max snorts a chuckle. "Nah."

"Ah… Women problems?"

"A woman."

I know who he's referring to. "I checked out her handiwork in my dad's office last night."

Max rubs his scalp. Lake Clark is the one person who gets him worked up that way. Personally, I believe he only wants her because he can't have her.

"I don't know, Lynx. She gets to me, and it's insane that I can't…." He shakes his head like he doesn't want to think about it anymore. He wants to say get over her. "What about you? Are you ready to make Penelope the mother of your children?" He blurts out a laugh.

The thought of becoming serious with Penelope makes my head hurt. I squeeze my eyes shut and pinch the bridge of my nose to relieve the pressure, but out of nowhere, Xena's sexy face and body come to mind. Recently, I've been masturbating to memories of our night together. I've been wanting a replay, but I've been too busy to make it happen. "Remember the girl Orion brought to Treasure's wedding? She was his assistant—Lilly."

"Yeah, I remember Delilah O'Shay. She's cute."

I nod in agreement. Cute is a huge compliment coming from Max. It's his way of saying she's beautiful but doesn't do it for him.

"She has a cousin I met on Wednesday night, Xena."

Max tilts his head to one side. "I mention Penelope, and you tell me about Delilah's cousin. Has the spell been broken?"

I scoff, offended. "There's no spell."

He aims the tip of his finger at my eye. "The only way you'll lose interest in her is if she stops playing fucking games with you."

I punch him playfully in the chest. "Screw you, man." Max knows I tend to lose interest in someone once they get interested in me. I don't know why it happens, but it does every time.

Max stumbles, laughing and pretending my weak shove knocked him off balance. Generally, he's a severe guy, even when being playful. However, he quickly recovers his typical serious attitude.

"I suspect something happened between Delilah's cousin and you," he says, frowning. "But tread lightly because Orion Lord and Delilah are married. They were married on the night before Treasure's wedding in Las Vegas."

That tidbit of information strikes me like a hard slap across my face. "Get the hell out of here."

Max nods and explains the details, which are crazy as hell. He's explaining behavior I would've never associated with Lilly. Orion, yes. Lilly, no. He also suspects the two don't know they're married.

"Orion and I met last week. We're going to be working together," he says. "And I want to get him under contract before TRANSPOT blows up. He'll be one Lord I won't have to worry about."

I shake my head in shock. "Shit, Max. You can't say that kind of shit to me out loud." He basically admitted he's going to use Orion as a pawn. "How did you find all that out about them being married anyway?"

"I keep tabs," he says like it's no big deal.

"Right..." I rub my ear nervously. Max and Achilles are why Orion and I could never be friends. We went to the same high school, Dorset Meacham Academy. Orion and I liked each other. So we kept it cordial and said hello to each other now and then. Then after the one and only occasion we played a pick-up game of basketball in the gym during lunch, word got back to his brother and my cousin that we were being civil. Max reprimanded me for being a traitor to the family. To add insult to injury, my father broke my heart when he said he would disown me if I associated with the Lords. That's why it's puzzling that he's allowing Achilles to control him through Treasure.

Orion must've faced the same sort of firing squad because he never spoke to me again. But he had friends who liked to screw with me for shits and giggles. His followers liked to yell, "This is Lord's country," in the corridors and write it on both my gym and hallway lockers. Orion never did anything to rein them in until Treasure, who likes to behave like she's older than me, paid him a visit.

"All I'm saying is now is not the time to rock the boat with anybody associated with a Lord. If you're not all in with this girl, Xena, then…."

"We had one night, that's all," I say before he can finish suggesting I leave Xena alone.

"I like how you're thinking," Max says, then claps twice. He skips backward, heading toward home plate while pointing at me. "Give me ten more minutes, and then you're up."

I watch him pick up his bat and get in position to hit. I don't like my decision to put space between Xena and me. I've been missing her soft skin against mine. Even the way she smells and tastes. And her sexy face. I like how nervous she was around me. The way her body shivered when she orgasmed. Heck, when I came too. Everything about her felt new. I want more of her, so maybe I should keep my distance because Max is right. I'm a disaster at relationships.

"Start her up," Max calls.

I take the remote out of my pocket, and when I press the start button, I again remember I have a date with Penelope tonight. It's good; she'll help put last Wednesday behind me. I don't need Xena in my life. I don't need to break the mold; for now, Penelope is the mold.

# FIVE
## XENA ST. JAMES

Thursday, 2 Weeks Later

My feet pound the pavement so fast I'm nearly
running. I knew from the moment I woke up, and
the electricity was out throughout the building yet
again, that the day was shaking up to be
catastrophic. I should move. Everybody tells me so.
Lilly even offered me her apartment before she
moved her things out. If I had said yes, I wouldn't
have had to pay any rent until September of next
year. That's almost an entire year of living rent-free.
My gut said to take the offer, but my pride said no.
Orion's company owns the apartment. Lilly might
love him, but I can't trust him yet. Also, I don't
want to run into Mr. Eleventh Floor again. What a

dick! Lynx Grove has actually banged me and then forgot about me. I hoped he would've proved my fears wrong. On the one hand, I can respect that he forewarned me before I opened up and let him in. *But still...* Oh boy, had Lilly painted him out to be someone he is not. He's a fuckboy. And the rule is never fuck a fuckboy twice, or else... The list of fallouts is long. I could catch an STD, even incurable ones. Or, given the deceitful and seductive nature of sex, I could accidentally think I've fallen in love with him, risking my heart blowing up like an atomic explosion—*bang!*

However, in moments like now, I kick myself for not being more rational than emotional. I should've taken Lily's apartment. When the electricity inexplicably shut off in the middle of the night, the heat went out with it. I felt like an ice cube between the blankets. At some point, I have to shop for essentials like thick winter comforters. It's entirely possible that my mom has subconsciously made me hate shopping because she sells things for a living. I can't stop myself from being contrary to her—another irrational but emotional trait of mine.

I groan, protesting my life, as I pass a line of actors waiting to be cast in the next season of Perfect Together—I work on that reality show. The prospective cast members, all young, beautiful, and eager to become a star, watch me with hope in their eyes as I sweep past them.

"How you doin' this morning, Zeen?" Si, the security guard, says before I reach the coveted entrance. He's watching me with the sort of pity reserved for someone who just got up after a hard fall.

I groan, rolling my eyes as he opens the door for me, and I sweep past him. Si chuckles. He once remarked that he's never seen me arrive in a good mood in the three years he's worked for the company. He was right. I hate this job. I should leave it.

"By the way," he shouts as my footsteps echo through the hollowed-out hallway. The space reminds me of the corridor sports players walk through before descending onto the field. "Greg wants you to stop by!"

I raise an arm, letting my floppy hand speak for me. Si laughs. *Here we go.* Earlier, I texted Greg, our show's head producer, my direct supervisor, and my ex-boyfriend, to inform him I was stuck on the train. He lambasted me in three consecutive replies, saying that it was my responsibility to anticipate the possibility of something like that happening. My job is too important. He said I'm already operating at a deficit. *Whatever the hell that means.* And of course, he added, I am paid well enough to find a place to live closer to work. He likes throwing how much money I make in my face. I regret every second of every day that I spent being Greg's girlfriend. What was I thinking? He has always been a douchebag.

I'm overheating as I stomp down the "unincor-porated" corridor. My office is on the sixteenth floor of the new super postmodern Industrial Entertain-ment Complex in Midtown Manhattan. Above the underground level, the building is primarily reflec-tive glass. The area we call the dungeon, where I am now, is three interconnected u-shaped hallways left over from the original structure built in the 1970s. One hallway provides access to the studios. One hallway allows access to above-the-line offices. The other corridor gives access to below-the-line offices where I work. The very important people like my mom access their offices on the very top floors through the modern lobby at the busy street level, entering under the grand marquee and being greeted by Lucien and Augustus, the dapperly uniformed bellmen. Their arrival is way fancier than this.

Luckily, my side of the building is far enough

from Greg's. Sometimes I can go the whole day without seeing his face, and those are the best ten to twelve hours I spend at this place. I don't even know how I was ever able to look at him on the mornings I woke up next to him or stomach him on top of me and inside of me. He's such an asshole. Greg is not unattractive.

On the contrary, he has a boy next door cuteness with James Spader, as Steff McKee in *Pretty in Pink* jerk tendencies. He's convinced his opinion is always the most important. He's undoubtedly pompous, and I just learned a few Wednesdays ago that he's ultra terrible in bed.

"I should really find another job," I whisper as the elevator stops climbing and the doors slide open. I've lost track of how many times I've declared that since I woke up.

It's nice and warm in this hallway, cozy even. It's colder on our side of the building. I say good morning to everyone I pass. As usual, in the a.m., people are clutching coffee and walking fast. There's so much work to do at a production studio in a day. That's why I'm so peeved that Greg is wasting our time. This is New York City. A quarter of the employees are late for work every day. There are always multiple train stoppages and traffic that grinds to a halt. Anything can happen. Last month, while walking, Judy in accounting narrowly avoided being clobbered to death by an air conditioner unit falling from someone's tenth-floor window.

I check the time on my cellphone before I enter Greg's office. I'm only twenty-three minutes late. He's just flexing his weak muscles and being a certified asshole. Now, I'm super peeved, which is why I push open his door with gusto.

"What do you want?" I growl, rushing into his office.

Greg withdraws deeper into his cushy executive chair, gleaming at me with a smug smile. "Late again."

I don't sit because I don't want him to think I will give him more face time than necessary. "You know why I'm late. I texted you."

Greg swivels from side to side, pinning me with his arrogant eyes. "You're the one who chose to live where the subway service is spotty."

I press my finger against my temple as I stare at his face. Look at him... He knows he can screw with me, and I won't do anything about it. I could complain to my mom, but he knows I won't. I try avoiding her more than I do him.

"I'm trying to figure out if that's even an appropriate thing for my boss to say?" I finally say.

I detect a hint of a smile on his lips. "You make enough money to live in this neighborhood."

He's baiting me, but I refuse to chomp down on his hook. "What do you want, Greg? Why am I here?"

"You've been late three times in six months."

I bristle. "I think that's a perfect record because I can name at least twelve other people that have been late more days than that. The only difference is you don't want to screw with them. You want to screw with me. Why is that Greg?" I let my icy glare burn him to the core. "Is it because I broke up with you?"

He stops swiveling to tap his pen on a notebook. The page on top has a to-do list scribbled on it. I spot my name written at least twice. I see he has me on the brain.

Greg eyeballs me, seething. "Don't flatter yourself, Xena."

He's still watching me with that expression I've come to loathe. It's not lust or even casual admiration. It's not even hate or dislike. It's judgment. And, as usual, it works. My anger rescinds into nothingness. I can't help but feel icky, like I'm a bad girl, and he's permanently right.

Finally, Greg narrows his eyes so intensely that he's squinting. "You have an essential job. You're almost above the line. If you can't hold yourself to a higher standard, then maybe you don't deserve to be a line producer. You were never late when you were a production manager. But then, you lived with me."

My anger's back with a vengeance. I feel a sheen of sweat on my forehead, and I'm light-headed as I clear my throat because I want him to hear me loud and clear. "I never lived with you. But I can recall several occasions when we were late together. Like one of the thousand times Fido defecated in my shoes or my purse, or the six or seven times your dog pissed on my coat."

Greg laughs dismissively. "That's quite a stretch, Xena. You went from a thousand to six or seven."

"Once is too much!" I shout at the top of my lungs. I'm shaking now because I'm beyond triggered. "You didn't even try to train him to respect my personal property. And you know what I think?" I step closer. I'm not myself. I feel like I'm having an out-of-body experience. "I think you liked it. Fido is you. You are Fido. You are projecting through him.

Poor Fido. It's you who wanted to piss on my shit, and you made that poor animal do it for you. He's supposed to be man's best friend, but you've weaponized him against me!"

Greg falls back against his chair, laughing mockingly. "What is that, Xena? Quack psychology from your cousin?"

I shake my head while glaring at him. He's so far from self-awareness. Talking to him further about this is pointless. The guy doesn't even believe childhood wounds can affect how you are today. I mean, that's just common sense, and he's just another person who refuses to look at himself and admit that perhaps he's fucked up like the rest of us.

"And I gave you money for those shoes," he adds.

"Only after I broke up with you."

"Who broke up with whom is debatable."

I open my mouth to lambast him, but I can't—I just can't anymore. Because my head hurts and my throat aches from shouting. I'm still shivering too. Gosh, I think I hate him.

"So, are you writing me up? Or are we done?" I'm tired of looking at his beady little face.

"You know I can't do that," he says, the picture of calm as he picks up his pen again.

I snort bitterly. He wants to mention my mom and Jane Chippy, who's VP of Production and Development, and she's my godmother. Greg always stops short of saying just that. *Wimp.*

He's reading what he's written in his notebook. "You missed adding the pre-production dinner to the show's budget."

"What?" I bark, intensifying my frown now that I'm in a worse mood than while stuck on the train. "There is no pre-production dinner. We don't even do preproduction dinners. There has never been a preproduction dinner. Now... I can budget for one, but don't sit there and pretend as if it's something I missed. Since we've never talked about a pre-production dinner, I never missed it." I'm trembling because I know he just wanted to say "missed" and apply it to me. That's him being judgy. And whenever he does this to me, I become eerily aware that Jojo often makes me feel this way.

"Calm down, Xena," he says, flopping his hand dismissively.

Now he's patronizing me. It takes everything in me not to shout, "No. You calm down!" But I choose not to give him the satisfaction of me further losing control while he pretends to keep it together.

I'm watching him examine me. I always thought his gray eyes resembled those of a cat. He looks so harmless, but he isn't. If I let him, he would pound my self-esteem into grains of sand. My chest rises high and falls low. He's not smirking outwardly, but inwardly he is. I know it. He relishes getting me worked up.

"A dinner. Got it," I say, impressing myself with how unrattled I sound, even though it is very Dr. Jekyll and Mr. Hyde.

"Tonight," he adds as he nonchalantly underlines something on the notebook page.

A bitter laugh escapes me. "Are you serious?"

"Dinner will be at *Treasures* at nine." He's looking at me as if daring me to have a problem with it.

My jaw has locked my mouth open as I watch his pen circle the word *Treasure*. "Treasure Grove's restaurant. Lynx's sister?" I'm asking, but the words aren't coming out.

"Who..." I say, unable to finish asking who made the reservation. Who's invited? I'm used to budgeting for wrap parties; larger venues are needed for those events. Also, Treasure is pretty pricy. I would have to figure out how to cover the bill.

"It's for the above-the-line personnel...." he clarifies.

I sigh with relief because that'll keep the cost low enough. Also, I'm not expected to be there.

"And you," he adds.

Gripped by disappointment, I go rigid. "Me?"

"I want you there," he says, fiddling casually with some papers on his desk.

"Why?"

"Because it's your job. That'll be all." He waves me away like I'm a peon.

I stand still for a few beats, and he's already tapping on his cell phone. Frankly, I don't have the energy to go another round with this guy. So, without another word, I turn my back on him and hope I don't run into Lynx Grove tonight at Treasure Grove's restaurant. I mean, really... What are the odds?

# SIX
## XENA ST. JAMES

14 Hours Later

I'm ready to put today behind me, but I can't because I have this goddamn dinner to attend. I'm not even hungry. After leaving Greg's office, everything that could go wrong went wrong. Plus, I had this nagging feeling that everybody I worked with knew something I didn't, and nobody was brave enough to tell me what that was. They're all so intimidated by itty-bitty Greg.

I grit my teeth because I hate that he's seen me naked.

Just so I could be on time for dinner at 9:00 p.m. because nobody does anything early in this damn city, I caught an Uber home from the office.

When I arrived at my apartment, the heat was on until after I showered and changed into a clingy, silk blue dress with black patent leather Mary Jane stilettos. Studying my image in the mirror, I denied that I went a step too far to look good for dinner because of my slim odds of running into Lynx Grove at his sister's restaurant. I don't even know why I care. I should stop caring.

I paid to take another Uber to the restaurant because it's chilly tonight and I wanted to arrive early enough to inquire about the reservation. I had gotten so busy in meetings with our costume and casting departments later in the day that I forgot to call the restaurant and ask who made the reservation. However, upon arrival, I was stunned to see that Greg had already arrived and had a very blonde woman with him. There's something about seeing the two of them together that makes me restless. That's why I haven't gone in yet. I'm standing about fifty feet from the restaurant with my hands shoved in my coat pockets while I shiver from the cold. I've never seen that woman before. However, she seemed to be conversing with George Cunningham and Liz Daughtery, both producers on the show, like they were colleagues. Also, Greg stuck by the woman's side like glue. And he kept glancing at the door as if waiting for me to walk in. He's going to put on a show as soon as he sees me. This I know for sure.

I groan inwardly. I wish I had trusted the right side of my gut and stayed at home. I knew Greg was up to something, but the randomness of his choosing Treasure of all places to have dinner tonight, made me throw caution to the wind.

"Xena," a voice calls from behind as if happy to see me. I bite down on my back teeth to keep from shivering as I turn to Marie Leeds, one of the writers.

Seeing a friendly face is a relief, so I don't have to force a smile. "Marie!"

Since Marie's a hugger, she hugs me.

"You're going to catch your death out here," she says, squeezing my arms

I keep going with my smile in response. There's no need to share that I'd rather turn into an ice cube than step into the trap Greg has prepared for me.

"Well, come on. Let's get inside." She hooks her arm around mine.

Admittedly, her body heat is so refreshing, even though it feels like a boulder sits in my chest as we head toward the restaurant.

"Preproduction dinner, that's new," she says. It sounds like she's leaving her comment open-ended, waiting for me to remark.

Maybe she thinks I know something about it. "Well, I'm just as surprised as you."

I feel her arm tense up. Wow, she's shocked that I didn't know about the dinner.

Marie's happy expression doesn't waver. "Well, at least it's at Treasure. I've been trying to get a reservation for months." She reaches out and opens the door. "After you!"

---

Ten Minutes Later

As usual, the person who's about to get the stick shoved up their ass is the last to know it. I hate the entertainment business. And when I walked into the restaurant, Greg pretended not to see me. He's been introducing everyone to Helena Johansson and saying cryptic shit like, "You're going to be seeing a lot of her around" and "You'll be able to rely on her."

I also learned that Helena made tonight's reservation. Apparently, she's a friend of one of the managers. Greg's been repeating that. I'm this close to divulging that I could've gotten a reservation here too. Granted, I would have to swallow my pride to do it. But if securing that reservation was going to be like pie in Greg's face, I would've called Lilly and asked her to ask Orion to ask his sister-in-law if she could reserve us a table. It might've worked. I'm pissed that he didn't give me the opportunity to try it.

I'm not wholly present, though, as we're being led to our table by the hostess. I tell myself to relax. I could be reading this all wrong. Maybe tonight is not about embarrassing me. I mean… Everything doesn't have to be about me.

"There are name cards on the table," Greg announces. He's watching me read the white paper placards with gold lettering.

I find my name and then glare at him. I was wrong. He intends to mess with me. I've been placed right across from him and Helena.

My head is spinning and swimming. It's too late to run away from whatever Greg has planned.

"Ooh," Marie, who's been seated to my right, says. She's excited about something. "Famous people alert."

I hadn't intended to look because all I can think

about is how to exit as fast as possible. But I allow myself to glance at who Marie's beaming at, and it's my bad luck that I'm staring into the eyes of Lynx Grove.

"That's Lynx Grove. His sister owns this restaurant, doesn't she?" Marie asks.

---

I ONLY REMEMBER to take off my coat because I'm overheating. Could tonight get any worse? A beautiful woman, who's more in Lynx's league than I am, sits beside him. She caught us looking at each other, so she leaned her shoulder against his and whispered something in his ear. The woman proved that he actually lied to me. They are obviously a couple. Marie said the guy, who turned around to see perhaps who Lynx was staring at, is Alex Shaw, a professional baseball player. I know that because Marie slapped me on the thigh and told me. I would hate Lynx more for being a liar if I had any more hate to give—Greg has absorbed all of it.

I'm still studying Helena, trying to figure out the deal with her. Why is she here? Is this Greg's way of showing off his new girlfriend? I mean, did he think I'd be jealous? Visually, Helena and Greg make a compatible couple because they're the same height and weight. I'm two inches taller than he is, which is probably why he always felt the urge to dominate me, and when he couldn't overpower me, he let his dog pee in my shoes. *Asshole.*

Now that our orders have been taken and I can't put all my focus on the menu, I try to avoid the exaggerated way in which Greg beams at Helena. I know better than anyone else; he's never loved anything or anyone that much. But Helena can't stop directing her curiosity at me. And then, there's Lynx, who I avoid looking at as though he's Medusa, and one glance will turn me into stone. This night can't get any worse, and my stomach's rumbling wave of anxiety won't disappear.

"He keeps staring at you," Marie whispers in my ear.

I'm aware of who she's referring to. I can feel Lynx's attention on me, and against my better judgment, I give into the cosmic pull I've been fighting and let my gaze venture across the restaurant to connect with his. I'm trapped in his stare, and actually, it's not so bad. Maybe I don't dislike him as much as I should. On the contrary, I'm grateful he showed me what expert fucking feels like. Although he's a cheater, his girlfriend must be completely sexually satisfied. *The asshole.*

Greg twists to look over his shoulder. Of course, he would wonder what has taken my attention off him. He must've found what he was looking for because he stands suddenly, obstructing my view of Lynx.

"People, if you haven't met Helena yet, although I'm sure you have. She's personable and likable." He smiles down giddily at the woman who's sitting next to him. But Helena presses her lips tightly. I think she's uncomfortable about being an unwilling participant in Greg's sideshow.

I fold my arms against my chest. Greg is definitely insinuating that I am not personable or likable. However, everybody knows that I am. I'm fuming, and keeping my breath even is becoming increasingly more challenging.

"She's been hired as Xena's co-line producer." He decides to look at me with a sinister grin, and I swear I see the devil in his eyes. "She's what's needed to help that part of production run smoother and more efficiently. That job requires a lot…." He tilts his head as his cunning eyes narrow a pinch. "More. And that's why we need two hands on deck."

The world around me feels like it's fallen into the background, and there is nobody in the restaurant except my enemy and me. "Four." The growl in my voice surprises me. The word came out of me like a rumble of thunder.

Greg's lips are parted like he wants to continue speaking, but he's watching me as though I'm a car crash he can't turn away from.

"My hands and her hands make four hands. Your math is wrong," I say, clutching the table's edge. My head feels detached from my body as I glare at everyone around me. "And nobody's going to stand up for me? Huh?"

"Xena get ahold...."

My finger shoots out and up like a missile. "Shut up Greg!"

My grimace stops on the people that I work with every day. "Help me out, guys. Help me the fuck out!" Because I need someone to finally stand up for me—someone besides the one person I can't count on anymore because she can't see beyond her new-love bubble.

One by one, my eyes beckon my coworkers to speak up for me for once. But no one seems to be willing to risk their job. I get it. This is an expensive city, production jobs are not a dime a dozen, and there's always a lesser or more qualified person waiting in the wings, ready and willing to fill our shoes. And maybe I can learn to play a harsher game at work. I could use my mom and godmother to my benefit. But alas, although my teeth are sharp, I don't have the will or stomach to bite and draw blood.

"You know what?" I bump the table as I bound to my feet. Now I'm glaring down at Greg, and it's just the way I like it. Greg hates that I'm taller than him. I shoot my arm out, pointing my finger at the people to my right. "Their silence speaks volumes. They're scared of you because you're a vengeful little prick. Even your dog is a projection of your shit!"

"Leave Fido out of this," Greg retorts.

"Ha," I scoff at how much that got a rise out of him. I don't care anymore. I don't need him. Screw him and this job. "Yeah… You're never going to change. Poor Fido," I say, shaking my head with pity. "He will die being you, and then you will replace and train the next Fido to be just like you too!" I raise two fingers in front of my face and jerk them as I growl, "I quit you asshole. Deuces."

Only now that I've decided to storm off do I feel Marie's hand on my thigh as if she's supporting me the best way she can. Her touch only reminds me of one thing. I'm not done yet.

"Oh that's mature of you," Greg says in that annoyingly calm but snarky way of his.

"Oh, and Helga, or Helena, whatever your name is." I snatch my coat off the back of my chair, building up to say the meanest thing I've ever said to anyone. "He's a terrible lay. I hadn't orgasmed since the day I met Greg, but he"—I point at Lynx, who's already watching me—"broke my dry spell in an earthshaking way."

I storm off, putting on my coat and distance between me and that table of cowards and one asshole. But I'm aware that I screwed up royally. I threw Lynx under the bus, and he didn't deserve that. We were two consenting adults the night we had sex, and he was upfront about our actions not turning into anything serious. I hope I hadn't made things sour between him and his date, who possibly could be his girlfriend.

I'm losing my mind. I'm losing myself, and it's been happening for quite a while. As I sweep past curious diners, one thing is for sure. Even though I feel like crap, I'm light on my feet, and perhaps that's because I've done what I should've done a long time ago and quit that horrible job of mine.

"It looks like she was pointing at you, Lynx?" Penelope says, squinting as she and half the diners watch Xena storm out into the chilly night. "And what did she say?"

I glare at Penelope, who's watching me demandingly. Firstly, she's not supposed to be here, and now I regret not sending her away when she and her friend Jess showed up.

I asked Archer Donovan, my head of player and owner relations for the Ramblers to dinner. I also asked my sister to make a reservation and put us in a quiet spot where he and I could talk. However, when Penelope and her friend showed up, we switched tables, and I decided to put what I wanted to discuss with him on ice.

"Excuse me," I say as I push my chair back.

Penelope puts a hand on my forearm, applying enough pressure to convey that she doesn't want me to get up. "Where are you going?"

"I'll be right back."

And I'm off to catch up with Xena.

---

I'M OUTSIDE, and cold air expands in my lungs as I whip my head from left to right. I spot Xena tapping on the screen of her cellphone. I take a moment to admire her graceful figure in a long trench coat. Her heels are slender, and her hair sits in a messy bun at the nape of her neck. She has the kind of sex appeal that happens without trying. I noticed that about her when I first admired her in Lilly's apartment. Then she told me I made her panties wet, and no matter how hard I tried to get that out of my head, I couldn't. That's why I returned to Lilly's apartment. I wanted her so much I would've burst if she denied me. I want her right now. I want her to get in the backseat of my car with me and let me take her to my place. I know what I'll do to her first.

Xena quickly looks up and over at me. She startles, and then I think she just rolled her eyes. I get it, she hates me for not calling and following up after we made love. I wish I had a valid explanation for ghosting her but I don't.

"Sorry about that scene I made in your sister's restaurant," she says as I approach her. "He just ugh." She closes her eyes to shiver.

I raise my eyebrows. *Is she apologizing to me?* Even though her eyes are watery and red, and her skin is drained of undertones, the city lights casting their glares across her face make her as pretty as an angel. I desire to touch her skin, kiss her soft lips, and whisper against her mouth, "Settle down, Beautiful. *You* have *me*," and that scares the hell out of me.

"I just…" She says, closing her eyes as I stop in front of her. She shakes her head as if whipping her thoughts out of her mind. "He's the problem, not me."

"That guy's name is Greg?" I ask, wanting to know more about her object of scorn.

Her fawn eyes grow wide with horror. "You know him?"

Damn, I want to wrap her up and draw her near. "No," I say, my throat warm and thick. "But you said, 'Shut up, Greg.'"

She looks even more terrified. "Oh, my God." Xena drops her head, covering her eyes. "I made a fool of myself." As she inhales deeply, she looks up again. "Greg is my ex-boss and ex-boyfriend." She grunts, frowning even more like she just remembered something. "My mom is going to flip out."

The cold has seeped through my shirt and nips at my skin. To warm my hands, I shove them into my pants pockets as I grin vaguely. "Jojo? I can't picture the pricetag lady flipping out."

"That's right." She sighs. "You're a fan. You know happy-go-lucky pricetag lady is an act, I hope."

I tighten my arms against my chest to keep from shivering and raise an eyebrow flirtatiously. "Now I do."

Xena studies me as if she's seeing something I'm trying to hide. Then, finally, she blurts out a laugh. "I told her about you, and you know what she said?"

I raise my eyebrows curiously. "What?"

"She said while tipping her whisky to me, and I quote, 'that shit didn't happen by osmosis, Sweetheart.'"

I laugh, picturing the pricetag lady drunk on whisky and taking a self-absorbed victory lap. And then, it's like the moon appears over a torrential sky when Xena also smiles.

We're gazing into each other's eyes, and I feel like I'm tumbling into her. *What is happening to me?*

"And I'm sorry about telling the world you gave me earthshaking orgasms. I really wanted to stomp on Greg's fragile ego."

"Oh," I say, piping up. So that's what she said. *Nice.* "Earthshaking?" *Shit.*

Xena's beautiful eyes expand. "You hadn't heard that part?"

I shake my head as I recover my voice. "I only saw that you were in distress."

"Well, I'm sorry I opened my mouth about it, being that you said you didn't want to have a relationship with me and...."

"I'm sorry about that," I blurt out because I don't want to hear her reflect my words back to me. "I was wrong to say that to you."

Her grunt sounds like agreeance. "It was definitely a jerk move, but I had sex with you anyway. Did your girlfriend hear what I said?"

I want to smile, but I stop myself. She's fishing. I can tell by the eager way she's waiting for my reply. I think Xena's still attracted to me, and I like it.

"She's not my girlfriend," I whisper, battling another intense desire to shiver.

Xena tilts her head to one side and eyes me suspiciously.

"She's not," I affirm. "I didn't even invite her to the restaurant. She just showed up."

Her sexy eyes narrow a bit more.

I squint curiously. "What's that look for?"

"She was showing the world you belonged to her, Lynx. So don't lie. And maybe the fact that I will never let you fuck me again will help you with the truth."

I step closer to her. "Is that so?"

A breath catches in her throat. "Yes," she whispers.

Her wide eyes are on me like they were when I pumped into her. There was too much going on inside me. All those fucking feelings I experienced. I had no idea where they came from.

"But," she starts, and I remember to breathe. "You said something that night."

"I said a lot." I want to kiss her.

"True. But you also said I turned sex into a power struggle and that you knew there was something about me."

She's waiting for me to say something. Oh, shit,

I'm hard. Because Xena doesn't get herself at all, maybe that's not good for me. She said I wasn't an angel, and I'm not. How can I reveal that what I desire and who she is fit together like missing puzzle pieces?

"You know what? Never mind," she says, kicking the toe of her shiny black shoes against the concrete. "I have bigger problems than what you think about me. I mean, as of now, I'm unemployed."

Her cellphone dings and she searches up the street.

Suddenly, I know what to do. "How about you work for me?" I'm taking my wallet out of my pocket. I'm glad I have it with me.

"Ha!" she scoffs mockingly. "I'm good, but thanks."

She doesn't stop me from finding my business card and handing it to her. "I'm working on something special and can use somebody like you."

"Somebody like me?" she says, frowning at my card as if it offends her.

"You're a line producer?" I ask, leading her away from whatever harmful intentions she thinks I might have.

"Was," she says, holding her hand up as a red

compact car stops at the curb before us. "And don't you own a sports team?" She shakes her head. "I don't know anything about sports."

I don't retract my card even though I can tell that's exactly what she wants me to do. "The job is not about sports. It's about something else." I glance over my shoulder and through the windows of Treasure. "It's why I'm here tonight. Listen, I'll pay you whatever you make now."

"Ha!"

"I'm serious. Take my card. Think about it."

Xena's pretty face watches me askew. I'm freezing my ass off, but I can stand the cold much longer to hang out with her for a few more minutes.

"How about I take you home?" I ask because my cock is begging me to convince her to stay in my bed tonight. It's saying, fuck Archer and Penelope. It has better things to do.

She snorts a cynical chuckle. "I thought you wanted to give me a job."

Her eyes are on my mouth, which is the only reason I know I'm moistening my lips like I'm getting ready to kiss her. Also, she takes my card, and that's a good sign.

"Lynx! You're going to freeze to death out here," Penelope bellows from the restaurant door.

Xena rips her gaze off me to see Penelope. I ignore Penelope. Instead, I experience loss as Xena opens the back door of the red car. "Okay. I'll think about it," she says. "Have a good night, Lynx."

She's quickly in the back seat, closing the door behind her. I'm focused on the diminishing rear bumper, committing the license plate to memory. But I don't feel the chill nipping at my body anymore. My cock is softening too. It knows it won't feel Xena tonight.

She'll call, I think.

She will definitely call.

# EIGHT

# XENA ST. JAMES

## Friday, The Next Day

I hardly got any sleep last night as I lay in bed, bothered by a flood of worries. I also kept staring at Lynx's business card. I held it in front of my face, studying the gold letters and how sturdy the paper was. I set it on the end table beside my bed and stared at it longer. I wondered if he wanted to offer me a job so that he could have sex with me again. But that's ridiculous. Surely a successful man like Lynx Grove wouldn't play so loose and frivolous with his business? And he said he's willing to pay me the salary I made at Rank Media. Thinking about how much money I won't make anymore placed a lump of doom in my belly. The bills I've accumulated over the years, mainly in credit card debt, are too high for me to be unemployed. But I'm not sure it would be appropriate to accept Lynx's job offer, even though it's a great offer. It's so tempting now that I'm standing at my mom's office door, summoning my courage before entering.

My mom called less than an hour after I got home last night and requested to see me in her office today at 10:00 a.m. I wasn't surprised to hear from her before the paint dried. News travels fast in the entertainment industry.

I suck in one last deep, long breath through my nose and tell myself to stop stalling. As I exhale, I open the solid, blond-wood door to my mom's impeccable office, which resembles a Pottery Barn ad layout. Before I barely have one foot over the threshold, and before the light from the gray sky invades my eyes, Jojo says, "Sit, Lovebug," as if she sensed me standing outside her office the whole time.

My body is tight, and my head swirls as I do exactly as she says. Only now do I realize she's on a phone call.

"Uh-huh," she keeps repeating.

I'm relieved we don't have to get into it right away. I have some time to relax a bit and restrategize. I think about what I want moving forward. I have savings in the bank. My dad, jazz pianist Hollis St. James, taught me how to save to live comfortably during rainy days. He says he made it big by learning how to store the extra. It got him through very lean times when money coming in couldn't keep up with money going out, and he didn't have to give up on his dreams and get a job to survive. I have about thirty thousand in the bank. Plus, I have a final check coming my way. That's another seven grand. My rent is thirty-three hundred a month. To save extra cash, I could live off one and a half meals a day and a lot of green tea. My cell phone bill is only eighty dollars a month. I don't need cable or television, period. I'm okay with reading books or playing my guitar to entertain myself. Plus, I go out with my girlfriends a lot. There's hardly ever a dull night when living in New York City.

"Jane, just email me the report, and let me deal with the rest," Jojo demands.

It's Jane Chippy, VP of development, my mom's best friend, and my godmother.

My mom glances at me as if chastising me for forcing her to have this little meeting she's arranged between us. "Yes. She's here."

The hairs on the back of my neck bristle at the realization that she and Jane have been discussing me. *Great… just great.* I fight the urge to glance at the door. I'm ready to go. When Jane and Jojo combine powers, I'm at a severe disadvantage. But I can't leave yet, so I stare at my mom, looking for any signs that she'll go easy on me. I don't want to fight. After yesterday with Greg, I'm tired of fighting.

I've looked at my mom probably a billion times, and her presentation never ceases to amaze me. Her chic business style feels effortless. Like today, she's wearing a brown silk blouse with a cowl's neck collar. The color makes her look regal. My mom always knows how to style herself to appear as if she's the most important person anyone will meet that day. And she probably has the price tag for the blouse tucked under the sleeves' cuff, ready to share it with the first potential shopper who compliments her on her outfit. Curious about how she put the rest of her ensemble together, I look through her glass-topped desk. Jojo's very sharp today in cashmere, off-white, wide-legged dress pants, and brownish gold closed-toe leather pumps. As usual, she's head-to-toe stylish.

Finally, Jojo drops her desk phone hard on the receiver. "What the hell happened last night?"

I will not get rattled. "I quit, Mom. I can't work for Greg anymore," I say.

She always closes her eyes when she sighs as if she's made so weary by the tiniest thing that disturbs her peace of mind.

"Have you read *In the Know?*" she asks.

I grimace. "The gossip blog? Why would I read that?"

First, Jojo observes me like she's just caught me eating every last Oreo in the cookie jar. Then, she puts her hand on her computer's mouse. Her fingernails are perfectly manicured, and the polish matches the color of her blouse.

Jojo cranes her neck forward and focuses on her computer screen. "I'll paraphrase. Last night Jojo O'Leary's daughter," she pauses to throw a scolding glance in my direction. "Xena St. James announced to patrons at Treasure, a popular restaurant in Chelsea that attracts the rich and famous... Pass that. Treasure Grove's hot... Pass that. Pass that...," My mother mumbles. When my mom arrives at what she's looking for, she throws me another chastising look again. "It says you announced that she hadn't experienced an orgasm until billionaire Lynx Grove gave her several of them."

I'm like a mouse facing down a hungry cat. Did I say that exactly?

"Are you denying this?" she asks, studying my intense frown.

"Well, I didn't say that exactly."

She makes that famished sigh again. "What am I going to do with this, Xena? I don't have time for this shit."

"I'm sorry" is all I can come up with.

"Sorry for what?"

"Embarrassing you."

Jojo's examination of me deepens until she grunts. "Right..." My mom knows I'm bullshitting. I'm not sorry at all. "Do you understand how fast unsavory publicity could tank my ratings?"

I stop myself from rolling my eyes. "Yes. I'm very well aware of your ratings, Mom. I've been aware of them my whole life." And with that reply, I fired the first shot.

Jojo wiggles her finger. "Don't get sassy with me. And you're not quitting." She casually puts on her glasses like her word is final. "I understand your issues with Greg. And I agree, he's a moron. If Burt weren't his uncle, he'd be panhandling on 42nd Street. We have a spot for you on my show." She's fiddling through documents like she's going to present me with a contract.

"No, Mom," I say loud and clear. "I don't want to work on your show because we'll end up killing each other. And I love you too much to kill you." And that's the stone-cold truth.

"It's not up for debate," she says dismissively. "You need a job, and this is where you work. And you're my line producer. We've sent Axel to...."

I shake my head vigorously. "No, Mom. No." I'm on my feet, suppressing the urge to run away from her as fast as I can. "I've got a job."

My mom falls back in her chair and eyes me suspiciously. "Are you lying to me, Lovebug?"

My eyebrows shoot up as I lie. "No," I declare in a high-pitched voice, trying to sound convincing as possible.

She folds her arms over her chest. "And where is this job?"

"A private equity firm in Chelsea," I say.

"Doing what?" she's quick to ask.

"Financial analyst," I reply quicker.

"For whom?"

"That's private," I press my lips in a defiant smile.

"For whom?" she says louder.

I shake my head. The thing is, I'm not making up the job. Before I tucked myself into bed last night, I skimmed the job market. I saw one announcement that initially caught my attention. However, the pay was commensurate to experience, which means they want to get highly qualified people through the door just to tell them the job pays peanuts. That's why I scratched the position off my list.

"For whom, Xena St. James," Jojo demands.

Luckily my cellphone rings in my purse, and I get to look away from her eyes which are playing a Jedi mind trick on me that's close to working. It's Lilly.

"Oh, they're calling me now," I say, glaring at the screen. "We're doing all the preliminary paperwork." I silence my device as I take two giant steps to the door. "But don't worry about me, Mom. I'll be thirty next April, which means, I'm already a whole adult who takes care of herself."

She scowls at my sarcasm and is about to say something, but thankfully her desk phone rings. I'm surprised it sat silent for as long as it had. Every single phone my mom owns is constantly making noise. She's the busiest person I know.

"Yes, St. Pete's next week," she roars into the receiver. I've pissed her off.

"Bye, bye, love you," I say as I'm halfway out the door.

I don't give her time to call my name. The door is closing behind me. My strides are long and quick, and the corridor seems to be extending because I can't reach the elevator fast enough. *No.* Not the elevator. I'll take the stairs.

But suddenly, my feet stop moving and closing my eyes, I squeeze the bridge of my nose. What am I doing? That's my mom I'm running away from as if I'm a petulant child. I don't like how this feels.

I look at the phone still in my hand. There's only one next move to make. I call Jojo. I'm sure she won't answer because she's on a business call, and her business always comes first.

"Hello," my mom says. Her tone is flat. She's obviously upset with me.

My eyebrows shoot up in surprise. I planned to leave a message, but instead, the words, "Sorry about how I stormed out of your office," gush out of my mouth.

"Your apology is accepted," she says in the same voice.

I squeeze my eyes shut as my feet want to take

me back to her. But then what? My stance hasn't changed. "Mom," my voice cracks.

"Yes."

"Can I please do this myself? Don't put me in this position. I mean, you raised a strong and capable woman. And yes, I've made some rash decisions lately, but I can do this on my own. That's all." I have no idea what I just said, but I felt it strongly. My heart knocks against my chest as I wait for her to tell me I sound ridiculous. I would love Jojo's approval, but I'm already walking to the elevator.

Jojo has been quiet for several seconds, and then she says, "Okay."

I stiffen. "Okay?" I can't believe she didn't come at me from a different angle.

"Yes," she says tightly. "As you know, I'm in St. Petes for most of next month, but I'll be back for Thanksgiving. You can tell me all about your new job as... What was it again?"

Oh shit, what did I say? I think hard and take what I hope is a lucky guess. "Financial Analyst," I sing optimistically.

"Good," she says right away, which is a sign that I had gotten it right. "I can't wait to hear all about how you like your job as a financial analyst."

# NINE
## XENA ST. JAMES

I can always feel the unseen contents of New York City on my face as I walk up Columbia Avenue. When I left my mother's floor and stepped out into the lobby of the entertainment complex, I found Lynx's business card in my wallet. Feeling butterflies flapping around in my stomach, I called him. He didn't answer, and I almost chickened out and ended the call without leaving a message. I could find another job before Jojo returns from St. Petes. I know a lot of people, and somebody always knows somebody who's hiring. But could I find a job that pays my current salary? Maybe—maybe not. I didn't want to chance it. So, I said, "Hi, Lynx. This is Xena. I'm curious about the opportunity you mentioned last night at the restaurant. I mean, I might be interested." And then I left my phone number.

I made it halfway to the subway station when my cell phone rang. It was him, and hearing his voice made me feel lightheaded. Lynx wanted to meet with me immediately, and now I'm taking a private elevator to the fifty-eighth floor of the building that houses his offices.

I'm nervous as hell as I watch the numbers change to 56 and 57. *How do I look?* I flatten my palms against my queasy stomach and then inspect my reflection in the metal panel before me.

"Shit." I smooth a wayward strand of hair on one side of my head.

I didn't think about dressing up when I left my apartment this morning. I figured the less ready for the office I appeared, the more my mom would get the hint that I wasn't going back to work for Rank Media. That's why I'm wearing slim-fitting black jeans, a black sweater, and a charcoal gray puffer coat with gray hiking boots. My curls are pulled back into a messy ponytail. This is how I look when Lilly and I go flea market shopping. We haven't done that in forever. Now I find myself missing my favorite cousin. I wonder if she and I will reclaim any parts of our former relationship. It seems her love for Orion has ruined us.

I'm battling another bout of missing Lilly intermingled with nerves of seeing Lynx again when the elevator stops with a ding. I plan to immediately find a restroom to make myself more presentable as the doors slide open. But before I can step out of the car, I'm being reeled into the most hypnotic eyes ever.

***

IT'S the complete picture that I'm faced with that has taken my voice away. Whenever I see Lynx, it's as if I'm experiencing him anew. He's tall, dressed in a nice fitting navy suit with a crisp white shirt and no tie. His hair is always a little unruly, and his eyes are naturally intense. Men should be made to earn the right to be so attractive. Especially one who informs a girl before experiencing the best sex of her life that he's not looking for a relationship, and neither does he spoon nor kiss. *Remember, Zeen...* This guy has more red flags than a ten-car pile-up at the Indy 500.

Lynx extends a long-fingered hand. "Hello, Xena."

The inside of my chest feels like it turns to mush when I complete the gesture. "Hi." I remember to smile.

His slow-building sideways smile gradually displays perfectly naturally, not artificially, white teeth. "You made it."

"I did." That came out too tightly. I don't want to seem nervous or even be nervous.

"I'm glad."

Neither of us has moved an inch since shaking hands. Oddly the elevators haven't closed me inside.

"So, um…" I maneuver around him as I step out and into the foyer. He rotates to keep me in sight. "I'm here about the job."

"I know."

Why am I nodding? *Say something, Xena.* "So, what's the job?"

He's doing that thing where I feel his eyes record every aspect of my face. I wonder if he reveres others this way. He's already struck me as an observant guy. I lift my shoulders, squeezing them together as I recall how unattractive I look at the moment. I want to say something else to distract him from looking at me that way, but it's his turn to say something.

"Right. My office is at the end of the hallway." He takes a step to clear the path. "After you."

I consent with a swift nod and then start walking. I want to cringe because I know he's getting an eyeful of me walking in my oversized coat with two pencil legs in bulky shoes. I'm definitely channeling Humpty Dumpty. *Grrr… I'm overthinking this.* How can I work for him if I'm so absurdly self-conscious around him? But I need a job, and he's hiring. That means I have to wear my big girl panties when I'm around him, and the crotch must stay dry.

# TEN
## XENA ST. JAMES

I meet Evie, Lynx's very pretty executive assistant. I thought for sure a man who doesn't do relationships has done her quite a few times, but she was wearing a fat diamond wedding ring with a gold band. Not only is Evie taken, but there's no hint of attraction in her eyes when she looks at Lynx—that's impressive.

As Lynx gives Evie instructions on how to onboard me after he and I talk, I take notice of the wooden block-style desk that Evie works behind— it's nice. She has two large monitors on each side of her 27" iMac computer. Six white armchairs are against the wall, separated by white acrylic end tables. To the right, a large conference room sits empty behind spotless glass. The windows beyond the large table with executive-sized chairs display a gorgeous city view of the immediate neighborhood. I like this space a lot. It has a great ambiance, and it feels rich. I don't know why I find that surprising. Lynx is by no means small potatoes. The man owns a successful professional baseball team. Also, he's from one of the wealthiest families in the world. I forget those things whenever I'm around him because he's so normal, even down to being an average commitment-phobic guy.

"Okay. After you." Lynx steps back so I can enter his office first.

He's the consummate gentleman, and I want to say that to him with an appreciative smile. But I must keep our interaction professional; after all, not going broke in a matter of months in this expensive city is on the line.

As I enter Lynx's office, I'm impressed by the 180-degree views of the city. His desk is made of the same wood as Evie's station, resembling a massive block with a tall-backed executive chair behind it. A tall metal floor lamp with a curved neck angles its silver shade toward one side of his desk. A full-sized bonsai tree is nestled in the crook of two floor-to-ceiling windows. I don't know, there's something very Lynx-like about the two decorative pieces.

"Have a seat over there," Lynx points his hand at a seating area with a plush royal blue velvet sofa, two matching armchairs, and a coffee table made of the same white acrylic as the end tables in his reception area.

"Sure," I say, confused about whether I should settle on the sofa or in one of the chairs. I glance at Lynx, smiling nervously. I figure I can't go wrong taking one of the chairs.

"Nice office," I say.

He sits in the chair congregating with mine. "Thank you." Lynx smooths his pants over his firm and muscular thighs. I'll never forget how much of a solid wall of muscle his body was when we screwed that night. "So, what I tell you today, stays between us."

I sit up straight, halting the act of lusting over him. He's ready to get down to business, and so am I. "Sure."

Lynx's magnetic eyes search my face yet again. I'm not sure he knows how often he pauses to pick me apart. *What is he looking for?* Perhaps he's seeking signs of whether I can be trusted. So, I press my lips, trying to smile convincingly until I realize how much I'm burning up under all the warm layers I'm wearing. "Sorry," I say as I unzip my coat.

Lynx bounds to his feet. "I'll take that for you."

Now that I'm out of my coat, I hand it to him, and he strides across the office to hang it on a coat tree. His physicality is perfect in every way. I bet women stare at him everywhere he goes. He must get hit on a hundred times a day. I wouldn't want to be his girlfriend. I think I dodged a bullet.

"Thank you," I say as he retakes his seat. I feel like I can finally be nice to him now that we're heading toward a strictly professional relationship. His impressive office and polished assistant—all is definitely forgiven.

Lynx smiles mildly. "You're welcome, Xena."

Suddenly Lynx appears to be all business as he clears his throat. "As I was saying. What I tell you and our business together must stay between us. And I've already figured out you're good at keeping a secret."

My eyebrows arch in surprise. "You have?"

He smirks like he's mulling over the punchline to a joke.

"What?" I'm extremely curious to learn what he thinks he knows about me.

"You haven't told Lilly about us."

"Oh. No. I haven't. But how did you know that?"

"I ran into her last Saturday while she was moving out of the building."

My shoulders slump. "Right. She offered me her apartment, and I probably should've taken it," I admit, thinking about how cold it was while I slept last night.

Lynx's eyebrows bounce as if he's processing new thoughts. "Are you looking for a new place to live?"

I exhale a long sigh past my lips, regretting not bulldozing past my pride to clench the keys to Lilly's old apartment. "I should be. Probably... soon."

Lynx grunts thoughtfully. I feel as if he has a response to what I just revealed because his mouth opens and closes twice before he abruptly readjusts in his seat. His back grips the chair like he's trying to sink into the cushion. "Why didn't you tell her about us?"

I shrug nonchalantly. "Because she doesn't need to know." I ponder how that conversation could've gone if I had spilled the beans to my cousin. "Plus, she would've wanted to discuss every angle of what happened and examine every moment between us ad nauseam."

Lynx's sexy mouth puckers thoughtfully. "Sounds fun."

I give him half a stink face. It does sound fun, but we should keep this all business. "I mean, did you tell anybody?" I'm confident he hasn't.

Lynx's hand shoots up to rub the back of his ear. "Yes, I did."

I yank my head back in shock. "You did?"

"I told my cousin Max."

"Oh," I say, keeping my lips stuck in the "O" shape. Max Grove knows I had sex with his cousin. Not only shit, but holy shit!

"Also, I want you to know I wasn't using you, Xena."

"Lynx," I utter suddenly to stop him from saying more. "It's okay. No harm, no foul. I just want to know what job you're offering me."

I feel dizzy under his scrutiny. I really didn't want to appear angry about what happened between us, but revisiting it makes me feel stupid but satisfied, and mixing those two sentiments makes quite a confusing existence. And right now, I don't want to be confused. I want to know what sort of work I'll be doing to make the same salary paid to me at Rank Studios.

"It's just…." I start, thinking I should take the

severity out of my previous remarks. He studies me carefully, waiting for me to finish what I want to say. "There's no use in stepping back into the past. We've trampled over those weeds, and now look where we are. I might work for you. And sex or discussing the sex we had, which I don't remember anymore, is the last thing we need to complicate things." Actually, I think there's one thing a woman will never forget, and that's the moment she experienced an intravaginal orgasm. He gave me three of them. So, I'm totally lying about forgetting the sex we had.

"I mean," I say, figuring I should further explain. "We had a one-night stand, and then that's it."

Lynx throws up a hand to silence me. "I understand, Xena." He said that in such a business-like voice. "So, I might sell my baseball team," he blurts.

The sharp change in subject feels jarring. "Okay." Nodding, I readjust in my seat until I'm wearing my all-business thinking cap.

"Nobody is to know what I just shared with you, and only four of us are privy to the information." He raises his thumb. "Max…" He raises his other fingers, counting up as he says, "my father, myself, and now you. Understand?"

My nodding feels frantic, so I stop doing it. "I do. Yes."

Lynx's naturally well-manicured eyebrows hover over his sultry eyes. "In your former job, you managed budgets and supervised operations and production processes."

"And a million other tasks."

"Like what?"

"Hiring, scheduling, putting out fires, reading and completing contracts, making reservations...." Fighting with Greg is on the tip of my tongue, but not only do I not say it because it's majorly inappropriate, but Lynx's penetrating gaze also silences me. There's something extraordinary about being in my position, being on the receiving end of his intense scrutiny. I'm the one who's captured his special attention. I wish he would stop looking at me that way, though, and I wish I didn't like it.

"Good." He clears his throat. "Very good."

"What's the job?" I blurt thoughtlessly. My nerves are getting the better of me, and I yell at myself to get a grip already.

Lynx rubs the back of his ear again. I've figured out he does that when he's nervous. And now I'm doubly worried as I wonder why the job he's offering me makes him so uneasy.

"When I graduated from the London School of Business," he says. "I had one goal: to take my seat in a high-level position in my family's business. I also thought that was my father's intention, but it wasn't."

I nod, letting him know that he has my undivided attention because I'm sure there's a moral to this story.

Lynx turns toward the windows to gaze off into the gray sky. *What a profile.* "Leo, my father, wanted me to start closer to the bottom while Max, who graduated a year earlier than me, was made co-CEO alongside him." He snorts bitterly, and the butterflies in my chest flutter as he sets his attention back on me. "I didn't find that fair, so I struck out on my own."

I'm on the edge of my seat and falling deeper into admiration of Lynx Grove as he tells me how his first major endeavor was the baseball team. He needed three-quarters of votes from existing owners to franchise a new club. He spent a year living in hotels, lobbying owners, convincing them that even though he was still in his twenties, he had what it took to be successful. To get the approval, he struck deals on top of deals. It also didn't hurt that he had a billion in the bank to back any losses, thanks to understanding how to invest his hefty family trust payments.

"But a few weeks ago," Lynx says, sounding like he's getting to the big point. "My father expressed that he's ready to step down and hand his key to the kingdom over to me."

I can't stop my jaw from dropping. "As Co-CEO of Grove Industrial Tech? *The* biggest tech company in the world."

"Yes."

"Wow," I mouth.

He's glaring at my mouth. I know it's not because he wants to kiss me because Lynx Grove doesn't kiss. I think it's just something he does, and it's like another nervous habit or something.

He rips his eyes away from me to grimace at his desk. "However, if I take the seat, I cannot own a competing business enterprise."

"But one is tech, and the other is professional sports," I say.

Lynx's eyes are back on me. It's almost like he's seeing me anew. I wonder what he's thinking until he says, "I know. It's not about competing interests. The issue is capital parity between two partners."

"Capital parity between partners," I say in a tone that asks for clarity.

"My family, the Groves, and the Lords. A merger between GIT and LTI will be announced soon."

"Oh."

One of his eyes narrows at my mouth again. I touch my lips. Right... They're forming an O. Maybe he thinks it's too expressive, too unprofessional. I sink my teeth into my bottom lip, and Lynx abruptly rubs the back of his ear as he tells me the demands of running his team, even though it's the off-season, it sucks up a lot of his time. He hasn't made a final decision about taking his father's seat, but there's a lot he needs to know about Grove Industrial Tech, or GIT, if, in fact, he chooses to give up his team.

"That means I need you to pick up the slack for me so that I can make an informed decision."

"I see," I barely say past my tight throat.

Lynx sets his magnetic eyes on me again, and my heart reverberates. Suddenly I admit to myself that working for Lynx Grove will not be easy, at least not in the beginning. I'm still attracted to him, but the more I see him, the less handsome he'll become. One day I'll be like Evie and have the ability to look at him like his striking good looks are not a big deal. I'm sure I'll be able to do it because I want this job. The executive-level duties are a challenge I welcome.

"I want you to keep track of any paperwork that lands in my hands from GIT. I'll have you sit in on most calls. You probably won't be able to make some, but I'll download you on what was said. I want you to read everything and tell me what you think. You'll be my second brain and second pair of eyes and ears. You'll accompany me to most business meetings that have to do with GIT. My cousin Max will be difficult. Don't take him personally. Also, we won't communicate by email, and none of our correspondence will be saved on a computer. Since your cousin is married to Orion Lord, and you and Lilly are close…."

"Less so these days," I say. "But still, I'll keep what I do here a top secret."

"Great."

I'm immovable as Lynx leans forward, widening his legs to rest his elbows on his knees. I try like hell not to view that enormous bulge between his legs. I want to say, dude, close your legs. How is a girl supposed to concentrate with something like that staring at her?

"I'd push myself to the brink and do all this myself. But I won't be at my best due to my issues with my father and family, which I explained beforehand." He narrows an eye and has the sexiest facial expression I have ever seen. "You see, Xena, I'm too angry with my family, which makes me emotional. I'm not saying emotions are weak. I built my club and made it successful because I love my players and my front and back offices. I love the league and other owners. I love Grover, who keeps the stadium grass in tip-top condition. And hundreds of others who keep my business operating at optimal levels. But anger, well, that emotion, will make me miss something significant. And I can't miss a thing if I choose to give up what I love."

I feel I will pass out from desire as Lynx and I focus on each other. All I want to do is maul this capable man's mouth. I want to feel his cock surge through me like a rocket. But I also have more clarity about the person he is. I thought he lied to me about not having a girlfriend. This man is no liar. I believe he's not in a committed relationship. However, I feel Lynx is all about the uncommitted relationship, which is why I must work on compartmentalizing our association into two categories— boss and possibly, maybe one day, we'll be friends.

"Does that mean my job will be temporary?" That has been worrying me.

"You'll have a job with me for as long as you want."

I grimace, worried. "What's my title?"

"How about *we* call you my Executive Business Manager?"

I chew on that for a second. Jojo will stay off my back if I'm Lynx Grove's Executive Business Manager. "I like it," I say jubilantly.

"But."

My smile fades.

"Until the deal is either done or I pass on it, when asked, you'll say you're working with me on personal accounting matters."

I wish I could look happy about that, but I can't.

"Is that okay with you?" he asks, perhaps reading the disappointment on my face.

There's no need to complain about my mommy issues. "No. It's fine." I sound fraudulently over-optimistic.

"So Xena, will you take the job?" he officially asks.

Our eye contact remains strong as I say, "Yes."

"Good," he says, throwing his arms up victoriously. "How much did you make at your previous place of employment?"

I tell him.

"I'll triple that, plus all medical."

"No," I say, shaking my head insistently. "There's no need to overpay me."

"Xena." He makes sure he has my full attention. "You'll be earning every red cent. I promise you that."

"Oh," I am barely able to say. His tone was so suggestive, which doesn't help my effort to compartmentalize. And he's staring at my mouth again, which makes me nervous.

"And there's something I'll need from you." Lynx swallows hard, and he hasn't stopped watching my lips. Is he going to ask for sex once a week? If so, would that be a deal breaker?

I'm waiting with bated breaths for him to say something. "What is it?" I ask impatiently.

Lynx readjusts abruptly in his chair. "So," he says, clapping his hands and then rubbing his palms together. "How about I be thorough and formally interview you?"

I don't think that's what he wanted to say. But I decide to go with the flow. I mean, I have to go with the flow. He's the boss.

I inhale deeply through my nose, filling my lungs and forcing the air out as I brace myself. "Okay."

Lynx chuckles. "Relax, Xena. You got the job. But I want to get to know you better."

We smile at each other, and I force my heart to keep it platonic.

"What do you want to…." I say.

"So…" he says at the same time.

We chuckle conspiratorially.

I point my palms at him, giving him the floor. "Excuse me. You're the one who's in charge of this interview."

His left eyebrow shoots up as if intrigued by what I just said. "Right. Xena, what makes you tick?"

I grimace as I ponder his odd question. "What makes me tick?"

He graces me with his mega-watt smile. "Yes. What do you like to do when you're not sitting in front of me interviewing?"

"Are we talking for work or fun?"

"Let's start with fun."

The answer is easy. "I like hanging out with my girlfriends, and sometimes I play my guitar." Then something occurs to me. "However, I hadn't had much time to do either since becoming a line producer. That job took a lot out of me." I picture Greg's face, realizing he made the work more arduous than necessary.

"You play the guitar?" Lynx asks, snatching the picture of Greg right out of my head.

"Uh-huh," I reply, smiling tightly.

"Wow. Your cousin dances, and you play the guitar."

"Well, I only play to relax."

"That's right, Hollis St. James is your father. Did you inherit your musical talent from him?"

I shake my head arduously. "I don't want to be a musician. As I said, I only play to relax or...." I press my lips. I'm not sure I want to divulge the rest.

His smirk is to die for. "Or?"

My eyes grow double in size. I almost shake my head and ask for a pass. But why the hell can't I just say it? "I've been known to angry play. I'm talking Taylor Swift and Alanis Morrissette times ten."

Lynx laughs, and I love the sound of it. "Have I been one to inspire you lately?" he asks, watching me askew.

I chuckle. "No, actually. I think it's because you were upfront with me. I can't be angry at someone who is...." I press my lips, stopping short of saying something that could be construed as an insult.

"Emotionally walled-off?" Lynx says.

He said that like he's heard it before. But I'm

shaking my head because that's not it. "No. Commitment phobic."

He grunts, and I can't tell whether it is a thoughtful grunt or it has a different meaning.

"By the way, I listened to your father's newest album last week," Lynx says, effectively changing the subject. "I figured since I know his daughter...."

I'm again awed. "You listened to my father's music because of me?" I didn't know I meant that much to him.

He's grinning like that's no big deal. "I had. And now I'm a fan of both your parents."

The weight of Jojo and Hollis bears down on me. I often feel uncomfortable when I have to think about my parents as my parents. My friends know not to go down that road, and my coworkers knew better too. Even Greg rarely spoke about them, but I think that was because he felt they made me better than him. The truth is, they make themselves better than me every day.

"You're not a fan of your parents?" Lynx asks.

I blink until he's back in focus. "Sorry, I'm a fan, especially of my father," I admit. "He's a phenomenal musician."

Lynx appears to be waiting for me to say more, and there is more to say. For some reason, I want to tell Lynx that I spent most of my life missing Hollis way too much. I never even wanted to tell Greg that. The thing is, I feel I can trust Lynx with that information. He won't throw it in my face and use it to judge as proof of my shortcomings. However, the level of intimacy between us is climbing too high, way too fast.

My cheeks warming, I screw up my face and then say, "I thought this was supposed to be a job interview."

He graces me with an easy smile. "It is."

Suddenly a series of loud knocks blast in the air, and I jump, startled. Life unfolds slowly as Lynx twists in his chair to see the gorgeous human who has entered without permission. And I'm watching her too, which is why my jaw has dropped.

## ELEVEN
## XENA ST. JAMES

I retreat deeper into my chair as the woman, who smells like a blooming flower garden, glides confidently into Lynx's office. She's beautiful and impeccable and has that mashup of Megan Fox and Mila Kunas thing going for her. I'm also trying not to stare at how perfectly she's wearing a tight black skirt suit that hugs her feminine figure in all the right places. And there's one more thing, I've seen her before. But where? A second ago, I had her complete attention, but now she's solely focused on Lynx, making me feel like I'm not in the room.

"Don't forget we have a meeting at the stadium at three," she says.

Lynx slaps a hand against his forehead. "Shit. I'm skipping it."

"You can't skip it," the woman says as if that's the most ridiculous thing she's ever heard.

"By the way," Lynx says, nodding to point at me. "Penelope, this is Xena St. James. She'll be working for me, and only me."

Penelope glances at me as if I'm someone who doesn't deserve her full attention. This woman has issues and is certainly not a girl's girl.

"Doing what?" she snaps.

She sounds like she has a lot of pull around here, and I wonder if she does, especially now that I can finally place her. She was the woman sitting beside Lynx at Treasure last night.

"Personal accounting, and this meeting is private." He's watching her as if expecting her to turn around promptly and leave us in peace.

Penelope folds her arms defiantly. "Well, Lynx, honey, you can't blow off this meeting because you're expected to take photos with my father, who will also be there—remember?"

"Ah," Lynx says, squeezing his eyes shut. "That's right." He looks at me like he's seeing through me. "Let me finish up here."

Penelope tilts her head like she's doing it involuntarily. She's no longer ignoring me. With narrowed eyes, she watches me curiously. "Haven't I seen you before?" She shakes an elegant finger at me. "Last night you were...." Her eyes dart to Lynx, and then she glares at him, admonishing him.

"Step out please, Pen," he insists. "I have to finish up."

Her lips twitch like she wants to say something else. Instead, she throws me one last look of warning before leaving us in peace.

I'm slightly rattled by what just happened and disappointed. However, I make myself get over it. Lynx is Mr. Uncommitted when it comes to love— our time spent together before Penelope showed up, with all the flirting and sharing, almost made me forget it.

However, now we're alone again, and he's struggling to maintain eye contact. "I'll have Evie show you to your office." It is almost as if he's relieved to avert his gaze from my face when he gets up and walks briskly to his desk.

"I have these for you," he says after taking a set of keys out of a drawer. "Lock your office if you're not inside. And no one else is allowed in your office but you."

He's back in front of me, and I stand up to take the keys from him. Then, our gazes meet and hold, and hold, and hold.

"It's okay," I finally say. "I'm not upset that your girlfriend also works for you."

"She's not my girlfriend."

I raise my eyebrows in objection. "Is that so, *honey*?"

His lips draw into a slight and resistant frown, "Yes. That's so."

I want so badly to call him out on his bullshit. I still believe she isn't his girlfriend, but she's definitely in a relationship with him, and I think it's sexual. I want to say just that, but he's my new boss, who was my perfect new boss until "Pen" showed up.

I break our intense eye contact by trying to focus on the floor.

"Right," he says, and then he's on the move. "I don't expect you to work today, but I will pay you for the full day." He opens a desk drawer.

"I can stay. I have nothing else to do."

Lynx freezes, pinning me with penetrating eye contact. I feel he's holding me captive because I can't move an inch. But my guess is he has thoughts about what I said, and I wonder what they are.

"If it's okay with you," I add.

He nods briskly. "It's fine."

Lynx gives me more instructions about what to

do when I sit at my desk. But first, Evie will provide me with a tour.

We stand outside his office, facing each other. Lynx holds his hand out, and I shake it. "We'll catch up soon," he says.

I ignore the sizzles of giddy energy rising through my arm. Thankfully, we quickly release our handshake.

"Evie. Time for her tour," Lynx says.

Evie stops her relentless typing. "Alright."

I grow rigid when Penelope re-enters the main suite. She sweeps right past Evie and me and into Lynx's office. It's as if she's sending a message. She belongs in Lynx's domain, not me.

My new boss nods at Evie and me one last time before closing himself inside his office with Penelope.

"Ready?" Evie asks.

I jump, startled. I didn't realize I'd been staring longingly at the space Lynx left behind.

I force the most delightful smile I can muster, realizing that it's official, Lynx Grove is definitely romantically off-limits.

"Absolutely."

EVIE TELLS me that LG Investments comprises one-half of the entire fifty-eighth floor. She says the operation is minimal, and only a handful of Lynx's employees work at this location, but the rooms and offices are enormous. Evie points out Penelope's office, which is near the elevator. She's VP of Corporate Communications for The Ramblers. Archer Donovan, VP of Player and Owners Relations, is across from her. And a third office belongs to Alex Shaw, a baseball player who's also the team's captain and Lynx's friend. Richard Chastain, Penelope's father, a co-owner of the Ramblers, has an office on one side of Lynx's suite. I can't help but mull over how the plot has thickened as Evie tells me Richard, who they call Rich, is never in, so I won't ever run into him.

"But they're all associated with the sports team," I say as Evie takes me to the lounge.

"The LG Capital Investments operation is Lynx, me, and now you. The others are here because they prefer offices in the city, so LG Capital Investments leases to the team."

Before I can respond, we enter the large and well-designed lounge. I'm awed by how stylish it is. A huge turquoise leather U-shaped sofa set faces a big TV screen. Two smaller, more intimate seating areas with matching chairs are placed behind them, and the light fixtures of metal rails hang over all the furniture. Also, the part I love the most is the white leather seating benches in front of floor-to-ceiling windows with killer city views.

"It's gorgeous in here," I comment.

Evie scowls at the face of her watch. "I know. I'll quickly show you the kitchen and then your office. Lynx gave you the keys?"

I nod rapidly, allowing her sudden anxiety to affect me.

We pick up the pace, and next she shows me a very modern kitchen with all the bells and whistles like a self-serving coffee bar with a variety of mochas, cappuccinos, and light flavors, medium, and dark roast coffee from several regions. A glass encasement of refrigerated food items displays all sorts of sandwiches and desserts. She invites me to eat as much as I like when I want. Also, most mornings, a hot breakfast is served in the kitchen.

We're at our final stop. Evie points at a door across from Richard Chastain's office. "You're here."

"Great," I say. The fact that I'm next door to Lynx's suite isn't lost on me. But I guess it makes sense. He wants to keep me close and away from his other business colleagues. "I can take it from here."

"Perfect!"

I hear voices, and we both direct our attention to Lynx's suite as he walks out first and then Penelope behind him.

Penelope comes to an abrupt stop. "That's her office?"

Lynx doesn't stop walking or look back. "Let's go, Penelope, or we'll be late."

If looks could kill, I'd be six feet under because Penelope gives me evil eyes before whipping herself around and storming off behind Lynx.

"Don't worry about her," Evie whispers. "She's territorial."

"Are they together?" I ask, figuring this is an excellent opportunity to learn more about Lynx's association with Penelope.

"I don't know. But..." She renews her smile. "Welcome aboard, and if you have any questions or need anything, I'm at your service."

I broaden my smile and say, "Thank you."

I watch Evie reenter Lynx's suite. Her short answer about Lynx and Penelope said a lot. I think Evie would've had no problem saying they were together if they were a legitimate couple. However, if they shared no romantic link, Evie would've easily said something like, "No, they're not together," and probably added they were merely business colleagues. But she said, "I don't know," and that answer is telling. I think she knows they get it on, but they've ascribed no label to their relationship. And that is more consistent with the Lynx Grove I have come to know—Mr. Uncommitted in the flesh.

Suddenly, there's another loud ding, and I yank my attention toward the elevator. For a fragment of a second, I hope it's Lynx, returning to tongue the hell out of me and assure me that I got his relationship with Penelope all wrong. But the elevator next to the one he entered with Penelope opens. A man exits. He's tall, dapper, athletically built, gorgeous, and watching me curiously.

*Oh no.*

I speed up the process of entering my office to escape Mr. Handsome's scrutiny. I don't need anyone associated with Lynx coming on to me. If I'm going to keep the peace with my new boss, I must keep our professional and personal lives separate, and that includes not screwing around with any guy who works where he employs me.

# TWELVE
## XENA ST. JAMES

*Holy moly.*

I thought I would be working in a space that resembled a broom closet, but instead, I'm met by a majestic view of east Manhattan, featuring skyscrapers of various sizes, colors, and textures. I have a huge wood block desk, the same size, and style as Lynx's. I have a seating area with a long black leather sofa, congregating with two matching chairs. In the center sits a white acrylic coffee table with a glass vase full of fresh and colorful carnations. Also, the same metal grate hanging fixture in the lounge hovers over my desk and the seating area. Earning a desk like this at Rank Media Studios would take me forever. My office is twice as nice as my mom's, who's top talent, and much larger.

I grin from ear to ear because yesterday's office had no view. It was also so cold that I had to wear several layers of clothing to the office and two pairs of socks on most days. But today... I remove my coat and hang it on my own coat tree.

I stand still, waiting for a chill to close in on me. There is none. I even have my own thermostat that's already set to 75 degrees. This space does an excellent job of retaining heat. It must be well-insulated. Finally, I rub my fingers along one of the white lacquer floating shelves holding office supplies. I get a spiral notebook and a red, black, and blue pen and then return to my new desk.

The chair doesn't creak as I carefully lower my rear end onto the seat. Ooh... It's comfy. I slide left and then right, and it moves as if it floats on air.

"Wow," I say, delighted that I hadn't let pride get in the way and make me ignore Lynx's offer. I've landed in an optimal situation here, and I pray to God that this all isn't an illusion, a house made of cards that will soon come tumbling down.

I'VE UNLOCKED my desk drawer and found the files Lynx mentioned. He wants me to examine the financials, all the products, developers, employees, everything. I started by studying the financials for the previous six fiscal quarters, which consist of balance sheets, income statements, cash flow statements, and statements of owners' equity. Hours have passed. The sky has purpled, and I'm starving. The last time I looked away from my work, I heard tapping on the door between Lynx's and my office. My chest fluttered as I said, "Come in," believing perhaps Lynx had returned. But Evie stuck her head in and said she was leaving for the day.

I take my phone out of my purse and power it on. I turned it off earlier while on the subway. I suspected that Lilly would call me again, and I was right. I have two missed calls and voicemails from her. I didn't want to speak to her until I sorted things out with Lynx. However, it's almost 6:30 p.m. I think I'm ready to inform her of my new job.

My stomach growls as I rise to stand. "Food first."

Suddenly, my desk phone rings, and I stiffen as I look at it. It can only be two people, Lynx or Evie, and my guess is that it's Lynx. I snap myself out of my hesitation and answer the call.

"Hello?" I say, sounding unsure.

"Hey. You're still there." *It's him.*

"Yes." I simper, so happy he's not around to get a look at the silly smile on my face. "I'm finding the financial reports quite gripping."

Lynx laugh is like a soothing sound selection on a white-noise app. "Listen, I won't make it back to the office today, but I'd like to hear your assessment of the financial reports first thing Monday morning. But I realized I don't have your phone number in my cell phone. Could you call the number I give you using your device so I can save it in my contacts?"

"Sounds good." I'm impressed by how professional I sounded. I race back to my desk. "I'm ready for the number."

"Were you leaving the office?" he asks.

"No," I reply, pen still ready to write. "I was going to grab something to eat and a coffee."

"You don't have to work all night, you know?"

I'll never admit this out loud, and I'm only vaguely admitting it to myself, but now that he's not returning, I'm ready to skedaddle.

"Thanks for the nice office," I say. "I was pleasantly surprised."

"You're welcome, Xena. But still, I don't unduly

overwork my employees. So go home, enjoy your weekend, but first, I need your number."

---

I ENDED my call with Lynx roughly five minutes ago. It's odd being able to leave the office so early. Even on Fridays, I'd work until at least 9:30 p.m. at yesterday's job. TV production is an arduous business. But I can't say that I hated the work. I just hated the person in charge of me. However, I decided to complete that phone call to Lilly before leaving.

"You're what?" she asks way too loudly.

"I'm working for Lynx Grove."

"Doing what?"

"Personal accounting." That came out more confident than I expected.

"How much is he paying you?"

Of course, Lilly will go straight to the money. "He's paying me well. I like the job, and you know how much I hated the entertainment industry."

I scoot to the edge of my seat to absorb Lilly's judgmental silence. "Accounting, Zeen? Really?"

I rub my suddenly itchy left eye. "Yes."

"But you're free for once. I thought you might

try pursuing music. And, if you need financial assistance...."

"Lilly, stop." I don't want her to get to the part where she offers me her husband's money.

Her famished sigh is loud.

"Come on, Lil, we're not our mothers." Kathy and Jojo are survivors who are constantly anxious that Lilly and I are one wrong decision away from the hard life they had to endure.

"I know. You're right," she says. "As long as you're happy." Then, my cell phone beeps, letting me know I received another call.

I check the screen. "Ooh, it's Nat. I'll call you this weekend," I say, hoping Nat has an offer that will save me from spending extra hours alone in my depressing apartment.

# THIRTEEN
## LYNX GROVE

Friday, 11:00 P.M.

I look around the room, which reminds me of an unfinished basement with one large floor-to-ceiling window stretching from one side of the room to the other. Everything in this space appears outdated and scratched up—the dated metal file cabinets along one wall, a buzzing refrigerator against another wall, the musty carpet, and in the center, a dry and chipped wooden conference table with ten chairs that are too large for the space. Max asked me here to meet potential buyers for my team. If he believes I'm selling to anyone who thinks this is a great place for a deal to go down, then he's out of his mind.

I turn to gaze out the window and over the floor below. "What kind of sketchy operation is this?" I ask Max. There is a lively party taking place on the main floor, but I can't hear a peep.

"This venue is rented for parties and meetings like the one we're having," Max replies. "I like this place because no one expects us to be here."

I extend my arms behind my back, experiencing the pull while enfolding my fingers as I read the scene below. "You got that right," I admit. It's been a long day. This subtle stretch I'm taking feels good.

A lot of the partygoers are wearing costumes even though Halloween was last week. But I wouldn't consider the costumes on brand with the holiday. Some people are dressed as birds, like parrots, canaries, cockatoos, and shit. Some are ancient Romans in sheets, sashes, and with gold leaves tied around their heads. I spot more Marilyn Monroes. The girl who escorted me to this room was costumed as Marilyn Monroe. I spot Playboy Bunnies, Hugh Hefners in pajamas and cigar jackets, and pirates. There are breakdancers, skaters, and men in drag performing break-neck dance moves. A live band is on stage. I don't know what kind of music they're performing because I can't hear them, but everybody seems to be having a hardy good time.

I tap on the glass. "This soundproofing must've cost a pretty penny." I turn to make another examination of the dreary room. "Max. This looks like a mobster spot, and I'm not selling to mobsters."

Max, who hasn't sat down either, folds his arms across his chest. "I'm not associated with mobsters, Lynx. You know that. We needed to discuss this business somewhere anyone who matters can't see us." He holds his palms up. "Don't you think this place covers the basis?"

My grimace shows how irritated I am. "Yeah, but I don't need you finding me a buyer."

"You're dragging your feet."

"I'm weighing my options and being diligent."

"What is there to be diligent about? CEO of GIT is the safest seat in the house. Your procrastinating isn't about diligence it's about something else, and you're running out of time."

"I thought I had until December first."

"November thirtieth," Max growls as if I'm frustrating him. "That's less than a month, Lynx. Selling your team is a process, and your team can't be on your balance sheet when you sign the contract to be CEO of GIT."

I can see the worry behind Max's eyes. For the past two weeks, he's been hounding me about getting rid of my team already. To him, it's no big deal. Set GIT and the Ramblers on a scale, and co-CEO of GIT is the heavier option. Also, Max thinks buying the time and making it successful has not only proven my point to my father but paid off.

I watch him with burning and narrowed eyes. I've told him a thousand times that I'm doing this my way. Not only that, but taking my dad's seat isn't a decision I've made yet. Maybe I'm still bitter about what happened after I graduated from business school. Leo can't take the holy grail away from me and then hand it back after I built my own empire. That just doesn't feel right. It doesn't seem respectful.

Thankfully before Max and I can get into it again, a group of men file into the room, and they definitely do not resemble mobsters. We eye each other keenly. Contrary to what Max knows, I have had a solid week of meetings with the potential buyers. I didn't tell any of them I was selling, I presented them with the unlikely probability that I would sell to them and asked, "how would they run my organization differently than I had." I didn't like their answers, which is why I considered them all wrong to take over my team. But as I watch these men, all around my height and in their fifties or sixties walk over to me and introduce themselves, I have a feeling that this group of potential buyers is different than the others.

———

## 1 Hour Later

The potential buyers are Joe Long, Anthony Smit, Collin Peterson, Jay Noelle, and Erik Austen, who are former players and legends of professional baseball and basketball. I've listened to their pitch. They've asked me the tough questions about how I was able to get the league to approve my franchise. And finally, I've done a quick, hard scan of their written proposal. They're waiting to hear what I have to say.

I'm tapping the table as I travel down every avenue of possibilities in my head.

"The league would never approve the sale," I say.

The men, who believe their popularity alone is enough to get them whatever they want in the field of sports, exchange surprised glances.

"I met with every owner in the league to get my three-quarter votes to expand. What convinced them to give me a chance is that I had sixteen billion in the bank."

"Don't worry about that," Max chimes in. "Our bank will handle capital backing. There are no excuses Lynx. These are our buyers, and you know it."

I glare at Max. "You mean my buyers. My team."

Max scowls at me like he wants to knock my block off. "You see what I have to deal with," he says to the men.

"What the fuck. You're like a junky eager to get his next hit by selling my business," I snap.

"Come on, Lynx," Max grouses.

"No. You come on."

Fueled by anger, I rehash what it took to give them a product to want to purchase. I'm on a roll, telling them how the owners were sure I would fail, but as long as I had the cash to fund the team, it was a win for them even at a loss for me. But I made the right hires. Even making the decision to hire Penelope, Rich's daughter. I tell them she's fantastic at her job. She convinced the entire state, being that Ramblers territory covers six cities, to believe my team belonged to them. We fill seats. And the league respects my business acumen. They know as long as I'm the owner, they're guaranteed success in Connecticut. But these guys are players. They're not businessmen. Even if Max gives them a billion-dollar cushion to fall back on, at this stage in the process, that won't be enough to make the league believe they have gas to sustain the life of the team.

"Then they wouldn't mind stripping it for parts," Max growls.

The other men at the table are jolted into shock. They're not used to how coldhearted my cousin could be when it comes to ensuring his control of GIT. They're seeing he doesn't give a shit about them or my team, or even me. He wants me to replace my father because Leo has become a thorn in his ass. He's been losing too many votes to Achilles, Hercules, and even his sister Paisley. Our mothers haven't been agreeing with the direction he wants to take the company either. Max wants to give the middle finger to all the corporate coopera- tion that's been taking place since our sisters married Lord brothers. Achilles and Hercules even have the ability to sway our fathers to vote for their interests. So that's why Max is chomping at the bit to onboard me. He needs me. And yes, I will have Max's back, which includes convincing him to see the light even when he's being a megalomaniac.

I shoot to my feet and take long strides to the window to think. I'm rendered speechless when I see a beauty on stage under a blue spotlight, playing guitar.

*Holy shit.* "I have to go," I say, snatching my coat off the back of my chair. I point at Max on the way out. "Let's put a pin in this for now. But if I sell, then you're my guys."

I'm out of the room and running down the musty hallway. I tell Marilyn Monroe who escorted me to my meeting that I need to get into that party. Without hesitation, she walks me past a line of party seekers who made it inside from the sidewalk but still have to wait in a long hallway to make it into the main venue. We sweep past two burly bouncers. I thank Marilyn Monroe, and she says something about joining me for a drink later. I ignore her as I move closer to the stage. The voice of an angel spreads through the air. It's Xena on stage, wearing a strapless top with black jeans and ankle boots. She has this slinkiness about her that's awfully sexy, singing:

---

*Wo-o-o-oh… We're such a terrible explosion, and we're not getting closer, we're moving in circles and washing away.*

*And I bet you didn't know that I had it up to here with you…*

*It could've been my fault because I hadn't been clear with you…*

   *Let's take a seat at the bar and I grab a last beer with you. so I can tell ya.*

*Let me tell you….*

---

In a heavy moment of pause, I'm drawn to Xena, caught in her allure as I rub my tight chest over my heart. She said she played guitar, but I could've never guessed she could make music at this level. She's actually making me feel something. And then her beautiful voice rises again.

---

*Wo-o-o-oh… We're such a terrible explosion, and we're not getting closer, I'm running away.*
   *From you.*

*Wo-o-o-oh... We're such a terrible explosion,
and we can't make it much longer, we're moving in
circles and washing away.*

*Wo-o-oh-Oh!*

---

The last big note has been sung and played. The entire nightclub erupts in applause, and before the hooting ends, she's making her way off stage. Damn, she looks good tonight. Shit. What am I going to do? I'm her boss, and now there's a line I can't cross.

I have to make a decision soon though.

Suddenly, Max walks up next to me and elbows me in the arm. "Is that her?" he asks.

I scowl at him.

"Xena?" he says.

I nod, wondering how he knew to ask me that.

Reading the curiosity in my expression, he says, "It's the way you're looking at her. Also, the fucking unprofessional way you ran out of our meeting."

On that note, I slap Max hard on the back. "You mean your meeting. See you soon." I'm off to find my new employee.

## FOURTEEN
## XENA ST. JAMES

My hands shake as I put the club's guitar on the stand for the next musician to use. I skip down the stage steps fast, keeping my head down. It isn't until Nat hugs me and says, "Oh my God, Zeen! That was amazing!" Do I begin to feel stable again. It's disappointing to admit to myself that I still have an awful case of stage fright.

"That was more than amazing," a man says from behind. I recognize the voice, but there's no way it's him.

I whip myself around, and my jaw drops. It is Lynx. "What are you doing here?"

"Whoa," Sarah, who steps up beside me and links her arm around mine, says. "You're LG Capital, Zeen's new job." Her gaping eyes dance around his face as if she's been bewitched by his unmatched gorgeousness.

On the way to the nightclub, the conversation briefly turned to the subject of my life.

Yes, I quit Rank Studio.

Yes, I had a new job.

LG Capital.

Of course, Sarah's heard of it.

Owned by Lynx Grove?

He's your new boss?

Yes.

He's hot.

He's involved with Penelope, his partner's daughter.

But you two had sex? That's what you said at *Treasure* last night. The blogs reported it.

Yes, we had sex, but it felt like it happened eons ago. He's shaping up to be a great boss, and I don't want anything to ruin that.

And then to change the subject, I mentioned Greg and how I picked up flowers from the mailroom he sent me when I got home. I told them I wanted to sing a song and dedicate it to his classic abuser's behavior and basic red roses. The mention of Greg shifted the conversation away from Lynx, which was a relief.

However, not in a million years would I have ever guessed that my girlfriends and I would be staring down my new boss on Anything Goes Night at The Bunkers.

And Lynx still hasn't answered my question. There's no way he's here to party. He has on the same suit he was wearing earlier today. There are offices on the top floor. Is he here on business?

Sarah shoots an arm out to shake his hand. "I'm Sarah."

The DJ has taken the stage.

He shakes her hand. "Nice to meet you, Sarah."

Now Nat's hand is outstretched. "And I'm Nat. And I heard you're Zeen's new boss."

Lynx grins. "I am."

"But you two also had sex," Nat adds.

I elbow her, embarrassed. "Nat!"

"Ouch!" She pretends as if that soft nudge I gave her hurts. It didn't, although she deserves for it to hurt.

"Join us for a drink!" Sarah shouts. She's grinning at me, nodding as if asking my permission after extending the offer.

"Absolutely," Lynx exclaims.

No. I can't have alcohol in my system while he lingers around us.

I frantically wave at him even though he's already watching me. "Lynx, can we talk?"

---

I'M LOOPY, and my feet feel like they're treading air while Lynx holds my hand, guiding me through the excited crowd. He has a tight grip, and so do I. As he continuously glances back at me, each eye-lock feels like a stab of attraction. This whole scene doesn't help me maintain a platonic distance between us. Then, we're outdoors, and the chilly night reminds me that I hung my coat on the back seat of my chair when I took the stage.

"Ouch," I say, pulling my hand out of his grasp as I hug myself. "I should go back in for my coat."

Lynx is out of his wool black duster lightning fast.

"We're getting inside my vehicle." He drapes his expensive coat around me.

Oh my God, it smells even more like him— citrus, sandalwood, cinnamon, and a hint of vanilla. The lining is silky and extra warm. I don't ever want to take it off.

"Thank you," I say as he opens the back door of a spotless SUV that shines under the streetlight.

It's too cold to hesitate, so I climb into the back seat. After closing me inside, Lynx races around to the other side and joins me. The dusky atmosphere makes this moment feel highly intimate. With dread, I watch a tinted window rise to the roof, separating us from the front of the SUV. Now we're truly alone.

We start to speak at the same time, and then once we realize it's happened, we chuckle.

Lynx graces me with my favorite sideways smile. "You first. Since this was your idea."

It was my idea, and I remember why. My eyes plead with him to understand me before I say, "I just enjoy working for you, and I don't want my girl-friends ruining things. Because they will."

"It's just a drink, Xena."

I shake my head adamantly. "But they know we had sex."

"Yeah?" He strokes his chin. "I'm surprised you told them and not Lilly."

I roll my eyes as I grunt grimly. "I didn't tell them anything. They are devout readers of *In The Know*." I can't believe he and I didn't discuss that before he hired me. I drop my head repentantly. "I forgot to mention that this morning. You know, they wrote what I said about you in the restaurant."

Lynx puts two fingers under my chin and carefully lifts my face. "Your skin is soft," he whispers. Then, his eyebrows flash up like he hadn't meant to say that.

What the hell are we going to do about all the sexual tension between us that refuses to dwindle? I want to ask him that question, but I'm afraid to.

"I also wanted to apologize for the shit I said to you that night," he says, his voice thickened by desire.

He hasn't removed his fingers, and it almost feels like he wants to kiss me. "The night we met?"

"Yes."

"What specifically are you apologizing for?"

Finally, he stops touching me, and my skin cools in the spot his fingers abandoned. "I'm apologizing for saying I don't do relationships and…."

"You don't need to apologize for that. Plus, I like to know where I stand with a man right away." I shake my head pleadingly. "It was just fun, Lynx. Let it drop."

I don't know what's behind why he's looking at me that way. But I feel I have to say something else.

"It was fun," I continue. "That's it. And now you're my boss, which means our sexcapade is in the past." I sound like I'm trying to convince myself of that more than him. If this moment is revealing anything, it's that I might be lying to myself. "And the kiss—" I squeeze my eyes shut, banishing a visual of me making out with his sexy mouth out of my head.

"I enjoyed kissing you too," he whispers before I can remember what I wanted to say about the kiss we shared at the door.

The words "I could tell" sit on my tongue, but I would officially be flirting back if I say them. And that is a dangerous thing to do.

"Because you said you didn't kiss," I whisper tightly.

"I don't."

I stare into his electric eyes. This man's looks are unreal. And I'm not the sort of girl who goes ga-ga over a guy just because he's attractive. But I can't deny there's something about Lynx Grove's head-to-toe appearance that makes my pulse race and pussy weep for him. I could do him right here and right now if I didn't need my job so much.

I point toward the sidewalk. "I should go. And I'll tell my girlfriends you couldn't stay for the drink."

"Do you want to know why I'm here?"

My eyes open wide as my brain tries to keep up

with the unexpected subject change. That's right. I want to know. "Yes. Why?" I sound as if I'm out of breath.

Lynx anchors himself deeper against the seat as he glares ahead. "Max secured buyers for my team. And I can't say I wouldn't sell to them. But as you know, I'm still not convinced I want to let go."

I take my hand off the door handle as I ease the urge to flee out of my body. "Oh."

Lynx extends his long arm across the top of the seat. "But I don't want to talk business tonight. We'll discuss it more on Monday. Tonight, I want to get to know you better. Sure, I'm your boss Xena, but I also wanna be your friend."

I grin at his bullshit. I want to applaud him and say well played as I study how close his fingers are to my face. Here's the undeniable truth: Lynx wants to fuck me, and I want to fuck him too. But I won't do it. I can't.

"What?" he asks, reading my expression.

I snort facetiously. "Okay," I say, ready to amuse myself by playing along. "How was it growing up in the home of one of the richest families in the world?"

"Lonely," Lynx replies without hesitation.

I inhale sharply between my lips as his eyes hold

mine captive. I'm also surprised he answered so candidly. I once saw a show where Max Grove was asked the same question and he totally death-stared the interviewer until the guy moved on to a question he preferred to answer.

"And you?" Lynx asks.

I cut a small smile. "I didn't grow up in a wealthy house."

His crooked smile reappears, and his sensual lips wear it so well. "But you were raised by the price tag lady."

I blurt a laugh. "Yes. I was."

"That had to be interesting."

"Didn't I tell you that's an act?" I ask.

He nods slowly and indulgently. "Yes. You did."

"My mom is ambitious and needs to project that onto me." I press my lips. I can't believe I shared that with Boss Pussy Hound, who I think I would let take another bite of me if I remain in this car longer than necessary.

I watch his fingers rub the leather seats. "My mother's ambitious too," he says. "She never had to be ambitious, but she is."

"Ah," I say because now it totally clicks.

He pins me with a curious gaze. "Ah, what?"

"You've been emotionally neglected. That's why you have an unhealthy relationship with sex."

Lynx's head lulls back as he laughs. I smile as I watch him. I love this face he's giving me. Gosh, he's such a beautiful man.

"Maybe I should ask a shrink about that," he says.

I shrug indifferently. "Maybe you should." Since I'm digging, and he seems to be okay with it, I also have another question regarding a rumor I heard about his family. "Oh," I say, shaking my finger as if what I'm about to ask just came to mind. It hadn't. The question came to me as I admired his face. "I heard your father married your mother because she resembles his brother's wife." I hold my breath, watching him, hoping I hadn't crossed a line with that one. I mean, it sounded like something I wanted to ask when it was still in my head. Now that it's out, I totally crossed the line.

"It's a story, isn't it?" he replies without relinquishing the power of his intense stare.

"Sorry," I say, wanting so much to see him smile again, which bothers the hell out of me. I thumb across my shoulder. "I should really get back inside."

"What are you apologizing for?"

His voice sounds a million miles away as my pussy thumps like it has a heartbeat of its own. "Good night, Lynx."

Lynx's tasty tongue moistens his top lip, then the bottom as he scoots closer. I'm rendered immobile by his stare. The door opens behind me, and cold air rushes in.

"I'll see you soon, Xena."

My heart hammers so hard that his voice sounded muffled. "Good night!" I say, the words heating my throat. I hop out of the car and slam the door behind me, running away from that entirely tempting situation with Lynx Grove.

---

I'M BACK INSIDE and at the table with my friends, who are yelling questions about what happened between Lynx and me above the music.

I insist nothing happened between us, and we just talked about business and what we'll tackle on Monday morning.

Sarah shakes her head as if rebelling against my claims. "No way, Zeen. You get him on the phone, tell him to come back, and you book that shit. Because he's into you."

"He's my boss, Sarah! I'm not going to jeopardize my job by sleeping with him. Because he's still a fuckboy," I say loud enough so they can hear me.

"Then fuck him," Nat declares. "And you never know!"

I shake my head, grimacing. "Never know what?"

"He could be the one."

I yank my head back so far, my ears crunch. "Are you serious? Have you listened to anything I said about the night we slept together? He said he doesn't kiss. He said he doesn't spoon. He said he doesn't do relationships. And now I'm working for him and in the same vicinity as another woman he's fucking. So, Nat, Lynx is certainly not the one."

Nat rolls her eyes dismissively. She thinks I'm being overdramatic. "He didn't even know you then, Xena. But now he's hired you."

I shake my head like I don't get what her point is because I don't get it.

"You know her type," Sarah chimes in, patting me on the back. "Men like Greg!"

I want to say that's not true, but it is true.

"You know you're still wearing his coat, right?" Nat asks.

"What?" I look down at myself. "Oh no."

My girlfriends burst out into laughter, and I'm frozen from indecision. I consider calling him to arrange a pickup, but then he looked so delicious tonight. I'm still ruffled by how close we got in the back seat of his car. I can wait. I'll see him on Monday morning. I'll return his coat then.

A cocktail waitress appears at our table as I move to take off Lynx's coat but then think better of it. I love the way the silk lining feels on my skin. The waitress serves us drinks we hadn't ordered.

"From the gentleman over there," she says, pointing at a man at the bar. She's looking at me. "He says he's a fan of your music."

I follow where she's pointing to a man dressed as a Roman emperor. A Roman costume is typical on Anything Goes Night since the empire had a reputation for debauchery.

"What the hell!" Nat exclaims. "You must be drenched in pheromones tonight, Zeen."

We all laugh.

"So what!" I shout as I raise my free drink. "Tonight is girls' night. Fuck the boys!"

We clink our glasses together. "We're fucking the boys!" my friends respond.

We down our drinks and then hit the dance floor. I refuse to take off Lynx's coat, though. It's too big, but I consider his coat sex safe—it's best to have him on me than inside me.

---

12 Hours Later

"Mm…" I groan. My head feels like I'm drowning as memories of last night replay. After we hit the dance floor, we downed more rounds of drinks, the fruity, tasty kind. We danced our heads off some more. We even skated. Sarah, who's a professional dancer, break-danced with the best. Struck by another memory, I sink my fingers against my temples. *Oh my God. Shit.* I sang another song. It went something like, *Go to hell, Greg, you fucking troll! You're the epitome of an asshole.* But first, I warmed up the crowd by telling them the story of Fido shitting in my shoes and urinating on my jacket.

"Oh my God…" I whisper. I'll never be able to show my face around those people ever again.

I threw up on stage. Nat and Sarah rushed me outside for air and a big laugh at me losing my mind. I never get so drunk and embarrass myself that way. And then, Lynx stepped out of his SUV.

He'd been waiting the whole time. We all got into the backseat.

*Right?*

Yes.

And then…

I gasp and sit up straight in my bed. "What are you doing here?"

Lynx Grove, dress pants on, white T-shirt untucked, and puffy skin under his wild eyes, sits in the rickety chair I keep in the corner of my tiny bedroom. He points to the ceiling grimacing at the water stain above my bed.

"Is that mold, Xena?"

# FIFTEEN

# LYNX GROVE

I love that sexy surprised look on her face. It normally shoots blood straight to my cock. But now is not the time. I gave her time to remember how I ended up in her apartment. She was probably too drunk to remember how I had Jovi drop her friends off first. Her friend Nat wouldn't let me drop off Xena last until I gave her my phone number, and I promised I wouldn't lay a hand on her friend and my new personal accountant without her consent.

*Speaking of consent.*

Xena had tried to kiss me as I took her shoes off. Her eyes barely opened, she said a lot I found shocking, and not in a bad way. I wonder if she remembers any of it. The last thing she called me was a heartbreak waiting to happen. I don't disagree with her. I've broken a lot of hearts, and I'm not proud of it. I've never had a serious girlfriend who was flesh and blood. I've been in a committed relationship with Ambition and don't know how to break up with her. But none of that shit is on the forefront of my mind. After putting Xena to bed, I toured her shoebox-sized apartment. The water runs brown, and the fixtures are rusted. I spent a long time trying to locate a foul odor that was the cross between a corpse and a landfill until the damn lights went out.

It was 3:00 a.m., but I stomped down to the front desk to ask what in the hell was going on. The girl on duty told me her name was Kerry and that the electricity goes out often. I asked if she knew where the breakers were and if she could take me to them. Kerry happily escorted me to the electrical room. I saw the problem right away. The breakers were too old for a building that houses as many units as this one does. Many structures in this city are ancient. And if time, attention, and a lot of money aren't put into modernizing them, then you have all kinds of problems like the one Xena's apartment is experiencing.

Then, I got carried away after thinking about Xena in bed sleeping under mold, showering in brown water, and being closed in with that fucking odor.

I considered calling my electrician and paying him to fix the issues immediately, but that would've been an overreach.

Instead, I asked Kerry to give me the manager's contact information.

"We're between hires," she said. "The last guy quit two weeks ago, and so far, we've had no luck replacing him."

"Shit," I muttered.

"Are you a new tenant?" I wondered what took her so long to ask me.

"No," I said, pondering what to do next.

"No?"

I glanced at her, and she looked frightened about the unknown. So I told her my friend lives in the building, Xena St. James.

Kerry went still. "Oh, her."

My eyes burned as I wondered what she meant by 'Oh, her.' But I also wanted to move forward and call George, my electrician. There was another option, but was I ready to offer it to Xena? Was it too much too soon? And then, I heard a series of gunshots that made Kerry duck behind her workstation, putting the final nail in the coffin. It wasn't easy waiting until Xena woke up. I couldn't doze off. It was cold as hell. And I didn't want to get in under the covers with her because that would've been too damn tempting. I have loads of emails Evie flagged for me to check, but I couldn't work either. All I could do was wait, walk, and wait.

Xena bends her neck to look down at herself. I can tell she's checking to see if she's fully dressed.

"All I took off were your shoes," I say.

Her eyebrows rise as she regards me cautiously. "That's just a water stain. It's not mold."

I shake my head defiantly. "That's not a water stain, Xena. It is mold."

She shakes her head dismissively, and I'm aghast.

"Why are you still here?" she asks.

"I was looking out for you." I feel like someone has to do it. "How long have you lived in this building?"

Her hair is mussed-up, framing her pretty face, and her lips are extra pouty. I'm suddenly held captive by her tight nipples pushing against the fabric covering her breasts. *What do they call the sort of blouse she's wearing?* Tube top. That's what it is. She's wearing a tube top. The only reason I know that is because of Treasure. When we were teenagers, I used her tube tops as headbands until she stormed into our home gym, yanked the thing off my head, and shouted, "Leave my fucking tube tops alone."

"I guess I had too much fun last night," Xena says as she spins her legs over the mattress, and her feet hit the floor.

"You haven't answered my question. How long have you lived here?"

She shrugs indifferently. "I don't know, six or seven years."

Suddenly, there are moans. A bed creaks, and a headboard knocks. It almost sounds like the subway is rumbling through the apartment upstairs. But it's not a train. It's sex. I point at the ceiling again.

"Is that…. Are they fucking for real?"

"They are fucking for real," she says, giving my words a whole new meaning. I lick my lips as her eyes fall over me. "Are you that pampered, Mr. Lynx Grove?" I'm slayed by the grin on her lips.

"Hey!" I roar. The fucking continues. "Hey!" I shout louder, and it stops. "She's trying to fucking sleep down here. If you don't respect her, I'll buy this fucking building and toss your asses out."

"Lynx?" Xena cries.

The thing is, I wasn't kidding. I've been thinking

about purchasing this shithole since I returned to the room. That might end up being option two.

"Your electricity went out last night," I snap.

She rolls her eyes tiredly. "I know. It's always going out."

"That's because the breakers need to be updated." It's time to stop lollygagging. I've built my case and added padding to my offer.

"Listen…" I rise to my feet. "Why don't you stay with me? I have more than enough space since my apartment comprises the entire eleventh floor. You'll have your own wing."

Her eyes are narrowed as she watches me as if I'm deranged. "Are you kidding me?"

I set my jaw and fold my arms over my chest. "No. I'm not. And if…" I think twice about what I plan to say next. I was going to say that if she's worried about living with me, I have a place on the Upper Eastside where I can stay. But I don't want to move into that residence. I want to live with her.

Xena bounds to her feet and opens the tiniest closet I've ever seen. "I'm not going to be your pocket pussy, Lynx."

The shock of her words slams into me like a punch. "What? My pocket pussy?"

I'm annoyed by that. Last night, before she fell

fast asleep, she kept referring to me as a fuckboy. I've never even heard that term. And when I asked her, "what the fuck is a fuckboy?" She had said, "You, Lynx Grove."

The creaking and the moaning upstairs start again, and I glare irate at the ceiling. The mold makes me doubly mad.

"It's a trade-off," Xena says nonchalantly, slipping on a robe. "You get to yell, and they get to fuck. And…" She shakes her head. "Sorry about the pocket-pussy comment." She means to end this subject with a diverting smile. "It was really sweet of you to stay and offer me your much better apartment."

"You know I went to the front desk last night?"

She jerks herself back, leaning away from me. "You did?"

"Yes. And, the girl who works at the desk…."

"Kerry?" she asks.

"Yes. Kerry took me to the…."

Her sexy mouth opens wide, and I let myself imagine how her lips would feel around my cock. "She took you?"

Frowning, I shake my fantasy out of my head. "Yeah, she escorted me to the electrical room."

I tell Xena about the outdated hardware. I also

tell her that the manager quit two weeks ago, and they can't find a replacement, which means it will be a while before they look into the electrical problem if they care to fix the shit. "There are just some slummy buildings in this city. The trade-off is cheap rent for a place to rest your head. But why do you live in this fucking dump? You make enough money to put yourself in a better situation." I've been dying to ask that question.

"Because…" Her lips twitch like she's ashamed to reveal the answer. But I'm waiting for the answer because I want to hear it. "My mom would never come to this neighborhood unless she absolutely, positively had to."

I'm speechless. Surely she's not living in squalor because of her mother. "Is she that bad?" I ask, now concerned that Jojo might be *Mommy Dearest*.

Xena squishes her face up as she drops onto the edge of her bed. That's actually where I want her. "Not really. But she can be imposing though, and controlling. That's all."

I sit beside her and see her eyes get a little wider. I'm affecting her, and I like it.

"There were gunshots too," I say, suddenly remembering those.

"Really?" she says as if it's no big deal.

Silence sits between us as the man upstairs grunts at orgasm.

Xena and I look everywhere but at each other.

"It's odd having you on my bed," she says.

"There dickhead," the man upstairs shouts.

I point upwards. "I'm going to end this guy."

Xena laughs. "You can't stop them from having sex, Lynx. It's not their fault the floors and walls are thin."

"How about we have a little sex of our own?" slips out of my mouth. *Fuck.* "Sorry about that," I say, raking my fingers through my hair.

"You're my boss now," Xena says, rubbing the tops of her thighs.

"I know. And I'm offering you a space in my gigantic apartment with a personal chef, heat that never goes out, your own wing, private elevator, big bed, nice views....." I glare up at the ceiling. "No mold. And I'm sure I have neighbors that fuck, but you won't hear them."

"You got Kerry to show you the electrical room?" she asks as if she hadn't heard a thing I said.

"Yes, Xena," I snap, annoyed that she's not focusing on what really matters.

She whips her head from side to side. "I've been

asking her about the electricity for months, and all she would say is that she didn't know anything. I mean, she could've at least told me that Ray quit. What's her problem with me anyway?"

"You're beautiful, and some women find that threatening?"

Xena narrows one eye like the concept of random jealous women confuses her. If I understand that concept, I'm certain she does too. But her girlfriends, Nat and Sarah, are knockouts. And I hadn't detected any competitiveness between them. Every single one of Penelope's girlfriends has tried to seduce me; a few even flat-out told me they wanted to fuck. My gut tells me that Xena's circle of friends is similar to Treasure's. They're loyal and aren't the jealous types.

Suddenly, more moans and headboard banging come from a different region of the apartment. I glare toward the living room.

"Is that…"

"Jess must've scored last night."

There's a loud clicking sound, and the electronic clock on her nightstand turns on and off.

"Xena." I know one thing for sure as I ensure she's looking me in the eyes. "I won't take no for an answer."

She holds my gaze for a long time. I'm close to asking her to at least let me put her up in a hotel room while I buy this decrepit building and then overhaul it.

"Shit," she whispers and then leaps to her feet. Xena flips the light switch up and down, and nothing happens. "This must be a sign," she says, staring at me with big beautiful fawn eyes. "You know what? When Lilly offered me her apartment, I was too proud to take it." Xena takes a deep breath, holds it, and slowly releases it. "You say it's the whole floor?"

I sit up straighter. "Yes. And you'll have your own wing. A chef, cleaning, plenty of space…."

"Okay," she says, closing her eyes tightly. "I'll do it. It's just time to do it." She opens her eyes and raises a finger with caution. "But it's only until I find my own place."

"Of course," I say. "Sure. Of course."

# SIXTEEN

# XENA ST. JAMES

## Late Saturday

*What a day.*

I can't believe I've done this, and I still feel uneasy about it. However, I have played the say "no" game for most of my life, and saying "no" to opportunity has gotten me nowhere fast. Of course, the thought of living with Lynx in a six thousand square feet apartment is nerve-wracking. But it's too late to turn back now.

My exit from the apartment I spent nearly a decade living in went way too fast. Lynx had to leave after he called movers that are associated with his baseball team business. A crew of diligent workers was sent to my apartment in two hours.

With my guidance, they packed up all my things. They were careful to indicate where items were initially placed. I donated most of my furniture because when I eventually move out of Lynx's apartment and into my own, I plan to start anew. My bed was taken to be stored at a Ramblers warehouse site. I realize how little I owned when it took less than three hours to vacate.

After sharing a goodbye coffee with Jess, where we agreed to keep in touch, I went downstairs to drop off my thirty-day notice at the front desk. Oh, how I wish Kerry were pulling a double shift. I wanted to give her a piece of my mind for being close-mouthed with me but loose-lipped with Lynx. I was the one paying rent, not him.

Instead, I chatted with Lisa, who's a hundred times nicer than Kerry. However, she's part-time, and we rarely run into each other. She confirmed Ray had quit. There was an ongoing dispute between management, and the owners and Lisa said I was smart to get out now.

"It's a mess," she said, shaking her head at the chaos. "A big hunk of steamy, stinky mess."

I agree with her because when I walked out of the building, destined never to return, for the first time ever I could smell something else besides the rotting trash outside my window. I inhaled and savored the aroma of foods and baked goods prepared by nearby eateries, intermingling with other scents like motor vehicle exhaust and turning leaves. The delicious fragrance reminded me of what I loved so much about the city, which is how vast diversity comes together to make a beautiful existence.

I was ready to hike to the subway station, carrying my heavy weekender bag and crossbody purse, but I didn't know that Lynx's driver and SUV were waiting to take me to my new residence. Boy, had he thought of everything or what?

When I arrived, I checked in at the front desk. The process was smoother than cream since I know everyone who works in the building already. I was always here when Lilly lived in her apartment. A guy named Anthony gave me keys and showed me to our private hallway and elevator.

"Private elevator?" I said surprised and then mentioned how Lilly used to encounter Lynx in the main elevator all the time.

Anthony said Lynx closed off access to his floor from the main elevators when the private elevator was fully installed about a week ago.

I thought, wow, my new living situation felt

bigger than my britches. And now I've just stepped out of the elevator and entered a foyer where the walls are made of white sandstone, the floors are white and gray marble, and an ostentatious chrome statue of twisted metal greets me upon arrival. The space is so upscale that it's hard to fathom that this is where I now live.

My feet are on autopilot as I step toward the wide-open furnished space that's as large as a ballroom. Lynx mentioned the views earlier, but I never expected these views. The iconic cityscape on the other side of the Hudson makes sense of why he chose to make the eleventh floor his domain. Because we're not so high in the air, I feel as if I am at one with my outdoor environment. I bet the picture I'm gazing at is stunning at night.

I step into the living room. The furniture is white and black leather sectionals, ottomans, sitting benches, and armchairs. The end tables and coffee tables are marble and glass. The lamps are twisted metal. All the faux fur white rugs are properly placed. I haven't even seen the kitchen or bathrooms, but I'm sure they have the styling and size of a five-star hotel too.

"Lynx! Are you here?" I call.

Suddenly, the elevator makes a noise. It's not a

loud ding. It's a soft, melodic chime. Grinning from ear to ear and ready to rake my new roommate over the coals for not telling me that he invited me to live in a palace, I look across my shoulder to see him when he steps out into the foyer.

"Oh, Lynx!" Penelope and I lock eyes, then she gasps so loudly that it sounds like she's sucking air. "What are you doing here?" She stares daggers at my Weekender bag.

And oh my Lord, I can't wait to answer her question. So I get ready to savor each word of "I live here."

Penelope gasps as if she's choking yet again. "The hell you do," she mumbles as she slaps the down button with the palm of one hand while her thumb stabs the screen of her cell phone.

I don't have to be a Jeopardy champ to know the answer to "Who does the disgruntled employee and fuck-buddy of Lynx Grove call after finding the new girl in his apartment who says she's his new roommate?"

I feel like I should say something, but she's gone so fast that all she leaves behind is the scent of her highly fragrant perfume. I smash my hands on my waist, wondering what in the hell just happened. First of all, does Penelope have free access to Lynx's apartment? Am I going to wake up some mornings to find them canoodling in the kitchen after a night of satisfying sex, at least as far as she's concerned?

My sigh turns into a yawn. What have I agreed to? My eyes burn as I turn toward a long and lit hallway. It has been a long day. It's late in the afternoon, soon it'll be evening. I catch sight of a yellow Post-It attached to the flawlessly painted white wall that says: Xena's wing, this way.

I gently snort as I smile. Leave it up to Lynx to make me feel invited after Penelope has done the opposite.

I peel the square sheet of paper off the wall, and a hand wave has been drawn under the directions with the name Cecily written beneath it. It's from Cecily in reception, she must've made the note for Lynx.

I spot another note and follow what's written on it. On the way, I pass a room with two walls full of books and a seating area. I keep going until I reach a massive bedroom. I'm in awe of the king-size bed with a pale wooden plank backboard that stretches high toward the ceiling. Behind it is a white chevron accent wall. Adjacent is a mural of black and white lines drawn in all directions. On the bed are fluffy pillows and pure white linens with a gold-dusted design. A gold-tufted sitting bench is at the foot of the bed. A matching sofa curves with the window's glass and behind it is my own spectacular view of the Hudson River.

There are so many more details to take in, but I'm shocked to see my suitcase sitting on a rack against a wall. Then, I walk around that wall and am floored by my massive walk-in closet and an attached spa-like bathroom. Among other items that have been delivered, hung, and folded neatly and put carefully on shelves and inside drawers is my guitar which is nicely placed on its stand.

"Holy crap," I whisper. I have officially moved out of that dump I should've vacated a long time ago. I can't wait to sincerely thank Lynx.

I find my cellphone in my purse, take it out and check the time on the screen. It's almost 6:00 p.m. Lynx said there will be dinner at six. But where in the world is he?

"You did what?" Max bellows.

Max was already angry when I arrived, but hearing I invited Xena to move in with me worsened his outrage.

"What was I going to do?" I ask, gesturing wildly. "Her building had no electricity. I heard fucking gunshots. I encountered three mice on my way to the front desk." I shake my head unrelentingly. "Don't bust me out for doing the right thing, Max." I stab myself in the chest with a finger. "I did the right thing."

Max glowers at me as he pours the protein shake he blended into a tall glass. He's in full workout gear and wearing a headpiece that lets him talk on the phone while running on the treadmill. I return his aggressive expression because I don't have regret. I'm excited. I can't wait to get home to see her.

I had to leave Xena alone in that Godforsaken apartment this morning because I had to attend several meetings at the stadium. But I called in a team of experts to help make her move painless. The last update I received from the moving company was that a six-person crew had picked up her things, packed them, and put them away in her closet and bathroom. Xena hadn't shown up before the team left our apartment. I hadn't been able to call and check in on her because I hit the ground running as soon as I arrived at the stadium.

I met with an architect to discuss expanding the luxury box and stadium seating and improving acoustics. I had to keep downing coffee to keep my head in the game. I was nearly out of it for the next meeting, which was the first of many to discuss trades and acquisitions. I felt like a hypocrite sitting around my guys, who were excited about putting together a winning team for next season.

Penelope poked her head into the conference room and said she wanted to talk to me before I left. I didn't get to speak to her because Max called and said he needed to talk to me right away.

He still hasn't told me why he insisted I helicopter from Connecticut to his private landing pad atop the skyscraper where he resides. Max's place is high in the sky. He has acquired the entire penthouse floor and owns the three levels beneath where we are now. One floor is a fancy gym, and another is an office space of cubicles, desks, and private meeting rooms. He uses it when he has teams working on secret projects. The area right beneath his penthouse sits empty simply because Max doesn't want anyone living that close to him. It's not because he's a snob—it's paranoia.

"Why am I here?" I ask because the stare-off we're in is a losing game for him. He won't get what he wants from me when it comes to Xena.

"She's Lilly's cousin, Lynx."

I sigh. He's unable to let it go. "I know."

"They're close?"

"Max, contrary to what you believe, people, and even the Lords, don't spend every waking hour figuring out how to get the best of you."

His eyes narrow to two straight lines.

I throw my hands up. I don't know what else to say to him.

"Penelope and Richard know you're selling your team."

My blood hardens. That can't be the case. "How do you know that?"

"She's been hanging around Londyn, making your mother happy to hear you might settle down with her, have kids, and shit." At least Max isn't so mad that he can't blurt a laugh at the end of that ridiculous assertion.

I can't stop shaking my head. "That explains my father's talk of producing an heir."

"Fuck all that," Max says, bringing his drink to his lips and then pointing it at me. "Lynx, Rich and his daughter will try to put the squeeze on you, and I don't need you panicking."

"Panicking?"

"Yeah. Panicking. I know you're into Xena, or you wouldn't have moved her into your...."

"She's my employee. And we're friends."

Max glares at me as if I hurled bullshit at him. "Uh-huh."

I don't know what the hell he means by "uh-huh."

He carefully sets down his glass. "You had sex with Xena about a month ago."

I shrug. "So what?" I'm on the defense because this is the start of Max making a point.

"You said it was one night only, and then you

hired her. But you still haven't fucked. And now you've moved her into your apartment." Eyes narrowed, Max tips his head. "Is there a pattern developing here, Lynx?"

Is there? I can't figure it out. I like Xena a lot.

"Listen," Max continues because I'm lost for an explanation. "My guess is that Lilly's cousin is a you-bang-it you-buy-it kind of woman. I've known you all your life. You bang it and you bang it, and you bang some more, and then you lose interest."

"I thought you were discussing Penelope, not Xena."

"You've already banged Penelope and finished up. But she doesn't know it yet. Don't let her wise up to your ways, Lynx. It's going to be you and me running the show. We used to dream about this shit when we were kids. Don't let your dick screw it up."

I frown as I rub my chest. I'm confused because I don't want to bang and bang and bang Xena and then toss her out like last week's newspaper. I like being around her, and yeah, I like having sex with her too. But that's today. I don't know what I'll feel in the future. Maybe I am a noncommittal asshole. I may have made a mistake by inviting Xena to live with me. But that dump she called home....

Max watches me, scrutinizing his words' impact on me as he consumes his drink.

"Do you have a plan for Rich?" he finally asks.

Still vexed by how I treated women in the past and these strange feelings I have for a beautiful, intelligent, and good-natured woman I met almost a month ago, I nod slowly. Richard Chastain…. "I'll handle the Chastains," I say.

But Xena—I can't wait to see how she looks in our place.

# EIGHTEEN
## XENA ST. JAMES

8 Hours Ago

I had washed in my humongous shower earlier without worrying about my elbow hitting the slimy shower curtain. It was amazing. Then, I wrapped up in my fluffy white robe and toured the rest of the apartment. I marveled over the high-end home gym, an ultra-masculine den with black leather furniture and design pieces made of onyx, and two more bedrooms with attached spa-like bathrooms. I wasn't even halfway through when I poked my head into a nice office, and then I took another private elevator up to our own rooftop sunroom encased in glass. I laid out on one of the lounge chairs and admired the colors in the sky.

It didn't take long for the feeling that I must do something to wash over me. I leaped to my feet and promptly returned to the apartment. Once inside, I smelled food, and since I was starving, I followed my nose, and that led me to Hugo, the chef in the kitchen.

Dinner was a traditional lasagne with antipasto and focaccia plated gourmet-style. As I ate, I felt tired, lonely, and worried that Lynx and Penelope were at it like rabbits. She's obviously the reason he wasn't home. And the way she stormed out of the apartment said she was on her way to convince Lynx that I am not the most suitable option for him; she is. I don't disagree. Apart, Penelope and Lynx have the sort of sex appeal that stops traffic, together, they can halt the world.

I needed to get out and numb my insecurity and the usual hopeless feeling that I have no idea what tomorrow will bring. Right on cue, my cellphone chimed in my pocket, and it was my girlfriend Tab inviting me to go out with her and a group of friends. First, though, she oohed and ahhed on a quick tour of Lynx's apartment.

On the way to a Broadway producer's birthday party, she asked a lot of questions about Lynx.

"No man lets you move into a place like that

unless he's into you," she said, adding, "And you can take that to the bank and cash it."

I admitted that I'm unsure how Lynx feels about me or even how I feel about him.

"We're going with the flow," I had said. "And now the flow says I need a job, and we both know I should've moved out of that hellhole long ago."

"True." Tab beamed at me teasingly. "Well, if you fuck him again, and I know you will, get a hump in for me."

I punched her playfully in the shoulder as we laughed. That ended any talk about Lynx Grove for the remainder of the night.

The best parties consist of creative people who love to sing and dance. They can go from sunup to sundown, doing precisely what they're good at. There was a lot of drinking too, of course, and usually, I could get blasted two nights in a row if it's the weekend. Mega party nights have been few and far between since I became a line producer, but on the rare occasions when work hadn't been an anvil tied to my ankle, I would party up a storm on Friday and Saturday night and then sleep at Lilies all day Sunday. However, I kept it tamed tonight since Lynx witnessed me drunk and not at my best the previous night. I don't want my boss to think I have an issue with alcohol. So I drank sparkling water with lemon, and although I danced and joined in on some songs, I couldn't banish Lynx and Penelope from my thoughts. I have to make peace with the fact that they see each other in some capacity, which means he's off-limits. I don't share men with other women, hashtag girl-code.

But now, as I ride up the elevator, leaning against the wall, struggling to keep my eyes open, I know that even though Lynx's apartment is magnificent, I should probably find my own sooner rather than later.

The elevator stops, and butterflies flutter in my stomach. Now comes the moment of truth. Will Lynx be home or at Penelope's? I bet she lives in a luxury skyrise with loads of wealthy people.

"Tomorrow when I wake up," I whisper as the doors finish sliding open. I'll start searching for my own place then.

However, I'm already missing the grand foyer as I pass through it on my way to the living room where flashes of television light illuminate the darkness. Hand over my heart, I feel so relieved to watch Lynx rise to his feet when he sees me.

He's grimacing like he's chewing on lemons. "Where have you been?"

*Has he been waiting for me?* "I went to a birthday party."

"I kept calling you until I realized you left your phone in your room. I was worried."

I can see that he's worried. His eyes look tired and red, and his hair is mussed up like he's been raking his fingers through his untamed curls all night. He seems extra gorgeous when he's wired up. And he's changed into a pair of red track pants with a white and blue Ramblers T-shirt.

"Yes, I left it here by accident," I say.

"Are you drunk?" He says drunk like it's a dirty word.

"No. I don't get hammered every night. Even if every time you've seen me out and about, I've either been drunk or raging."

His eyebrows shift up and down like he's processing what I said, then subtly, a small smile appears across his lips. "Sorry I wasn't here to help you settle in. I got delayed."

"Penelope?" Saying her name makes my insides recoil, and I don't like the feeling. Never has another woman made me feel this way. Is it jealousy?

It's as if he's encapsulated by a haze of bleakness when he says, "No."

"No?"

"Why do you sound surprised?"

I twist my lips, wondering if I should say something.

"Spit it out, Xena."

"She was here earlier," I say with a shrug.

Lynx closes his eyes as he sighs. "That's why she's been calling me like crazy."

I try to hide how pleased and surprised I am. "You haven't spoken to her today?"

"No. What happened when she saw you?"

Groaning, I absentmindedly walk to the sofa and take a seat. I have to sit down for this, and Lynx sits too.

"She asked what I was doing here. I said I live here, and she said something like, 'the hell you do.'"

Lynx nods, but he's looking at me like he's seeing straight through me. "Sorry about that, Xena. I want you to feel comfortable in this apartment. It's now yours just as much as it's mine."

My face says, "dude, that's not true."

Lynx chuckles. "It is."

"Everything in this apartment is way out of my price range."

"Are you averse to being given nice things, Xena?"

His voice was so sexy it made my heart and other parts flutter. But I don't know the answer to his question, but I want to ask him something that's been bothering me all night.

"Will I have to worry about running into you and Penelope in the kitchen, perhaps, postcoital or something?"

He looks at me incredulously. "What?"

"I mean, I understand you're a virile young man, who probably has a vivacious sex life that includes Penelope...."

"Stop, Xena," he says, waving a hand. "That's not how it works between Penelope and me."

I wait for him to explain, but after several seconds of silence, I realize he won't say more about the intriguing statement he just made.

"Then how does it work?" I ask because I *need* to hear it.

Lynx eyes slowly narrow until their slits. "Sporadic."

"Sporadic?"

Lynx rubs his chin. "I thought you were more like her. But you're not."

I yank my head back. "I'm certainly nothing like her."

"I know," he whispers as if it surprises him.

But now I think I'm offended. "What made you believe otherwise?"

"It's what you did."

He had the same look in his eyes when he knocked on Lily's apartment door three weeks ago.

"What did I do?" I ask.

"You tightened around me."

*I tightened around him.*

My eyes grow wide as I remember. "Oh," I strain to say. "That."

"Yeah. That." His smile is naughty enough to make me wet, like the first night we met. But we can't do that again, not while I live with him. And certainly not when he's my only source of income.

I look down at my lap, shaking my head. "I don't know what got into me." Suddenly, I look up. "Actually, I do. You were just such a controlling asshole, so…" I shrug.

Lynx's eye contact is deep and prolonged. "So you took control."

I'm rendered speechless and motionless. I'm certain the answer to how he thought I was more like Penelope has already been revealed, but my ability to dissect his words is momentarily out of service because of my intense lust.

I hop up to my feet. "I'm going to go to bed."

I'm leaving. I have to get out of this living room, or I'll end up in his bed in less than twenty seconds.

Lynx quickly stands, towering over me. "By the way, how was dinner?"

I blink several times. Dinner? That was almost nine hours ago. "Good," I say in a high-pitched voice.

"Hugo said he made lasagne."

My head feels like it's floating above my neck as I nod.

"Um, listen." He runs a hand nervously through his curls. "Sorry about bringing up that night. You asked."

"I know," I say, figuring I should work harder to cool my lust. If this is going to work, I can't get all hot and bothered whenever we have adult conversations. "Oh, and listen, thank you for letting me move in so quickly. But I'm going to look for another place starting tomorrow."

"What. No." I can hear the pleading in his voice and see it in his eyes. "Come on, Xena. This is the perfect setup we have here. At least..." He's raking his fingers through his hair again. "How about we take it one day at a time? Plus, I like you being here. I like the company."

The vulnerability in his eyes makes my heart

thump harder. I admit to myself that I am not closer to becoming more platonic with Lynx. I'm also not closer to being able to look at him through the same lens through which Evie views him. Even now, he smells scrumptious. He must've showered. I want him on top of me and inside me so much that giddy energy stabs through my chest.

"There has been a development regarding selling my team," he whispers.

I nod lightly. "There has?"

Lynx is as stiff as a board as he observes me closely. Then, he releases the tension in his shoulders. "How about we talk about it over breakfast or brunch? Here, in our kitchen. When we wake up."

I can't stop my slow smile from blossoming. Gosh, I like him an awful lot. I wish it were easy to fall in love with him.

"Okay," I finally say.

His smile matches mine. "Good night, Xena. I hope you sleep well on your first night in our apartment."

Help me because my heart is doing backflips. "Me too."

"Oh," he says as if he just remembered something. "And you look amazing tonight. I'm surprised you didn't bring someone."

Oh shit. I nod stiffly. What he said confirms that he will bring women home on some nights, even Penelope.

"But…" He takes two steps in now he's closer. "How about we make a pact."

"A pact?" I barely say.

"No sleepovers until we get this deal done."

I love the sound of that. My throat is so tight because he's too close for comfort, and I'm only barely able to say, "Okay."

Hands in his pockets, Lynx tilts forward. His sensual lips are near my ear. "Good night, Xena."

I hear myself say goodnight, but I can't sense the words leaving my mouth. I'm walking to my bedroom. I feel his eyes upon me, but I'm too anxious to turn to see whether it's all in my head. Plus, I don't want to know. I can't know—because if I knew, I might turn right around and ask if I could sleep with him tonight.

And so, after crossing the threshold to my room, I close the double doors, and through the tiny slice, my gaze meets Lynx's.

# NINETEEN

# XENA ST. JAMES

### Late Sunday Morning

I blink until my heavy eyelids open all the way. Low gray clouds and a dimming effect on the windows mute the light in the room.

"Umm," I moan, smiling. It has been years since I've slept like a baby.

I thrust myself up into the sitting position and push the soft sheet and heavenly duvet down my legs. *I feel good—I feel real good.*

I reach over for my cellphone and look for the time.

"Yikes!"

I'm on my feet and scurrying into my walk-in closet, which I am in love with, and throw on my fluffy white robe. However, I pause to briefly consider wearing something shorter and silkier, but that would be too obvious. Plus, I'm in the process of weaning myself off wanting Lynx in a sexual way. So I keep the longer, bulkier robe on, then quickly brush my teeth and wash my face. I'm halfway down the hallway when I hear Lynx arguing with a woman whose voice definitely belongs to Penelope.

Lynx says, "This is how you wanted it."

"Not anymore," she replies.

I stand very still and silence my breathing in the seconds of ensuing silence.

"I don't know what to say, Penelope," Lynx says in a tone a girl who's in love with a man hates to hear from him.

"Are you fucking her still?"

I stiffen because they're talking about me.

"I'm not fucking anybody."

"You're fucking me!" she says extra loudly.

Lynx starts speaking, but his voice is cut off abruptly. I hear the faint sound of my cellphone chiming, telling me I have a text message. I run back to my bedroom and swipe my device off the nightstand. It's a message from Lynx: Sorry, I missed you. I have a training session. Lunch is in the warmer. Talk Later.

For some reason, I don't believe him. But that's okay, Lynx's argument with Penelope and his text message serve as a reality check, one that I need to remember, he is not the man for me.

I GET DRESSED COMFORTABLY and warm enough to spend a day away from the apartment. I don't know what's in the plans yet, but something usually materializes. It's rare that I'm home on Sundays because I hated my old apartment and spent as little time in it as I could. This Sunday, however, I would rather stay inside and play my guitar and then binge a new TV series on Netflix, perhaps something Italian or French. Also, I could lounge on our private rooftop and read a book. But to a greater extent, I want to avoid facing the aftermath of that conversation I heard between Lynx and Penelope. I need to process their words and run as far away from those mushy feelings I had for Lynx before falling asleep.

Thankfully, my dad calls from Los Angeles, and our conversation takes my mind in a different direction. He has a show at the Hollywood Bowl this evening and asks if I want to fly out and tag along for a few weeks of shows.

I sneer at his interesting offer. "You spoke to mom didn't you?"

He chuckles. "You caught me."

"I have another job, you know."

"That's what Jojo says. But, I don't know Peanut maybe it's time you come join me for a while. Your mom had you at the studio for how many years? It's my turn now."

I blurt a cynical laugh. "When did you start luring audiences who are interested in angst and rage?"

Hollis cracks up, and I tell him about a performance I gave on Friday night that apparently was Grammy-worthy. It was a song I performed after my sober act, so I can't remember it.

"It contained such words as Greg and troll."

"Then you left that guy in your dust for good?"

"Yep."

"Peanut, listen." The silence that follows says it's time to get serious. "I know I've been selfish. It's too late to go back and be different, but I want you to know if I could, I would. That's why I want you to come tonight. I wanna spend more time with you.

You're becoming a young woman, and soon you'll be telling me you're ready to marry some bloke. And I don't want your choices to be reflections of my massive fuck ups."

I over process everything my dad said, trying to figure out where all of this is coming from. "Wow, Dad that's very insightful of you."

His breathy chuckle is full of emotion.

"But you're a little late for this talk. I'm almost thirty, and I've already pulled apart and put together all the ways my daddy screwed me up."

"Yeah, yeah, I know."

"I love you," I say to take the sting out of what I said seconds ago.

"I know you do... What's that Jim?" he asks abruptly. I'm suddenly aware that his attention has been called away. He won't say, *give me a second, I'm talking to my daughter.*

As I wait for the muffle words in the background to end, my phone beeps. But I take a moment to let myself feel what's happening within me during two very intense seconds. Hollis is sending me a message that he loves me but what's going on around him is more important than giving me his full attention that will bring our call to a satisfying end. And I am relieved that Lilly has called so that I don't have to experience the grief of being second-bested by my father.

"Dad, I gotta go," I say before he can. "It's Lily calling."

"Ah, Lilly Belle. Tell her I love her. I'll call you soon."

"Alright," I barely say before his side of our call goes silent. As usual, the show must go first. But the sting of the abrupt end to my phone call with Hollis is already fading.

I click over to connect with Lilly. "Hey."

"You okay?" she asks.

I release a deep breath through my nose. "Yep. What's up?"

"What are you doing today?" She sounds as if her life depends on my answer.

---

1 Hour later

I'm seated at a table with Lilly and Orion. We're having lunch at *Bon*, a French bistro a few blocks from where I live. Lilly said they were in the neighborhood for sunup to sundown street bazaar.

It has been awkward, to say the least. For

instance, Lilly has been leaning against Orion's muscular arm ever since we were seated. It's like they're Siamese twins. It's still so odd watching them together. I mean, Lilly used to hate Orion Lord with every fiber of her being.

"I guess it's true what they say," I say after the waitress takes our order.

"What's that?" Orion asks.

My comment about hate being the bedrock of love stays stuck on my tongue as I think about that in real-life terms. "Nothing," I say, shaking my head after reconsidering my comment. Actually, there is no love in hate. People hate humans they've never met, and there's no love in that.

"You sure?" Lilly asks, sinking her arm deeper against Orion's. "Because Orion is all ears. Right, babe?"

I narrow an eye suspiciously. "Okay. Spit it out."

"Spit what out?" Lilly asks.

"What do you want to say to me?"

Lilly tilts her head toward Orion. "Babe, go ahead. Start."

I make a face. Start? What the hell is happening?

Orion looks very serious. "Xena, I want us to be friends. I'm here to assure you that I love your cousin very much. I've always loved her, even when I didn't treat her with the respect she deserved."

I'm trying to keep a straight face and not burst out into laughter. Although I believe Orion, he sounded like he was reading from a script prepared by Lilly. But the part where he prattles on about her brilliance and kindness was not orchestrated by Lilly. He says she is quick-witted too, which he finds to be a turn-on. I'm seriously listening to the man articulate a list of my cousin's positives, most of which is news to me. Does Lilly have a quick wit? When did that happen?

"Okay," I say, waving my hands because I've heard enough. I lean across the table, pinning my focus on Orion. "Orion, take care of our girl and her quick wit." A laugh escapes me as I sit up. "I trust you will." That's the best I could come up with.

"Xena, this is serious," Lilly chastises.

"I know," I say still laughing. "But quick-witted? Come on." My humorous moment stalls when my attention is captured by Lynx and Penelope entering the restaurant. Lynx sees me right away. He has on dark blue track pants with a black T-shirt. Penelope is wearing tight athletic pants and a tight matching jacket. It looks like they just came from the gym together. So, it's apparent I was wrong to think he was lying. He said he had training, maybe he was training to do some sort of physical event. I'm happy to believe that Lynx told me the truth. That's why my hand raises and my fingers wave weakly.

Lynx says something to Penelope, and now here they come.

Lilly has turned around in her seat to view who's stolen my attention. Her face lights up when she sees Lynx, and she bounds to her feet. "Lynx!"

They hug, and Orion stands to shake Lynx's hand like they're old friends. Penelope smiles at me as if to say, "hey bitch, I see you." The fact that she views us as competitors is written in her eyes. And I'm not the kind of girl who fights with other girls over a boy, and I won't start now. She's the one he's been hanging out with all day. Plus, the argument they had earlier was intense and revealing. She's the clear winner.

Lily's attention bobs between Lynx and Penelope. She's waiting to be introduced. When it's clear he will not formally present the woman he's with, Lilly says, "Roomies, huh?" Now her gaze shifts between Lynx and me.

Penelope's sigh is more like a huff.

I force a smile, trying to make light of it all. "I'm living in the lap of luxury." I want to add that it's temporary, but then I recall the deal I made with Lynx.

"And your her boss too," Lilly adds, grinning like it's her wedding day as she purposely rubs it in. My cousin isn't at all clueless that she's getting under Penelope's skin.

Lynx puts a hand on Penelope's shoulder. He's touched me that way on several occasions. Watching it from this viewpoint, it's evident that his action is strictly platonic. It's a relief.

"Penelope," Lynx says extra loudly. "Great run today. But I'm going to hang out here for a few."

Penelope's eyebrows shoot straight up and hold.

Lynx focuses solely on me. "We came to grab a cappuccino."

I smile weakly, letting him know that I'm grateful for the explanation.

"Then I'll see you tonight. Remember, we have dinner with my parents," Penelope chirps.

Her face leans toward Lynx, and to avoid seeing what I believe what will become a kiss, I aim my eyes at my lap. Soon, Lynx plops down in the empty chair beside me. Orion asks him how's the team.

Lynx says it's off-season, so things are less hectic but still busy. Orion understands.

"Alex Shaw was a winning acquisition for you," Orion says.

"Yes, he is." Lynx suddenly stiffens as if he remembers something. "By the way, congratulations to you both on your recent nuptials."

"Thank you," Lilly and Orion say, snuggling closer. I didn't think they could get closer, but they somehow managed it.

"So, Lynx, is that her?" Lilly asks.

"Her?"

I avoid looking at Lynx, but he sounds baffled by the question, perhaps because it lacks context.

"The friend you said you are in love with."

I feel warm under my black sweater. I can't believe Lilly is bringing that up right here and now. She's being naughty.

Lynx readjusts in his seat, and I watch his hands with fingers enfolded drop on the table through the corner of my eye. "I'm not in love with anybody, Lilly."

He has the same tone he used when he denied his relationship with Penelope to me.

"But you said you were in love with a friend, and that's why we couldn't take things further."

Oh my God, I can't believe she's doing this.

Orion seems unbothered by Lily's cross-examination of Lynx. He actually appears eager to hear Lynx's answer. It's as if they're teaming up on him, which is something Greg and I used to do when we've been gossiping about someone, and now we have a chance to get some answers.

I can no longer avoid looking at Lynx, who has a blank look on his face. It's clear he's not enjoying being in the hot seat.

"Things change," he says.

Lilly nods thoughtfully. "Right. Did things change after or before I left you two alone in my apartment? Because I think you've been lying to me, Zeen. I, we..." She shrugs a shoulder against Orion. "Think you slept together, which explains why you're now working for him and living together. So just tell the truth, Zeen. I want to hear it."

Well, she's no longer glued to her hubby. Lilly has perked up and is way too invested in hearing my answer, which is really none of her business now that I think about it.

Lynx and I raise our eyebrows at each other. When he shrugs, I get the message. Revealing the truth is up to me. But telling the truth isn't easy. I can never let myself forget the shit Lynx said about not wanting to be in a relationship and not kissing or spooning. And yet, I had sex with him anyway. If I tell Lilly all of that, she would judge me from here to kingdom come. I sort of feel like after Lynx hired me, and yesterday morning when he woke up in my bedroom at my previous apartment, we were granted an opportunity to start over.

"We became friends that night, and that's all," I say.

"But did you have sex?" Lilly rapid-fires her question.

Thankfully, our waitress comes to our table and asks us if we need anything else. Of course, she notices Lynx is a new addition and asks if she can take his order.

"Actually, I'm going to head out." He looks at me. "Penelope and I were practicing for the Paws and Claws marathon." He's obviously further explaining why they were together and dressed like the hot couple at the gym.

"Our mothers are sponsoring that event," Orion says.

"Right," Lynx mutters and puts a large and warm hand on my shoulder. "We'll talk later."

I gaze into his eyes as I nod. I make sure the butterflies in my stomach stay grounded.

Despite Lilly giving him the fifth-degree Lynx hugs her and shakes Orion's hand one last time before walking away from us. I watch him go. Lynx has the posture of a man who's sure of himself. It's sexy. I am not sure of myself at all.

"Pss," Lilly whispers.

I rip my attention off Lynx as he strides past the window and set my focus on her.

"He gave her the cheek when she tried to kiss him. Just thought you should know."

---

I COULDN'T FORGET that Lynx has a date with Penelope tonight. He may not be in love with her, but they are definitely in a relationship that is more than friends. Anyway, instead of going home to see him after he's dressed up for his evening out and looking yummy, I accompany Lilly and Orion for their second stroll through the street bazaar. At a certain point, I get enough of them kissing and being handsy. I call Tab who says I can hang out with her.

After saying goodbye to Orion and Lilly, I take

the subway to Tab's place in Williamsburg. To my disappointment, she left out the part where we were hanging with her boyfriend Derek as they shop for a new townhome in his same Williamsburg neighborhood. The two of them are not on the same page. His taste is similar to Lynx's, although much more sterile, and hers is more cluttered like mine. She wants something that's traditional. He wants a place that has been gutted and updated from top to bottom.

I bow out of the search at the fourth brownstone where neither is willing to compromise. Frankly, I can't believe their relationship has lasted this long. He's a Wall Street hedge fund manager, and she's a Broadway dancer. Not only are their tastes clashing but their friends are like night and day different. I leave them arguing about a soaking tub as opposed to a golden-toed claw-foot bathtub. When I make it back to the building, the doorman tells me that I have a guest.

"A guest?" I ask, wondering if it's my mom until I remember she left for Tampa this morning to prepare for tomorrow's first live show.

Then the doorman points out my unexpected guest, and my jaw drops.

# TWENTY

# XENA ST. JAMES

Greg isn't alone—Fido is on a leash. The dog's tail wags like crazy as he turns in circles because he's so excited. I'm shocked Fido misses me so much. His eagerness confirms Greg was the problem and not the lovable dog who's being affected by a deranged man.

"You live here now?" Greg grumbles.

I frown at the look on Greg's face. It's as if he's swallowing baking soda. It's not like the expression is alien to me. It's reserved for when I've done or am doing something he doesn't like.

Every part of me wants to ignore his question and then storm off to the front desk and tell them never to let him back into the building. Instead, I squat down and pet and rub Fido's belly since our reunion will be short-lived. I forgot how much I love the little bulldog when he's not being naughty. After all, when he went to the bathroom on my things, he was only doing Greg's bidding.

"Greg, what do you want," I say, ending my brief but intense love affair with Fido as I rise to stand.

"Are you living with Lilly?" Of course, he ignores me.

"No."

He scowls at a guy walking past us who's dressed nicely and smells good. I forgot how jealous Greg can be, especially when the competition is the apparent winner, which is odd because Greg could hardly keep his eyes to himself whenever we went out. He'd be speaking to me while staring at another woman. And then, at some point, he'd make a judgmental comment about her, like, "Isn't it too cold to have your boobs out for the world to see?"

But at the moment, I'll hand it to him, Greg has shown up looking his best. He has on gray cashmere dress slacks and a cream-colored sweater under a gray trench coat. Greg has always been a great dresser. I think it's one reason why I used to be attracted to him. He obviously knows I used to like it when he dressed up, which means he's trying to win me back.

"This building is too far from Rank Studios," he grouses.

I shake my head hard because that's his way of saying, *you still work for me. Sure, we had our big blowout, but you know what to do—get your ass back to your desk.*

A time existed when I would've been biting my nails, expecting and waiting for this moment to occur. However, I take stock of how I'm feeling and am surprised. Finally, I feel as if I have truly moved on.

"You didn't answer my question," I say. "What do you want, Greg?"

"Okay. You win."

I frown, pondering the words 'you win'. I win?

"Are we going to talk about this like adults?" he adds during my prolonged silence.

Suddenly, the door opens to Lynx and my private hallway. My jaw-droppingly hot roommate appears, and he stops in his tracks as we lock eyes. Greg is nicely dressed tonight, but he's no match for the strapping man wearing a long black duster coat showing just enough leg to see that his dress pants and shoes are nice and expensive.

"Everything okay, Xena?" Lynx asks, scowling at Greg.

Greg rips his attention off Lynx to give me a dirty look. "Who is that?"

It's like he's chastising me for being associated with someone he's intimidated by. Have I truly given this man that much power over my life? "He's Lynx Grove, my boss and new roommate," I reply.

Greg's eyes and mouth grow double in size. "Are you kidding me? You're fucking your boss again?"

That's exactly what I needed to hear to gain the proper perspective. "Go away, Greg," I growl and take a step toward the hallway. Greg grabs me by the arm.

"Hey," Lynx roars as he strides in our direction. "Take your hands off her!"

Lynx doesn't have to say it twice. Seeing the big hunk of a man barreling toward us, Greg lets go of me immediately. I step in front of Lynx to keep him from physically confronting the more petite man.

"Xena, please. I'm on my knees," Greg begs.

He's what? I turn to see that he's indeed on his knees, gazing at me pleadingly.

"I need you. I miss you. Move in with *me*."

I can't say I'm surprised he's doing this because this is how we operate. Yep, it's been three days since the restaurant incident. He never believed I would quit Rank Studio. He always took me for someone who couldn't stop doing what her mother wanted. But here he is, begging the old Xena St. James to show up and give him what he needs.

My mouth is open, and my lips tremble. Inquiring about what happened between him and Helena is on the tip of my tongue. I only want to ask if another woman is making Greg happy by jumping through his hoops so I won't have to worry about him. It's sad when I think about it—this notion that it's my job to make an unhappy person happy. Maybe I've been projecting onto Greg while we were together. If I could dispel his misery, then I could banish my own. But my efforts never worked for either of us.

"Here. Let me walk you to the elevator," Lynx says, curling an arm around my waist as he leads me away from my ex.

*Gosh, he smells so delicious.*

"Xena, honey, please," Greg pleads.

But I don't look back as Lynx and I escape into our hallway. Out of sight, out of mind, although Greg yells that he's not done yet as Fido yaps. I release myself from Lynx's tender hold on me. It felt so good being in his arms, but I have to remember that he's looking good and smelling divine for Penelope. They'll definitely have sex tonight. She's going to make sure of it.

I force the fakest smile I ever made. "I'm fine, Lynx. Go to your dinner. I'm fine."

Lynx's gaze flicks across my face. "Are you sure?"

I can hardly perceive that I'm nodding. "Yes."

His hand flies up like he wants to touch me, but he quickly drops his arm. "Enjoy the place. Have you seen the swimming pool?"

I hadn't finished my tour. "No." My voice almost cracked. It's great we have a swimming pool, but it's the last thing on my mind. My sinuses burn like I want to cry, but my brain forces my tears to stay put.

"It's on my side of the apartment."

"Okay." That came out too tight.

Lynx narrows an eye. He looks worried. "Are you sure you're fine?"

Shit. I've been standing here too long because I forgot to push the up button. So I press it hard. "Yes, Lynx. You can go. I'll be fine."

Suddenly, Lynx is hugging me. I close my eyes as his sensual lips kiss me affectionately on the forehead. My heart races to the moon as I turn my wavering smile away from him and enter the opened elevator as fast as possible.

When I turn to face the hallway, Lynx is already gone.

I make it to the apartment without shedding a tear. The weekend has been way too long, and I desperately want to cry because my heart hurts.

I fall face down on my perfectly made bed, realizing my room has been cleaned. Wow, maid service. I jolt my body around to lie on my back and gaze at the ceiling. And still, I want to cry. But…

Holy shit! I sit up and stare out my perfectly lit Hudson River view. "Am I unable to cry?"

# TWENTY-ONE
## LYNX GROVE

The Chastains keep a historic luxury apartment on 5th Avenue. Like many mini-mansions on that street, the building was built in the late 1800s and turned into luxury apartments in the 1920s. Richard and his wife Margaret kept as much of the original design as the degradation of time would allow. There's too much wainscoting, old wallpaper, coffer ceilings, and checkered marble floors for my taste. When I'm inside this place, not only does it make me feel like I'm trapped in an oversized casket, but it wreaks of Gilded Age gluttony. The smell never fails to get on me. When I'm on my way home, it'll fill the cab of my vehicle. The odor will torment me until I shower it off.

I've been seated at a table in their windowless dining room for nearly an hour. My mother would tell me what I'm doing is rude, which is checking my watch, but I don't have to worry about hearing her tsk because she's not here.

Sitting at the head of the table, Rich's large jaws chew a mouth full of prime rib. I can tell he's been trying to read me since his butler seated us at a glaze wood table that resembles the one my grandmother donated to the New York City Historical Relics Society after my grandfather passed. My grandfather used to love old shit like this too.

I arrived with a strategy in mind, and that is to say as little as possible. I want Rich to do all the talking. I also want him to get to the point of why he invited me to dinner. Penelope, who is sitting across from me, can barely look me in the eye. Every now and then she and Margaret will pass each other a look. So far, the topic of discussion has been the stock market and my plans for the team next year, which was his attempt to lure me into confessing that I might sell the Ramblers before the season starts.

I just finished listing a group of players we're scouting and articulated their strengths and weaknesses. The darkening in the way that Rich regards me is perceptible. He thinks I'm bullshitting him, but I'm not. I haven't decided to sell what I built from scratch, so I'm still operating like I have a World Series to win next season.

"So," Rich says, jerking his shoulders back to improve his posture. "When are you going to make an honest woman out of my daughter?" He chuckles like he's joking, but he isn't.

"Dad," Penelope scolds weakly.

"Londyn agrees," Margaret, who hasn't had anything to lend to the conversation until now, says. "She's over the moon about a union between our kids. You're perfect for each other, don't you think?" Her large blinking eyes settle on me.

I nod, thinking it's a great move to make the usually taciturn mother and wife their mouthpiece tonight. I can see it in Margaret's eyes, though. She's eager to be associated with my family. She wants to refer to me as her son-in-law and access all the philanthropic boards my mom sits on so she can turn her nose up higher than her snooty friends.

However, my mother has never been invested in who I'm to marry. But then I recall that conversation I had with my dad about heirs and shit, and now I'm starting to wonder if she's turned on me.

Margaret and the rest of the family are waiting

for my answer. I could be blunt and say, hell no. But this is a test. My answer is equivalent to a policy that makes the stock market go wonky.

"Penelope and I have been great colleagues. If it weren't for her, we wouldn't have gotten eyes on our team so quickly. Those eyes have stayed and increased, and that's all due to her effort to"—I face Rich—"make the Ramblers a success."

Rich's eyes narrow a smidgen, and his smirk is slight. I can hear his thoughts. He's thinking, what a way to bullshit a bullshitter young buck. The thing about our business arrangement is I've always known I made a deal with the devil. Rich is all about money and power, and he's into getting maximum output for minuscule input. But regardless if I sell or not, tonight has revealed the time has come for us to draw our pistols and duel it out.

"But yes, I like Penelope in other ways too." I shift anxiously in my seat. "But marriage isn't on the top of my list...."

"Why not?" Rich roars.

"Because hell, I'm only thirty-one, and Penelope isn't my girlfriend."

"Then date." He points at his daughter. "My girl is top choice. Do you know how many players ask about her? How many Wall Street hedge fund managers and CEOs like yourself? She's a treasure to have by your side, just like her mother."

I'm not shocked he said that shit out loud. Rich's mindset matches his stale decor. I let my attention float over Margaret, who blushes as she rubs the side of her neck.

It's easy to see that she hasn't been fucked good in at least twenty years. She should count herself lucky because Rich is into leaving high-end call girls sexually unsatisfied. But Margaret, although worn from worry, is a beautiful woman.

I'm rubbing my ear on purpose. I've figured out that Rich has learned it's something I do when nervous. I want him to believe I'm ruffled and he's having his way with me.

"Indeed," is all I say.

"Alright." Silverware clinks against porcelain as Rich drops his meaty hands on the table. "I heard you're selling the team. Is that true?"

I hold my composure, even if I want to sigh with relief. Finally, we're getting down to the nitty-gritty.

"Who told you that?" I ask.

"Does it matter?"

"It does," I say with a nod.

Rich glares at me with one eye narrowed. I know what he's thinking. He's thinking, you answered my question by not answering my question.

I could've lied, but I wanted him to know the truth. It's time to smoke him out and figure out what the hell he really wants.

He and Margaret make eye contact, and then he rubs his triple chin. "They weren't going to give you the team until I came on board."

Ah… Great move reminding me that I should be grateful. But I don't give a fuck. That was business back then, and this is now.

"True," I say. That's it. He's next.

He points a hand at his wife and daughter. "You know I have a family to feed."

I stifle a laugh. Not in a million years have I ever thought he would say that. Rich is desperate. But I know what to say next because it's the reason why he's beating around the bush.

"And we have a contractual agreement. I can't sell my team…"

"Our team," he cuts in, his voice ringing loud and clear.

I lick my bottom lip as I repress the yearning to remind him he only owns fifteen percent, which he paid peanuts for, and I have stipulations in the contract regarding his big discount.

But I don't want to send him in the right direction with this lawyer because the first shots have been fired, and we are at war.

"Listen, I'll buy into Grove Industrial Tech for five percent of your shares, and you can do whatever the hell you want with that team."

My grandfather taught me that the most powerful men in the world know how to keep their cool when it matters. I have to be the lion, and he's the cheetah. He has to sense that even though I can maul him to death, I'm being peaceable. That way, I can buy the time I need to stalk him slowly, then, in a surprise attack, pounce.

So I pick up my knife and fork and cut into the tender piece of meat. "I don't know who told you I was selling my team and what that has to do with GIT, but they should talk to me before spreading rumors."

I calmly put the prime rib in my mouth and chew as if unbothered by our conversation. It helps that it tastes good.

Rich eyes me skeptically and then grunts. "True or not, you know my terms."

I look him in the eye and conjure a shit-eating grin. "Marry your daughter and give you a piece of my family's fortune." I meant for that to sting.

I wink at him, and he grunts, smirking. I shouldn't have said that. *Shit.*

---

THE HOUSEMAID, dressed in a black and white uniform from the 1950's hands me my coat as I enter the foyer. The butler holds the door open and waits dutifully for me to exit.

I've almost escaped, but Penelope has been stalking me like a wildcat in estrus.

"Lynx," she calls before I can clear the threshold.

After dessert, I said goodbye to the family but asked to use the bathroom before leaving. I told the butler, who escorted me, that I had changed my mind. But shit, Penelope still found a way to catch up to me.

I turn to face her as I button up my coat. "Yeah."

Her eyes widen as she senses my annoyance. "I apologize for the couple's talk. I didn't know my dad was going to mention us."

"There is no us, Penelope," I say.

"Is it because of Xena? Are you seeing her?"

Maybe. I don't know yet. And that's the truth. "It's because you and I have never been in a traditional relationship."

Penelope eyes grow even wider as she panics. "William, Elena, you can be excused," she says to the butler and maid.

Without a word, our witnesses disperse, leaving us alone.

Penelope re-garners eye contact with me. "You know her mother's an orphan, right?"

"Whose mother?"

"Xena's."

"Jojo?" I say, surprised and impressed.

Penelope sighs as if I'm missing the point. "She's not on your level, Lynx." She burps a laugh. "She peddles those cheap clothes on the Home Shopping Emporium and the price tags, classless. She's laughable. That's not how Groves or Chastains behave."

I always knew Penelope was a snob like her

mother. I watch her sour expression. It's as if she's still reacting to her feelings about self-made, go-getting, sexy-as-hell Jojo O'Leary. I stop myself from revealing that before I met the daughter, I would've fucked the mother in a New York minute. Shit, those curves, and Xena has them too.

I also want to give her a Grove family history lesson. Where in the hell does she think we came from? High society? Everybody knows my grandfather is from a working-class neighborhood in Oakland, California. He grew up with a family who survived pay-check to pay-check. Everything was more challenging for my great grandparents—bank loans, home loans, having entrepreneurial spirits, and getting a lift to making their dreams possible. But my grandfather figured shit out. He allowed himself to accept a world where it's easier for some and harder for others, and that's just the way it is. Once accepted, he knew what he had to do. My grandfather found Hugo Lord, a man with inherited wealth, who wanted to make his own mark on the world and recognized the genius in Charles Gregory Grove. My grandfather used Hugo's name and entitlements to open doors that had been closed to him, and now here we are.

Everybody knows that story, I thought. Penelope

is no dummy. Perhaps she's grasping for straws. Perhaps she's lost the account of her own father's humble beginnings. Regardless, Jojo's scrappiness would make her the perfect fit for my family and a mother-in-law I can be proud of.

I prolong my examination of the look on Penelope's face.

"Do you stand behind the shit you said about Jojo O'Leary?" I can't wipe the troubled frown off my face.

Penelope hangs her head in shame. But I don't think she's remorseful about what she said; she regrets what she said because of my reaction.

"Goodnight, Penelope." I open the door.

"Wait," she says.

I face her.

"I do regret what I said. That's not how I think about people. I'm just scared, Lynx."

I nod at her silence. I can see her desperation. I don't know what to say to her, so I finally tell her good night before entering the chilly night.

———

THE LIGHTS ARE out when I arrive at the apartment, and it's quiet enough to hear a pin drop. I was hoping Xena would still be up, especially after the drama that ensued before I left. I want to ask her about her mother and learn more about Jojo's story. The more I learn about the well from which Xena rose, the more I'll know about Xena. She's been hard to pin down, and I've started thinking she's not attracted to me anymore. Recalling her ex, it's clear aren't important to her. I've been trying to distance myself from the horny asshole who just wanted to rip through her fucking sexiness that night. I've given her a lot, but I'm not sure it's enough to change her mind about me.

I make it to her bedroom door, it's open, and I take it as a good sign. Maybe she's been listening for me.

"Hey," I whisper.

"Hey." She sounds drowsy.

She's up, and I crack a smile. I want to ask if I can climb in bed with her, but we know how that would end. I want to be inside her again, but is she ready for that? Am I ready for it? I wouldn't have been asking myself those questions before the night I met her. Making love to her was the end of me. I've wanted to explain to her what I mean by that, but I don't know, maybe one day.

"How was the rest of your night? Did you take a swim?" I ask.

The only light in Xena's room comes from the dim-lit hallway, but when she sits up, I get a good look at her nipples and her fleshy but perky tits through whatever that thing is she's wearing. Damn, I want to choke on her fucking tits right now. I'm hard.

"It was okay. I'm just… I'm tired. I slept. How was dinner?"

I lean against the doorjamb and try to tame my beast. "It's true, Rich knows I might sell my team, and tonight he laid out his ask."

"His ask?"

"Five percent of GIT."

Her burst of laughter is cynical, and I love that she knows that's the appropriate response.

"What are you going to do?"

*How about you leave that bed, come to my room and sit on my cock?* "I don't know yet." *I'll kiss you, Xena. I'll fucking tongue you until your lips ache.*

"Wow," she says tiredly, raising an arm to scratch her head.

I stand up straight. "Okay." The volume on that was way too loud. But her tits are pointing right at me, and I don't think I'll be able to resist her if I stand here any longer. "How about I set your alarm? I figured we could walk to the office together."

"I set my cellphone."

"No, no, no," I say, shaking my head adamantly. "Turn yours off. Experience mine. I promise you'll want to."

## Monday Morning

It's a gentle transition from sleep to awake as the genre of music played at the end of yoga practice lingers in the air. Lynx was right. I do prefer the calming sound to the pounding chiming of my cellphone. I can get used to opening my eyes this way. As usual, I first reach for my device and take in a screen full of texts from Greg.

I groan, sitting up with relative ease. Without reading one message from my ex, I know he's written gripes about what happened in the lobby yesterday, my new job, and my new roommate, and accusing me of making wrong decisions that hurt him.

Suddenly my attention falls to my bare arms, and it dawns on me that my room is warm and comfy. My senses mark this moment because there's something so perfect about it, so novel. I'm not getting up and going to work after a torturous night of being cold and preparing to make the subway while freezing as I get dressed. I hurl my legs across the bed to sit on the edge of the mattress.

I hum a melody I just made up in my head as I delete Greg's texts one by one without reading them. I also block his cellphone and desk phone numbers. He and I are done.

My device rings, and the name across the screen makes me press my palm over my dancing heart.

"Hello?" There's an air of caution in my tone.

"Hey. Are you up?" Lynx asks.

"Yep."

"We'll leave at nine."

"Aye-aye, Boss." Yikes, I'm more jubilant than I usually am in the mornings. All it took was a one-night stand with a billionaire because if Lynx hadn't offered me a job, I'm pretty sure I would be on the subway, heading to my old job feeling miserable.

Lynx chuckles like he knows he's responsible for

my response. And he should take credit for my newly found contentment. I may owe him my life.

"See you soon, then," he says.

I keep Penelope in mind as I search for something to wear. She's definitely going to dress like a siren today. I'm not a big fashionista like her, but I know how to shop for garments that flatter me, and I have a closet full of them. I select a silk print flower pantsuit by Dolce & Gabbana. The pants are skinny capris, and the jacket is long and fitted at the waist. I found the ensemble while vintage clothes shopping at the flea market with Lilly a few years ago. My shoes are also designer, closed-toe, two-inch heels, and they will not go eight hours without torturing my feet, so I put a comfy pair of flats in my purse. Also, I apply enough makeup to notice that I'm wearing extra mascara, eyeliner, and matte dusty-rose lipstick.

As a testament that I got my look right today, Lynx's eyes expand as he watches me stroll toward him up the hallway.

"You look stunning," he says as his gaze continues to pour over me.

My cheeks warm, and I feel we should hug or kiss. But I tap down that mysterious urge that always wants to physically connect with Lynx Grove as I also allow myself to get an eyeful of him.

"Thank you. And you look fantastic too."

We're trapped in an eye lock as we both wear giddy smiles.

"By the way, breakfast will be served at the office."

"I know," I reply breathlessly. "Evie mentioned breakfast in the mornings."

Our staring deepens until abruptly cut off after Lynx says we should go.

---

ON THE ELEVATOR ride to the lobby, Lynx reveals that he's seventy percent sure he'll sell his team, and that's up from thirty percent.

"What spurred the increase?" I ask as we walk through the lobby. He puts a hand on my back to guide me closer as a woman races past us. Gosh, I love the sensation of his gentle caress on my body. My racing pulse is evidence of that.

"Rich's five percent ask for starters."

I furrow my brows as I ponder my next question. "But I don't get it." We step outside, and a nippy burst of wind hits my face. I feel Lynx's presence inch closer. I like walking next to him because he's tall and strong. He makes me want to snuggle against his hard body and wear him like in-season Armani all day long.

"What don't you get, Xena?"

His voice this morning is smooth and sexy, like butter. Or maybe it's me. Maybe he's made me horny.

I clear my throat and focus. *Platonic, Xena. Remember, platonic.* "Why are you nickeling and diming your interest? Are you really that indecisive?"

I look up at him for a reply. I may have been a bit too harsh by using the word "indecisive." I'm watching his face to see how he's reacting to what I said. So far, I'm coming up with nothing.

"It's a big decision," he says.

"I know, but we're talking about you becoming CEO of Grove Industrial Tech. I mean…" I press my lips, thinking maybe I'm digging too deep. Greg would've exploded by now, telling me in several ways to mind my business.

"You mean?"

Even with the heavy clouds dimming the morning light, Lynx's beauty still shines. Then he smiles encouragingly, and I feel my expression mirror his.

"I've known guys who are overly into sports, and you don't strike me as one of them. From what you told me about how you came to acquire your baseball team, didn't you do it for the challenge and not the game itself?"

Lynx is observing me with an intense gaze. My heart races when he licks his sexy lips. And just before he says something, his cellphone rings as we reach a "stop-walking" sign.

"Hey, Max," Lynx says, answering the call.

We start walking and Lynx places a hand on my back to bring me closer as a group of teenagers in school uniforms rushes past us a bit too closely. I glance up at him and offer a smile to convey my appreciation. If I were with Greg when the young men narrowly missed knocking me over, Greg would've roared, "Hey, watch it!" Even though all the boys were double his body weight and size, he still would've behaved as if he could take them in a fight. The guy has a sense of entitlement that I never entirely understood. But after avoiding getting his ass kicked by a group of teenagers who would've written him off as a crazy little man, he would spend the next fifteen minutes complaining about how kids nowadays have no respect. I would've been livid, thinking, *I wish they would've kicked your ass. And you just embarrassed the hell out of me, you asshole!*

Gosh, it's refreshing to be walking with a man who has class and self-control.

"Maryland, today, eleven-thirty, we'll be there," Lynx says.

Ripping myself out of my thoughts, I glance up at him, and he's already watching me.

"Xena and I," he says.

His eyebrows pinch together as he listens to whatever Max is saying.

"I know," he keeps repeating. I suspect he's being chastised about me. Lynx did reveal that Max knows we slept together.

"Is that it?" Lynx is short with his cousin. "Alright, later."

My shoes are torturing my feet faster than I thought they would. Thankfully we're almost at our building. I'll swap them out for my more comfortable pair when I'm in my office.

Lynx slides his cellphone back into his coat pocket. "To answer your earlier question, yes, I like the business of running a sports team more than sports." He takes a quick sideways glance at me. "That was very astute of you to notice."

*The problem is, I notice everything about you, Lynx Grove.*

Instead, I ask, "Was that a compliment?"

"It was."

Rather than smiling foolishly at him, I focus on the octagon designs on the pavement. But it's refreshing to have an honest conversation with an open-minded man who doesn't take everything I say personally.

"So, we'll helicopter to Maryland in about half an hour. Eat a quick breakfast, and then we'll head out."

I nod, but I cannot stop thinking about our conversation before Max's phone call. "So, what are you going to do about Rich?" My inquiry brings me closer to the individual I truly want to know about.

Lynx thinks deeply with a serious face. "I never expected Rich to be this unmanageable."

"Does he know about the relationship you have with his daughter?" And score one for me!

Lynx quickly glances at me with a sideways glance. "Do you mean the relationship I had with his daughter?" He emphasizes "had."

"Are you implying Penelope and you are a thing of the past?"

"What do you mean when you say 'thing'?"

I take a look at him. Lynx is stalling. If only he weren't my boss. My answer can be boiled down to one word, fucking. But I can't say that to the man who employs me. I need him to take me seriously. "Sex," I say.

Lynx blurts out a nervous laugh. "Xena, Penelope is my employee and does a great job for the organization." He looks at me as if deciding whether to trust me with what he has to say next. "Also, she's spoiled by her father, which is why I must keep her happy."

"Hmm," I say as we reach the revolving door to the building. Lynx steps back so that I may enter first.

He's so close as we walk through the encased glass that my backside feels tickled by his energy.

We stride through the busy lobby on our way to our private hallway. I'm starting to notice how everything about Lynx includes elements of exclusivity. I guess that's what I would do with a billion dollars, buy as much peace and tranquility as possible.

Lynx's mouth is close to my ear. "What did you mean by *hmm*?"

I shrug indifferently. "I meant nothing by it. And I sort of understand."

"And what is it that you understand?" Lynx uses his keycard to unlock the door.

The magnetism in his seductive eyes is hard to resist. I don't think he knows he's a naturally sexy person. I force myself to think of him as a good big brother. That's the only way I can keep my lust in check in his presence, especially since it sounds like he's willing to jump through Penelope's hoops to keep her father happy. That is what I understand, but it's something I don't want to say. I don't want Lynx to think I'm okay watching him give Penelope precisely what she wants.

I stab the up button before he can. "That business isn't always a pleasure," I say instead.

As we ride up to our floor alone, I watch Lynx as he ponders what I said. It's as if he's looking into my eyes but seeing through me. His intense gaze makes it difficult for me to maintain steady breathing.

"Xena." His voice is barely a whisper.

"Hmm," I chirp.

Despite his claim of not kissing, I can feel his lips pulling mine towards his.

"Things are moving faster than I had planned," he whispers.

"Mm-hmm?"

The ambiance seems dense and electrified, almost like a powerful magnetic force draws us closer. I must fight these feelings.

Lynx rubs the back of his neck. I think he's forgotten what he wants to say. But I'm staring into his eyes, waiting with bated breath for something to happen. What will happen?

Then, the elevator stops, and the doors slide open. Despite feeling lightheaded, I manage to divert my gaze from Lynx's perfect features and notice three individuals standing in the hallway observing us. One person is Penelope. Lynx, who is still a bit flustered, introduces me to Archer Donavon, a tall and remarkably attractive man. I'm a bit absentminded as I shake his hand. Mainly because I identify the older gentleman before Lynx tells me his name; he's Richard Chastain, Penelope's father, and he doesn't shake my hand.

# TWENTY-THREE

# XENA ST. JAMES

*That was interesting.*

Lynx said he'd stop by my office to collect me after I had breakfast. I caught Penelope glaring at me as if to say over my dead body, and her father glared at me with the same look. Wow, what a pair.

I think they're all in Lynx's office right now. Even though we share a door, I can't hear a peep from the other side of the solid wood. But now I'm in the employee dining room plus kitchen scarfing down the yummiest Dungeness Crab Eggs Benedict I've ever eaten. It's so lovely in this room too. The chair I'm sitting in has a soft leather back, making it so comfortable. The blond wood tables lighten the mood, and the abstract paintings hanging on the walls add a bit of fun. I don't think a time ever existed when I've been this relaxed at this time of day. I usually work feverishly, managing three tasks simultaneously and at least five within an hour. The jury is still out on whether I miss the work I used to do or not. I love this moment, though, and I can't take my eyes off the street below beyond the window. Manhattan is such a busy city. I love being part of the foot traffic.

Suddenly the door opens, and I turn to see Penelope glaring at me as she folds her arms over her chest and says, "Xena, let's talk."

---

## 3 Minutes Later

I guessed right about Penelope. She's dressed to appease Lynx today. Her baby blue pants are tight but very high-fashion, and her sweater is the same color, but a cut-out in the front displays her toned abs. The weather is definitely too cold for that sweater, but fortunately for her, the temperature in our offices is perfectly set.

I'm sitting behind my desk, but she insisted on standing.

"Penelope, how can I help you?" I ask, thinking we should get the show on the road already.

She folds her arms. "I don't know what you have planned for Lynx. But you should know that he's taken—by me."

Wow, she went there without delay. And frankly, I do not want to argue with a girl over a boy. I'm not in the business of doing that. But I can't stop myself from stirring the pot. "He told me he's single," I say, throwing that out there, and paying close attention to how it lands.

Penelope's pretty head slowly tilts to the side. "Is that so?"

I drop my elbows on my desk, steepling my fingers. "It is so."

She nods as if pondering what I just said. I want to applaud her. She's good at being subtly bitchy.

"I may have waited a tad bit too long to seal the deal. All the fucking we do....." She sighs as if famished by just thinking about it. "On his desk. In his car. In my bed. In his bed. In that room you're sleeping in, for now. It's a lot." Her laugh is disingenuous. "A girl can get pregnant really fast—don't you think?"

I'm shocked by all the loaded shit she just said. *In my bed?* Does she even know where I sleep? I doubt it. Penelope is trying to ruffle my feathers. I've seen this act before. Hell, I worked in reality TV! Penelope's performance reminds me of a terrible plot line in a horrible soap opera.

"Are you truly pregnant, Penelope?" I'm sure she can hear the doubt in my tone.

Her blinking turns rapid. I don't think she expected me to ask her that question. "No. But..." She raises a shoulder coyly. "He knows."

I paint on a fake smile. Lynx has stepped in horse shit, screwing around with this one. She's dangerous and has no integrity. Penelope is the kind of person who will do whatever it takes to get what she wants.

I look her in the eye, needing to convince her before she does something she can never take back. "You don't have to worry about Lynx and me. I just work for him."

"But you fucked him," she shoots back.

My mouth is caught open. I don't know what to say. I'm still speechless when a knock on the door that separates my office from Lynx's cracks through the air.

Penelope points at me and glares at me with a final look of warning before quickly escaping my office. Interestingly, she doesn't want Lynx to know about our conversation.

I clamp my lips until she's gone, fighting the urge to shout, "See you later, Penelope."

But again, this is not a battle I want to fight right now. So, when she's out of my office, I rise to my feet, walk over and put my hand on the door handle. I can feel him on the other side. We shouldn't still have this kind of connection. But I also love that he didn't just barge into my office. Greg always raced in without being invited.

I take two deep breaths, steady my welcoming smile, and then open the door.

*Damn it.*

I'm yet again blown away by the energy that often flows between Lynx and me at first sight.

"We should go," he says.

I force myself to appear unstirred by his mere presence. I smile and say, "Okay." Thankfully my voice sounded as clear as a bell.

## TWENTY-FOUR
## XENA ST. JAMES

We're inside a cozy helicopter. This piece of machinery must've cost a pretty penny. I've taken helicopter tours before while on vacation, but this is not the kind of aircraft used for sightseeing expeditions. Our ride is smooth and nearly noiseless. And mixed with Lynx's delicious cologne is a permeable scent of new leather and a hint of berries. But despite our very comfortable environment, I've been uptight since leaving the office.

Penelope's threat to claim she's pregnant if she doesn't get what she wants still vexes me. I should say something, but then what? He's already stuck between a rock and a hard place with Penelope and her father. I decide to stay out of it since Lynx is a functioning adult who can take care of himself.

"What's on your mind, Xena?" Lynx asks, interrupting my thoughts.

"Nothing," I enthusiastically claim, overcompensating for my anguish.

His eyebrows ruffle as if he sees right through me. "Alright then. So tell me, which of GIT's future products should be on my radar."

Thankfully, I'm not so worried that I can't do my job. I start with the semiconductors, giving Lynx the detail sheet to review. I brief him on ten more products that will result from this revolutionary technology called TRANSPOT. Then I arrive at my favorite, a bio-usage product that will allow lab researchers to experiment on 3D images.

"Personally, it's my favorite because it could banish the cruel practice of using living organisms for experimental research. What a game changer," I claim.

Lynx looks thrilled by my enthusiasm. "I like how excited you are about the possibility."

I readjust in my seat to get ahold of myself. "Well, it's impressive technology. It's unreal actually."

Lynx nods, smiling nostalgically. "My grandfather used to say greatness will occur when we find that one revolutionary product that will enhance our survival."

I grunt musingly. "Find and not invent?"

Lynx raises his eyebrows twice. "That's very astute of you to ask, Xena. And yes, find. My grandfather would sit with my sister, my cousins Max and Paisley, and myself to engage us in vigorous talks about the links between what is known, what we think we know, what's possible, and what is yet to be found."

I've been nodding like a bobblehead because I comprehend Lynx's grandfather's viewpoint. "He was a visionary."

"He was much more than that. He knew what to envision and how to make it a reality."

"How did TRANSPOT come to be?"

Lynx presses his lips into a hardline. Jeez, the man hasn't one unattractive facial expression or angle. However, the look on his face tells me all I need to know.

"Top secret?" I ask.

He shows me one of my favorite looks as he nods. It's a gentle, open smile that says he likes me as a person and colleague. And I love that Lynx has no problem showing me how fond he is of me. It validates that we can be and are friends, and if he's a friend, then maybe he needs to know what Penelope said earlier. I would've already told him if he were one of my girlfriends.

"By the way," he says. "Do you mind if I ask a personal question?"

Thoughts of Penelope fade away as my eyes expand as I anticipate what that question might be. "Um, no, I don't mind." There's a hint of uncertainty in my tone.

"Someone told me your mother, Jojo O'Leary, is an orphan. Is that true?"

"Oh," I sigh, releasing the tension in my body. I have no idea what I thought he would ask that made me so nervous, but I'm relieved the question is about my mom and not me. "She's not an orphan. But my grandparents did abandon my mom and aunt Kathy to join a religious cult." I tilt my head to beam at him. "But I thought you were a fan. Jojo's true fans know her tale of woe."

Lynx grins uncomfortably as he scratches the side of his neck. He needn't say more. My mom is sexy. I get it.

I squeeze my eyes shut as a chill flushes through me. "I'll never live down the fact that I slept with a guy who lusts after my mom. It's so creepy."

When I open my eyes, Lynx moistens his lips in that sexy way of his.

"Your face is very expressive Xena," he says.

"But so is yours," I counter.

Lynx scrunches his gorgeous eyebrows. "Is that so?"

"It is so."

Goodness, we're once again beaming at each other, and I lose my train of thought for a moment. Right, he asked me about Jojo.

I cough to unfreeze my throat. "So my mom was thirteen and my aunt Kathy was fifteen when their parents, Leanne and Barry, abandoned them to join a cult."

I tell him that my grandparents, Barry and Leanne, worked in the entertainment business in Hollywood, California. Barry was a sound engineer, and Leanne worked in central casting. Theirs was the typical Hollywood story. Barry, born and raised in Toledo, Ohio, and Leanne, from a small town in Maine, descended on Tinseltown to become big stars. But instead of being in front of the camera, they landed careers behind it. Then they met, married, and had two kids. Although unfulfilled by their jobs, they were paid well, which was why they could make a full-cash purchase of a house in North Hollywood. And to make extra cash they rented their backyard casita to a young set designer name Mina St. James.

"Hmm… St. James?" Lynx asks.

"That's very astute of you to ask, Lynx," I say lightheartedly, returning his earlier compliment.

We chuckle as a wave of refreshing feelings washes over me. It's so easy to converse with Lynx. Greg would've turned my little joke into an argument about how I was mocking him. I would defend myself, and then we bickered until I was too emotionally drained to continue. Then I apologized to make him shut up.

"Anyway," I say, getting to the end of the story my mom likes to recount whenever she's giving an inspirational talk about the making of Jojo O'Leary. "Needless to say, Mina freaked out that the owners of the house split. Then two weeks later a group from the cult showed up to the house to claim it because my grandparents had given them all they owned."

"Woe," Lynx says.

"Yep. Tale of woe."

My smile falters as his weak chuckle reminds me this is the first time Lynx has heard the story. He's not as desensitized to it as I am. It's definitely time to get to the bright side of a bad situation.

"Anyway, instead of allowing Jojo and Kathy to enter the system, Mina gained custody of them. She was only twenty-five but she looked after them until they went off to college. And that's the story."

Lynx's frown deepens. I don't think he's satisfied with the ending. "What happened to your grand-parents?" he asks.

I groan as I roll my eyes. Thinking about what happened next never fails to make my insides feel heavy. "Leanne ran off with the cult leader and had two more children, and Barry married another woman. But my mom and aunt Kat had nothing to do with them until the day their parents died."

"Then you never met them?"

I shake my head.

Lynx grunts curiously. "What about Mina?"

"You mean my aunt Mina, hence the St. James last name?"

"Your aunt?"

"Mina's my father's older sister. And she lives in the Palisades with her husband, Luis, and they have two children."

Lynx nods as if he's pondering everything I told him. "Well, that was a fascinating tale of woe."

I chuckle. "And now you can consider yourself an informed fan of Jojo O'Leary." My chuckle turns into a look of horror as the aircraft swings, and I grab the edges of my white leather executive-style seat.

"Relax, Xena," Lynx says with an assuring smile. "I won't let anything happen to you on my watch."

I keep my cool but wonder if he's making eyes at me. It's hard to figure out if he's being his naturally charming self or if he's flirting.

"Thank you," I say way too sweetly.

"You're welcome, Xena."

See…. Again, I'm confused. Was that a flirt?

LESS THAN TEN MINUTES LATER, we landed atop the glass tower GIT building in Baltimore, Maryland. Max was waiting inside the rooftop hallway as we entered the facility.

I try not to blink so I won't miss a thing about Max Grove's appearance. I've never seen him in real life, and in the flesh, the man puts the H in handsome, although he's very austere. Even when I shake his hand, his grave expression doesn't change.

We're walking fast with Max talking fast as he leads the way. I'm happy to be still wearing my flats. My feet would be killing me while trying to keep up with two long-legged men if I wore my sexy high heels. As they say, sexy is never practical.

Max hasn't stopped briefing us yet. He's all business, telling us we'll first be shown a demonstration module of TRANSPOT's semiconductor technology. He asks Lynx questions about the technology. Lynx is being quizzed by his cousin, which I find very Greg-like. Thanks to me, though, Lynx has all the answers.

The entrance to the lab is state-of-the-art. It's designed like a modern science and art museum with recessed lighting, sleek carpeting, and large paintings of the company's top products affixed to smooth, light wood walls. Employees zip past us like they should be wherever they are going five minutes ago. Most people avoid looking in our direction, perhaps due to our intimidating tour guide. I wonder if Max Grove is as dire as how everyone reacts to him. He hasn't paid attention to me since saying hello. If I were the sensitive type, I'd feel sour about it. But I consider myself the asshole whisperer. I love Jojo, but she can be an asshole. Greg is a major asshole. Showbiz in general is an empire of asshole sharks. So I wonder how sharp Max Grove's teeth are? And when he bites, does he suck blood too?

His ears must be itching, sensing that he's on my mind because he turns to frown as if admonishing me for my curiosity as we arrive at a door protected by a large man in uniform. The guard is even armed—wow.

"This way, Miss St. James," the guard says, waving me to a metal detector. I'm not surprised he knows who I am. My guess is that Max is thorough and efficient.

"Max? Do we need to do this?" Lynx grouses, clearly offended for me.

I raise a hand to signal peace. "It's okay. I understand." I truly understand. The grand scope of this place demands seriousness. So I step on the pads and raise my arms above my head as I clear the scanners. I turn one way and then the other. Lynx and I share a moment of eye contact. I didn't mean for that to happen. I glance at Max to see if he noticed.

He noticed.

Next, we give the guard our cell phones and my purse stays behind too, and then we venture inside.

# TWENTY-FIVE
## XENA ST. JAMES

The demonstrations are over, and Lynx and I are eating lunch in the executive dining room at the top of the building. We're two in a handful of people dining in a restaurant that resembles an expansive futuristic-looking space station. The tables are set far enough from each other that conversations remain private as soft elevator music hums in the background.

"Oh my God, that was unreal," I exclaim, still reeling from how impressed I was by the demonstrations.

I'm also eating the best crab cakes ever, along with brown butter risotto and roasted corn. This is all too fantastic—the ultra-modern atmosphere, the gourmet food, and what I was privy to in that lab, unreal.

"The dishware made by TRANSPOT's light technology? Wow. Weather-tempered walls and even better, the ability to build solid structures by programming them on your app?" My eyes have doubled in size, and I'm throttling my hands, trying to make my enthusiasm contagious because Lynx had the same stony expression throughout the presentation. I thought he was putting on a poker face to keep Max guessing, but now I'm not sure.

"This is sci-fi movie shit that's going to happen for real." I aim my finger vigorously in the direction of the lab downstairs. "Because I just saw it."

Lynx's smile is stiff as he grunts what I think is a perfunctory chuckle.

"For sure you were impressed too, right?" I ask.

"It was impressive," he replies in a flat voice.

"But?"

He shrugs indifferently. "But nothing."

"Nothing?" I shake my head in surprise. "You can't experience what we've just experienced and say, 'but nothing.'"

Lynx snorts a chuckle. I focus on his two fingers tapping the tabletop anxiously.

Instead of taking another bite of crab cake,

which I've been devouring like my first meal after being rescued from a deserted island, I set my fork down and ask, "What's going on with you?"

Lynx's face cycles through several expressions before he settles on a heavy look of contentment.

"I'm taking it all in, Xena. On one side of the aisle, I own a professional baseball team that I must consider." He surveys the high-tech, high-end restaurant. "And being here. Even being offered this position, it's loaded."

"Loaded?"

"This morning, Rich double-downed on allowing me to sell my team only if he's in five percent on my shares of GIT."

"Oh," I say, although I'm not shocked.

"That's not all."

"No?"

"He's asserting that I get serious about being with his daughter."

I'm now aware that I can no longer keep my conversation with Penelope a secret from Lynx. "I have something to tell you."

He frowns as if sucking on lemons. "What is it?"

And so I tell him about Penelope's threatening to claim she's pregnant to keep him.

Lynx shakes his head dismissively. "That could never happen." He sounds so sure of himself.

"But you had sex with her, right?"

"Yes. But…"

We peer at each other as his eyebrows jump slightly. I feel he's working out whether to trust me with whatever comes after 'but.'

"But?" I ask because I feel like I've been waiting an eternity for him to finish processing.

"I never came with her." He sounded as if he barely had enough breath to make his claim audible.

My eyebrows shoot up in shock.

Lynx circles his shoulders, loosening them up as he sighs. "Not with any woman in a long time until…." The intense way he stares at me says it all. "You."

The revelation leaves me breathless. I feel as if my head is floating away from my body as his gaze holds me captive.

"Me?" I whisper.

He rubs his chin. "I orgasmed with you, and it shocked the hell out of me. And it happened more than once." He's nodding as if visualizing his goliath-sized cock indulgently moving in and out of me, each stroke bringing me mysteriously closer to climax.

It's taking me a moment to recover my voice, but since we're discussing the night we had sex, I've wanted to ask if there was a method to get a girl to the finish line in such a stellar fashion. I'm also still processing the fact that Lynx Grove just revealed that he hadn't had an orgasm while having sex with Penelope, but he had more than one with me.

"All three times?" I can't believe I asked.

"All three times," he confirms.

"Oh."

I'm staring into his intense eyes, recalling how his body trembled and the sound of the quaking grunts he made with his mouth against my face when he came, and he came hard. Was there something extra powerful in how we locked eyes after it was over, our breaths crashing, fighting the urge to make out passionately because Lynx doesn't kiss?

*Don't forget that Zeen. This man has commitment issues.*

So I pull myself together and guide the conversation to what's important now. "So um…"

"Are you rattled by what I said?" His eyes are tapered as he studies me.

I don't think rattled adequately defines what I'm feeling. I'm shaken to my core, but I can't let him see it. I'm sure my smile makes me seem cool, calm, collected, and in control of my vag that's steadily reaching for him. "Not at all." *Great, that came out clear.* "That was then, and this is now. You're my boss and roommate, and now we're friends. I think. I hope. Are we?"

# TWENTY-SIX

# LYNX GROVE

I never answered Xena's question. I don't take her for someone so oblivious. She knows I like her. Can we be just friends? I'm not sure we can. I could've pushed that point, but as long as I'm indecisive about selling my team or going all in on the family business, I can't piss off Penelope or Rich. As a result, I may have to accommodate Penelope every once in a while. And that means loosening boundaries by taking her to dinner occasionally and keeping her happy without physical or sexual contact. I don't think Xena can handle that. Not only will she feel disrespected, and rightfully so, but she'll judge me until she can never be with me because that will make her feel safe, proving I'm another guy she can't rely on. But I know one thing:

big moves must be made either way. And Penelope will be a thorn in my side until I handle her father.

And I've always been fond of having my cake and eating it too. While viewing today's demonstration, I asked myself what Charles Gregory Grove would do about the decision facing me. Would he stew in indecision? He wouldn't. I want to keep my team and take my rightful seat as co-CEO of GIT. And, with an enthusiasm that burns hotter than lava, I want to be done with Richard Chastain.

The helicopter takes to the skies smoothly. I peer intensely at Xena's pretty face, watching her sleep. Her beauty is striking. Yet I've met many beautiful women. Penelope's beautiful. However, there's something about Xena's features that makes her stand out to me. Or maybe my attraction to her runs deeper than what meets the eye. Since she moved in, I've smelled her in the elevator, hallways, and kitchen. The scent of Xena St. James is peaches and strawberries with a hint of vanilla.

I believe Xena is sleeping instead of talking to me because she's upset I hadn't confirmed that I wanted to be her friend. There's no way I'm going to let her friend zone me. But hearing Jojo O'Leary's story clarified why Xena is the way she is. Jojo taught her never to rely on anyone to make her happy. That's why Xena was with whatever the hell his name is—Craig or Greg or whatever. He gave her nothing. He took from her. And I'm not talking about money, he took her time, attention, loyalty, and happiness. But here I am, giving her shit that I've never offered any woman. I'm not sure she understands that I like her. Most women in her position would've darn near jumped on my cock by now. I've heard the term "book him" regarding getting involved with me, and I'm pretty sure Xena doesn't want to book me.

Xena opens her beautiful doe eyes, and her penetrating and curious gaze momentarily takes my breath away. I'm glad she caught me staring at her. Maybe she'll get the picture and understand why I didn't reply to her comment about the two of us being friends.

I'm on the verge of addressing the issue of our friendship when the pilot communication button dings, flashing red.

"Yeah, Branson," I say, answering his call.

"Bad news…"

## Two Hours Later

We were forced to land at Carroll County Airport in Westminster. My cellphone won't stop ringing as Xena and I wait in a private hangar. The distance between us still looms. A lot of time has passed since Branson swore the mechanical issue would be identified and resolved within the hour. He said it could've been a sensor error, but he couldn't take a chance and fly us back to the city regardless of the system's warning.

The news of the possibility of me selling the team has finally reached Archer, who lets me hear it for not telling him earlier.

"I'm disappointed, Lynx. That's something you tell a friend, especially one who works for you," he says as I pinch the bridge of my nose, trying to release the pressure in my head.

I turn to Xena, who's on a call, pacing like crazy. I frown, wondering why she's so worked up.

"I know," I say. "Sorry about that."

"Are you fucking selling the team? Tell me now, Lynx."

"You want the truth?"

"Is there an option to lie?"

"There's always an option to lie."

His laugh is biting. But I power through his displeasure and tell him I don't know yet.

Archer remains thoughtfully quiet as I watch Xena end her phone call and drop her head back as if vexed by something. *What the hell is going on with her?*

"Then what option are you leaning more toward, Lynx?"

She's watching me as the answer comes as clear as a bell. "I'm going to have my cake and eat it too."

"What?" he snaps.

"Chill out Archer. The Ramblers belong to me, and that's never going to change. I'll talk to you tomorrow." I end the call.

"Hey," I call, double-timing over to where she stands, shoulders hunched over as she squeezes both sides of her head. "What's going on?"

She jumps as she looks at me with beautiful eyes wide with worry, and her sexy pillowy lips stumble a bit before she says....

## TWENTY-SEVEN
## XENA ST. JAMES

I fling my arms as I panic and try not to hyperventilate. "I have… I'm supposed to…."

Lynx's long and strong fingers have me by the shoulders. "Xena, take your time."

I just ended a call with Jojo, who reminded me of a promise I made several weeks ago.

"I'm supposed to stand in this stupid One-date auction for Jojo tonight." I moan like a child who's trying to talk instead of cry.

"You're standing in an auction for your mother?"

I open one eye, and I'm too afraid to open the other because that'll prove this is indeed happening. "That's what I thought too."

"I'm confused. That's what you said."

"Well, that's what I agreed to. I thought I would stand in for my mom, and whoever wins the final bid will go on a date with her when she returns from Tampa, but I got it all wrong, and now it's too late to back out, and if I don't make it to that podium on time, then...."

I'm out of words and short of breath while frowning at Lynx's smiling eyes. Of course, he would find my nervous breakdown amusing.

"So you're on auction for a date with you?"

I squeeze my eyes shut and rub my throbbing temples. "Mm-hmm. And the event starts in less than two hours."

"Xena?" His voice is calm, like a therapist talking his client off the ledge.

I open my eyes and watch him under the visor of my hand. "Yeah…"

"Take a deep breath."

Usually, I hate it when someone tells me to take a breath while I'm panicking. He doesn't understand. My mom is counting on me. But Lynx is right. I should calm the hell down. So I inhale deeply through my nose and let my shoulders loosen like a rag doll as I exhale.

"It's my mom," I say because I can hear her in my head saying, I asked you to do this one important thing for me, and you had plenty of time to prepare, but you've become so wrapped up in your own life that you've forgotten about my one little ask.

"Xena, this is not a life-or-death situation here. So don't worry about your mother. She will still love you if you make or miss the auction block."

I watch him with wide eyes, trying to absorb everything he's saying, but his words slam into my mental brick wall. I know all that already, at least intellectually, but I can't feel it.

"Lynx," the pilot calls. "We're ready to load up and carry on."

"See, all better," Lynx says, eyebrows high and nodding as if he's talking to an unstable person.

I hang my head, embarrassed he had to see this part of me. "Yeah," I breathe.

The tips of Lynx's long fingers lift my chin, and I can't avoid gazing into his eyes.

We tumble deeper into an intense stare. My heart swoons and my lips are anxious.

Lynx's mouth opens, and I can hear him swallow. Then, his smirk slowly appears. "We should get you to this important event you can't miss."

Not only did he chicken out by not kissing me, but he reminded me that nothing's changed. He's a man who's unable to kiss a woman, or at least he won't let himself kiss me.

---

BEFORE BOARDING, the pilot explained that one sensor overheated, and that caused the air-pressure warning to flash. Even though the aircraft is in tip-top condition, it's protocol to land and inspect the helicopter whenever a warning-light pings. And now we're on our way to The Big Apple. Lynx has asked the pilot to land as close to the Continental Hotel as possible. After calling in our destination, the pilot said he could do better than close; we're touching down on the hotel's rooftop helipad.

Mostly I've avoided direct eye contact with Lynx, still ashamed about my nervous breakdown in front of him. Luckily his cellphone hasn't stopped beeping, calling his attention to new messages he continuously answers.

"So Xena, what was that back there?" he asks, eyes still glued to his screen.

"Huh?" I say, shocked he's speaking to me. His thumbs still haven't stopped tapping out a message.

"This thing with your mother?" He looks up, catching me in a state of dumbfounded confusion.

Sighing hard, I close my eyes, knowing that I must start from the beginning. This is my chance to explain that I'm not so manic. "While in the hangar, my mom called and asked where I was and …."

"I'm referring to your reaction," he clarifies.

"Oh," I say and clamp my lips.

Lynx tilts his head as if studying me from a different angle. "Can I say something to you?"

I nod stiffly.

"Your mother will still love you even if you tell her no. If you don't want to sell yourself for a date, then don't do it. She'll live."

"I know," I say, abruptly adjusting in my seat. "I am entirely codependent with Jojo. I'm still in the process of learning how to exist independent of her. Taking this job and leaving Rank Media was a huge step toward me finally growing up. It's just been so hard, and it's taken too long."

Lynx nods understandingly. "If you think I see less than a strong woman when…." Lynx pinches his mouth as if stopping himself from saying something he shouldn't. Then he clears his throat, signaling that he's starting over. "I'm trying to say you're only human, Xena. Intellectually, knowing what to do and emotionally putting it to practice can be as far away as the earth from the sun."

"I love that," I whisper past my tight throat. I love that he just captured what I feel.

At first, Lynx is stiff as we fall deeper into each other's gaze, then he abruptly nods and claps loud enough to signal a subject change.

"Well, I can't wait to see you on that stage," he says, wearing an amusing glint in his eyes.

I'm shaking my head while wagging my finger. "What? No. You can't come." I absolutely cannot have Lynx Grove watching me standing on that stage. "Plus, it will happen so fast. I'm supposed to step on the stage, and within seconds, Jane Chippy, my godmother, who's also VP of Production, will bid twenty-five thousand, which is my mom's donation." I swipe my palms together, then claim, "All done."

"That fast, huh?"

"Yes. That fast." I sound overly sure of myself.

His slow smile builds. "What about all those guys who have a crush on you?"

I burst into laughter and then look over my shoulder to ensure I didn't disturb the pilot. "What guys?" I say more quietly.

Lynx looks at me askance. "Xena?"

"Lynx?" I say, challenging him.

"You can't be that oblivious."

"Oblivious to what?"

"How hot you are."

I scrunch my face. "Hot?" I shake my head vigorously because this conversation is going in the wrong direction and I want him to get something through his hot, thick skull. "Plus, you can't go inside because you don't have a ticket." Those words feel like they've failed to make an impact as soon as I finished speaking them, but I still feebly stand by them.

Lynx folds his arms over his chest as if he's the king of the world. But then, he spreads his legs farther apart—his bulge. Oh my God, it's so hefty that I force my peripheral vision to stop trying to force me to gawk at his bulbous package and focus on his handsome face.

"Xena," he says with a cocky laugh. "I can go wherever I want."

My jaw drops probably because I know as far as this auction goes, Paige, who manages the event, is not going to bar Lynx Grove from attending. But still... "I didn't take you for the entitled type."

"Entitled? Me?" he says as if that's ridiculous.

"It's the nature of the business, babe. It's a charity event, and I have money to give and bid on…"

I aim my finger at him because I want him to hear me loud and clear. "Do not do what I think you're going to do, Lynx."

"And what am I going to do?"

"Bid on me. How pathetic will that be? My boss bidding on me, and after that scene I made in the restaurant last week, I'm sure the gossip will spread like wildfire about how I… How you and I…." I press my lips. Oh shit. I've become deeply intertwined with arguably the world's most eligible billionaire bachelor. I can picture the teaser: Lynx Grove, owner of the Connecticut Ramblers and newly appointed co-CEO of Grove Industrial Tech, is now involved with a woman who does nothing remarkable with her life, and on a good day she'll wear makeup and comb her hair.

"I see." Lynx shrugs innocently. "Aren't there other beautiful women on the block?"

It takes several seconds to realize that I've turned rigid. My chest tightens as I reject the notion of Lynx purchasing the company of another woman. But I play it coolly. He mustn't know he just got to me. "I'm sure there will be loads of aspiring models and actresses to bid on tonight.

There always are!" Gosh, I put too much sweetness on that last part. I'm sure I sounded as fake as my creepy smile.

"But?" His eyes are narrowed. Lynx is clearly screwing with me right now.

I fold my arms. "But nothing."

He washes me with that sexy askance look of his until it fades into a syrupy smile. "Xena, I will honor your request. And, as an addition to our agreement not to bring one-night stands to our apartment, I will not bid on any of your former work colleagues."

My lips separate, but I stop myself from informing him that some of the super gorgeous participants aren't technically my work colleagues.

"Yes," Lynx sings, prompting me to let out the truth which still sits on the tip of my tongue.

I blink hard, expelling the comment as I shake my head. "Nothing, Lynx," I flop back against my comfortable seat. "Just go home or wherever the night might take you." Hopefully not to Penelope's bed. "You're making this a bigger deal than it's supposed to be, and the event is not that important in the full scope of things." *Oh goodness, what in the world did I just say?*

Lynx inclines toward me as he says, "Xena."

The mischievous look on his face nearly takes my breath away. "What?"

"I'm coming."

We leer at each other in our usual manner. There was something so sexy about the way he said, 'I'm coming.'

---

LIKE MYSELF, I believe Lynx needed a moment to cool off after the heated and silent exchange between us. He sent several text messages. He grinned while tapping a few of them. I wonder if he decided to take my advice and go wherever the night takes him. *And he said I was hot.* Has he seen the way I dress? The messy bun in the back of my hair that barely contains my curls will never stay neat. I admit, I look pretty attractive today, but a lot of work went into this appearance I put together. And frankly, I'm ready to snatch off everything I have on, jump into stretch pants and a hole-ridden, over-stretched, oversized T-shirt, and eat a cheese pizza while binging a British detective show on Netflix. But first, I'll have to wash off all the makeup that sits heavily on my skin. I feel embarrassed that I went out of my way to compete with Penelope to win Lynx's attention. Jojo always reminds me that when it comes to men, I'll lose them how I win them. So, if Lynx is only attracted to how I look and my pussy, then those traits are quickly replaced by another pretty face. And there are almost four billion vaginas on the planet. But she also taught me that the right partner would love me through and through, and I'll feel the same about him. She mainly brought those words of wisdom to my attention whenever Greg's name or David, who was before Greg and behaved similarly to him, came up.

"Are you okay?" Lynx asks with his attention pinned to his cell phone.

Am I staring at him? He lifts his head and pins me with his come-hither grin.

*Oh no—I am!* "I'm fine," I mumble as I rip my eyes from Lynx to view the glowing landscape as we approach Manhattan.

What in the world is wrong with me? I must remember that just because we have chemistry and some attraction, and I like him as a human being, Lynx Grove is not interested in anything serious. And frankly, after finally being completely free of Greg, maybe I should follow Lynx's lead. I've been with Greg for six years. Perhaps, I should let myself be single for a while.

That's what I'll do—be single.

"Why are you smiling?" Lynx asks.

I snap my attention to him. He's not even looking at me; how does he know I was smiling?

"I'm not smiling."

He looks up. "You're not smiling now, but you were a few seconds ago."

Lynx chuckles lightly, and I follow suit.

"Just finish texting, dude," I say jokingly, pointing at his cellphone.

He resumes tapping out a text message. "And keep smiling at nothing fair maiden."

I snort a chuckle as I continue admiring the city that's only a hop, skip, and jump away. I feel good even though I'm about to be a part of one of the most embarrassing occasions of my life. I think it's because Lynx will be with me. However, I'm refusing to accept that as fact.

———

WE LANDED on top of the mirror-glass tower hotel. The fact it was so easy to get to the venue is a mixture of blessings and curses. Lynx is here, and he isn't going to hang out with a hot date, evident by how closely he walks beside me and his unyielding intention to enter the ballroom with me. I enjoy feeling his presence by my side. I feel safeguarded by any crap the night might try to throw at me. I don't expect to run into Greg. He never attends this event. He says it's archaic and stupid and often spends a fair amount of time condemning my mom for lending her celebrity status to the cause.

But Lynx's presence is so reassuring. I've been wondering if I could go all casual, have sex now and then, and be his "friend" until he finds that one woman he doesn't articulate woeful warnings to before fucking her. But I could end up in Penelope's shoes if I let him play with me the same way he plays with her. And that could be a suitcase full of regrets.

I take that bit of wisdom and run with it, as it seems I'm hugging and greeting every person we come across. I never stopped to consider how many people I've gotten to know over the years while working at Rank Media. Even though they're not wagging their tails and balancing on two feet with their paws held high, they all have the eagerness of a puppy being fed bacon treats while waiting to be introduced to Lynx.

We're saying hello to Marie and her husband, Kelly. Our hugs are over, and now Marie gleams eagerly at Lynx. She probably knows more about him than I do. But still, she's hinting that I make the appropriate introductions.

"Marie, Kelly, this is Lynx Grove, my new boss," I say, but I'm not finished. "Lynx is with me because we flew out of town for a meeting this morning. And..." I snicker as if I'm amusing myself with this story, which I've relayed at least a dozen times. "The helicopter alert system signaled that it had some mechanical issues. It didn't, of course, but we were still sidelined for over an hour. We barely made it here on time, and I thought I would miss this event altogether, but"—I throw up jazz hands—"here I am!"

The skin between Marie's eyes puckers as she nods and says, "Mm-hmm." One would think her husband would be uncomfortable by how his starry-eyed wife is behaving, but he's just as dazzled by my new boss.

"Excuse me," I take the liberty of checking the time on Lynx's expensive watch since it's the fastest way to get the information I need. My eyes expand after realizing I have less than ten minutes to report to the stage. I transition from clutching Lynx's wrist to gently squeezing his solid bicep—gosh, he's so strong. "I have to go gather with the other cattle. So have fun tonight!" Marie and I hug and kiss each other on the cheek one last time.

In a shocking move, Lynx curls an arm around my waist. "I'll come with you."

Now that my pulse is racing and tingles flutter through my body simply because he's holding me against him, I quickly step out of his embrace. *I mean, wow, where did that come from?*

"Nope, you can't. Participants only," I sing, then swiftly turn to face the main doors. But before I can take my first step, I lock eyes with Greg, the last person I want to see tonight.

"Isn't that your ex?" Lynx asks, his breath tickling my ear.

I find myself leaning against Lynx's muscular body for support as Greg stares daggers at us. He's not alone; Helena's with him, and he was holding her hand, but he just dropped it.

"Uh-huh," I can barely say because I would rather walk in the opposite direction. Greg isn't above causing a scene in front of everyone who knows us.

"Come on. I'll escort you to where you need to be." Lynx's arm is wrapped around my waist again.

I nod, accepting the support as we sashay into the main ballroom like a real couple. All eyes are on us, and I want to explain that this is not what it looks like. I can hear their thoughts in a few months when Lynx Grove is reportedly hooked up with a real girlfriend. "I guess that was a fling between them," they'll say about us. "He so leveled up, didn't he?"

"By the way, are you going to run that script all night long?" Lynx whispers in my ear.

I jump slightly. "What script?"

"I'm your boss. The helicopter had mechanical difficulties, so I'm here with you?"

"Isn't it the truth?"

"Yes, but you don't have to tell everybody. You don't like me being here that much?"

I just caught sight of Jane, conversing with Libby, her assistant, in front of the hallway that leads to the room where I should be already. She's seen me too, and her eyes roll up and down my form disapprovingly as she finishes with Libby. I have maybe a second to say, "Actually, you just became my lifesaver, and so..." I smile up at him and wink. "I'm now glad you're here."

"Xena, sweetheart!" Jane Chippy calls excitedly.

I paste on a smile. "Showtime," I say to Lynx. And then, speaking like a ventriloquist, I follow up with, "And be ready to get the hell out of this place when this is over."

## TWENTY-EIGHT
## XENA ST. JAMES

I felt like I'd been caught in a whirlwind until now. I finally have a moment to breathe. In true fashion, Jane deemed me not presentable enough to stand on her stage.

"Flats, Xena?" she said, looking at my cute shoes as if they were covered in dung.

I spoke fast as I explained how the heels I wore this morning hammered the bottom of my feet with every step I took. The flats were comfortable and were the only reason I could stand on her stage at all and make a fool of myself.

"You're too beautiful to make a fool of yourself," Jane replied.

"It doesn't matter how I look anyway because

you'll bid twenty-five thousand, and then I'll be done, right?"

There was something about the way she said, "Sure, Sweetheart," that worried me.

There's also something about how she had a slinky, silky, spaghetti-strapped cocktail dress that was as blue as a cloudless sky ready for me to wear that made me suspect she wanted me to win an actual date.

The garment fits perfectly, of course. I was also given black, scrappy stilettos, which are wreaking havoc on my toes, and Jane tasked Libby, her assistant, with fluffing out my locks. Then I was made to stand in line and wait my turn to be humiliated.

In front of me is aspiring model Ainsley Michaelson, a cast member of Surviving Modeling, a reality competition show Rank Media produces. Behind me is a girl I don't know, who's holding the attention of Jeff Riley, a man we refer to as "Hot Camera Guy."

"Oh my God, Xena, it's you!" Ainsley exclaims after doing a double take of me. Her Twiggy eyes grow wider as she looks me up and down. "I didn't even recognize you. I thought you were one of the girls from another show. But gosh, look at you."

I'm genuinely lost for words. I feel like Jane and Jojo set me up. Like, they are actually setting me up. They've done that before, tried to set me up with "a nice guy," who's usually a preppy-looking man with no backbone.

"And was that Lynx Grove you arrived with? Are you dating him?"

My head shakes as my tongue remains stuck against the roof of my mouth. Should I say no? I don't want her out on stage prancing just for him. What if he can't resist Ainsley's long legs and perfect face? I can picture him licking her as he licked me. The night we had sex was all about the sex. Maybe that's what kind of guy he is. A shiny new vagina will take his attention entirely off me. He'll probably ask me to move out by the end of the month. And then…

"No," I finally say, concluding that if Lynx puts all the affection he's showered on me recently onto another woman, then I won't have to wait for him to disappoint me. "He's just my boss."

"Your boss?" she screeches, smiling as if a photographer prompted her to show her perfectly white teeth. "He works here!"

"No, I quit on Thursday night."

She's about to say, "Oh," I think. However, Libby calls Ainsley and tells her she's up.

Libby snaps her fingers. "Hurry, hurry, hurry, Ainsley, chop, chop." Then Libby aims her finger at me. "And you're next, so get ready."

My nerves suddenly get the best of me, and my back slams against the wall as I massage my temples. I don't think I can do this.

The woman to my right stops flirting with Hot Camera Guy to rub my back consolingly. "You'll be fine, Xena. Don't worry. You're going to get loads of bids."

I look at the woman, and I don't recognize her, but she knows me. That's how things are at Rank Media. People know me because I'm Jojo's daughter, but I don't know them.

But "loads of bids" remain stuck in my head. Now I wish I hadn't warned Lynx not to bid on me. But nobody will go over twenty-five thousand dollars; I don't think. That's a lot of money. My mom is probably in Florida right now fantasizing of the moment the auctioneer announces that her astronomical donation was made from far away. And look people, "Meet my daughter, who loathes being on this stage but knows I'm in charge, and she will forever jump through my hoops!"

The ballroom erupts in applause. Has Ainsley finished already? If so, that was fast.

"Xena, you're up," Libby calls, trying not to be too loud.

My head is light, and I feel like I'll either throw up or pass out at any moment. All around me, people whisper about how Ainsley went for fifty-thousand dollars.

Who has that kind of money out in the main ballroom to throw at a charity auction but Lynx? It had to have been him. My eyes tear up because he failed a test I wasn't aware I was administering to him until now. Men suck, especially Lynx Grove.

My toes are killing me, but I'm not feeling the burning anymore. I just want to get this over with already. Maybe I'll Uber back to the apartment so Lynx can go off and fuck Ainsley. They'll probably do it in the Presidential suite of this hotel.

Good lucks follow me as I step onto the stage and meet all the eyes watching me from around poshly designed cocktail tables covered in shimmering gold cloths. People are smiling and having fun. I don't want to search the faces, and I certainly don't want to find Lynx's.

"Meet the lovely Xena St. James, daughter of our cherished Jojo O'Leary, who can't be here tonight," the auctioneer says. I have no idea who he is, but he sounds like a game show host. "And Xena's father is the famed musician Hollis St. James. Let's just say in addition to her stunning beauty, a date with Xena St. James can be very interesting. Let's start the bidding at Five hundred dollars."

I stick my glower on the auctioneer, a middle-aged man lucky enough to have a mop of hair. I feel like raising my hand and asking him if we can start higher to get this over with faster.

"Two thousand," a man bids.

I search the room, trying to find who said that. Then I see a man whose paddle is up. He appears to be in his fifties, not bad looking but going on a date with anyone as an outcome of this event wasn't the plan.

My head jerks from left to right as I search the crowd looking for Jane. Where is she? I'm aware that I look pain-stricken, but I don't care.

"Four thousand," someone says, and I tense up. Oh no, that was…

I glare at Greg, who has his paddle held high, leering at me. He looks vengeful.

"Ten thousand," another guy bids.

"Jane!" I call out, panicking.

I follow the sound of the loud chuckle to my left, and it's Lynx, who appears to be thoroughly enjoying my misery.

"Sixteen thousand," Greg bids.

I wish he didn't have the money, but he has it. He and his family are loaded even though ordinarily he's cheaper than a polyester suit. But he's proving a point. He wants to force me to pay attention to him. What can I do? Renege on my obligation to this charity event. I'll never do that, and he knows it. I'll be forced to go out with him.

*God help me.*

"Jane!" I shout at the top of my lungs. Where the fuck is she!

"Twenty-thousand," the fifty-year-old man says. Maybe he's Jane's proxy. She could've stepped out to handle business and left the bidding to…

"Twenty-five thousand dollars," Jane says.

I jerk my head toward the sound of her voice. She's to my right sitting all the way on the outer edges of the venue.

I put my hands in prayer and mouth, "Thank you to her."

She winks.

"Thirty thousand," Greg shouts.

I gasp. My head spins so fast that my vision blurs.

"One hundred thousand dollars," Lynx bellows.

I clutch my chest as I sigh in relief. Also, he didn't bid on Ainsley because each donor can only bid on one participant.

"Two hundred thousand dollars," Greg shouts.

"A million," Lynx responds without pause.

The audience erupts in gasps and loud applause. Everybody rises to their feet and continues clapping.

Greg has turned the color of a red apple as he stares daggers at Lynx, who's grinning at him cockily.

"One million going once, going twice...." The auctioneer slams his gavel. "And the winner is Lynx Grove, owner of the Connecticut Ramblers!"

Clapping like a happy seal, I beam at my new boss, new roommate, and the man who saved me from the torture of enduring Greg.

## TWENTY-NINE
## LYNX GROVE

The smile on Xena's face is worth more than the million I paid to see it. So this is what she looks like when she's blissfully happy. The dusky atmosphere in the back of our hired car can't even dim her light.

I handled the financial transaction portion of my bid, and then Xena and I escaped into the night. She hasn't since stopped talking about the look on Greg's face and how my win destroyed his fragile ego. She said watching him lose in such an epic fashion felt cathartic.

"He deserved it," she said. "Every bit of the humiliation he earned."

Her long, shapely legs are crossed at the knees, and she's sitting on her rounded hip, facing me. The hem of her dress is hiked up high enough to reveal a peep of her thigh's lean muscle. It's distracting. She's distracting.

"Nobody would've bid higher than Greg if you hadn't been there," she carols for the second time. "Therefore, I take it back. I'm over the moon that you came. And you, Lynx Grove,"—she pats me on the arm—"are my consummate night in shining armor."

My jaw is tight as I rub it. Something has been nipping at the back of my mind, and I figure it's time to ask about it. "Are you still in love with that guy?"

Xena jerks far back enough that her head nearly slams into the window. "No!" she exclaims and then repositions herself. "I don't even hate him. Well, not anymore. Or maybe I never hated him. I certainly don't like him. He's annoying, mean, and extremely selfish. You know he arrived with a date, but he didn't care about her feelings."

I watch her closely as she stares at me. Whatever this is I feel when I look at her mystifies me. I've always been hypervigilant about not being with a woman full-time, but everything about Xena is easy. Talking to her is easy. Sitting in silence with her is easy. Living with her is easy. Working with her is easy too. I don't know where to put these feelings I have. They're different and new, and I'm confident I want to keep them.

"I know…" She sighs, resting her head on the seat. "I should stop gloating. This is not a good look."

Her eyebrows raise as if asking me to confirm her comment about herself.

I fight the urge to trail my fingers down the side of her face where glares from city lights illuminate. "Feel free to take as many victory laps as you like."

"So, when are we going on this date?" she asks, wearing a beautiful understated smile.

"This date?"

"You bought a date with me, and according to the auction terms, I am to grace you with a date."

"One million dollars should buy me more than one date. How about we make it two and one starting tonight?"'

She sits up straight. I don't think she knew how close she had been leaning toward me. But I like her close. "Tonight?" she sounds surprised.

"At our place."

Her eyes widen as if she believes I'm insinuating we have sex. Making love to her would be nice, and it's long overdue, but nope. I don't want Xena to retreat to her side of the apartment while I go to mine.

"We could share a bottle of wine, watch some Netflix, eat plenty of snacks, and just hang out."

Xena's hand floats up to touch her chest. "Oh." Shit, I love her sexy surprised face. And then she smiles and says, "That'll be fun. Okay!"

---

## 3 Hours Laters

We've consumed one and a half bottles of Chateau Lafite Rothschild's Cabernet Sauvignon—the expensive shit. The big-screen TV in the main living room is off. It was on a while ago, but we kept talking over the episodes of the show we were watching, which is why we turned it off. The glare of the city flows in from the windows facing the Hudson. Xena sits against one arm of the sofa, pajamas on, feet on the cushion. I'm on the opposite end, facing her, legs outstretched and crossed. I've never chilled like this with a woman other than my sister. The excellent wine has made Xena's tongue much looser than usual. I've learned she doesn't like singing and probably would've never picked up a guitar or tried to belt one verse if she hadn't missed her father while growing up. She said Jojo hates it when she makes music because she sees it as a sleight against her.

"I'm the one who's been here full-stop, she reminds me," Xena said with a slur.

I would cut her off from taking another sip of the wine, but she's regulating herself. She hasn't touched her half-full glass in a while.

Xena sighs and her eyes flutter close as she rests her head on the sofa. Her neck looks soft and kissable. I want to taste her skin. "Gosh, I'm talking too much."

"No, you're not," I quickly reply because I don't want her to be quiet.

"What about you?"

I sigh impatiently as my cock grows another inch or two. It's been hardening and softening all day. At some point, Xena and I will have to figure out what to do about the attraction between us because it's becoming difficult to ignore it. "What do you want to know about me?"

"What's really up with Penelope and you? Have you ever loved her?"

*Shit. Not that question.* I lift my glass of wine off the table and take a big drink. I can lie and make something up. But I'm okay with telling her the truth. "I don't know."

"You don't know what?"

"We sort of naturally fell into our roles."

"What roles?"

Damn, she's quick with the comebacks. She's not as drunk as I thought.

"The game I told you about." I set my glass down. We're venturing into the conversation of sex, and I don't want to start something we're not willing to finish.

Xena nods thoughtfully. "Right. She denies you, which makes you want her more, but how do you end up doing it? I mean, you play and play and play, and then you fuck. How does the fucking begin?"

I rub the back of my ear, picturing myself bending Penelope over my desk, pulling her skirt up, and thrusting my cock inside her. That memory used to get me hard, but it does nothing for me anymore. But as I watch Xena's waiting expression, I can't stop shaking my head. I don't want to talk about sex with another woman.

"Why do you want to know this?" I ask.

Her eyebrows shoot up. "Hmm?"

I suspect she wants to hear about Penelope to maintain emotional distance from me.

"I don't know. It just happened, Xena. It doesn't happen anymore," I reply, regardless of not wanting to answer.

"I'm sorry. I don't want you to feel ashamed of..."

"It's not that," I retort, dropping my feet on the floor. "I'm not ashamed." I turn to look at her, stopping short of saying that I don't want her to use my words to create more distance between us.

"Then, why don't you kiss?" she asks.

I pin my attention on her sensual, cherry lips as I absorb a question that seems to have come out of nowhere. She just can't let that shit go. However, I'd never considered kissing anyone so much until I met her. "I've never been into it," I whisper. My throat feels hot, and my cock is as solid as steel when I rise. I'm tired of this song and dance of ours. "But..." I say, standing over her with an arm extended. I'm confident Xena can see in my eyes what I want, and she knows what to do because her soft hands take mine.

I help her to her feet, and Xena's parted lips point at me. My hands slip down her back, and taking control of her waist, I bring her closer, grinding my cock against her to give her an idea of what's on my mind.

Eyes wide with anticipation, Xena swallows a shivering breath. I bet she's dripping wet. First, I run my tongue across her lower lip. It's supple, and she tastes like four thousand-dollar wine. Her trembling breaths flutter against my mouth, and I like it because Xena is putty in my hands. I must take my time. I've wanted to savor her for far too long.

I'm now ready to show her what I think about kissing her. Our dazed eyes remain fixed on each other as she lets me inside her mouth. *Shit.* A whimper escapes me as the pleasure of softness and the taste of her sweetness spread through my mouth. Our tongues wrap around each other with fervor.

*Fuck!* "Xena?" I whisper and then dive back into her mouth to deepen our kiss.

"Hmm?" she moans.

"How much do you like your pajamas?" I ask, my words pressing against her lips.

"Not much," she whispers.

I rip the oversized shirt apart, and buttons fly and clink as they hit the floor. I knew she wasn't wearing a bra. Her perfect tits are exposed, and I take the closest one deep into my mouth, pushing my tongue against her hard knot. Her nipple turns more solid, and when it's as firm as a pebble, I suck and suck, taking her down on the sofa, sucking like I want to drink her dry. Because Xena must understand how long I've craved this.

If I had explained the game I'd been playing with Penelope for far too long, then Xena would know that she's why I'm unable to amuse myself with the other woman. I wouldn't masturbate when I played with Penelope. I would let my desire for a woman build and build while Penelope teased me by showing skin, brushing against my cock on accident, which was on purpose. Her hands all over me, she'd squeeze my biceps, my thighs, my ass, and even my dick. But I wouldn't beat off even if I wanted to. I would force myself to wait until I couldn't stand it anymore and then fuck Penelope as if my life depended on it. But once I was inside her, pumping, I was ready for it to be over. That's why I never came.

I can't tell Xena that on the night we met, I was deep into the game of teasing and combusting with Penelope. When Lilly introduced me to her cousin, I thought, *fuck, look at her*. I tried to keep it cool with her, but then she said I made her panties wet, and I could hardly keep it together after that. I took my father's call, and he asked if I would meet with him at his office on Saturday night. At the end of our call, I thought I would show some self-control and returned to the eleventh floor. But I couldn't keep still. I kept walking back and forth to the elevator, trying to talk myself out of what I did next. Xena wouldn't understand how her raw sexiness and those mysterious pheromones she emitted and still oozes, cold-stopped whatever I had with Penelope and led me back to Lily's apartment.

I grab a fistful of her pajama's waistband and pull. I want them off. I'm ready to make her scream.

The tip of her breast is hitting the back of my throat. If only I could swallow her whole and keep her inside me.

She cries out in pleasure because my fingers are surrounded by her wetness, warmth, and sweet walls. In and out, I pump my fingers, but I need her pussy against my tongue just as much as I'll burst if I don't get inside her already.

*Ding-dong!*

The elevator is ringing, but nothing will stop me as I separate Xena's thighs and press my lips against her satiny skin. I lick and take tender bites up to her pussy.

*Ding-dong!*

Xena whimpers and whispers indiscernible words. *Yes.* That's what I want her to do, enjoy this so much that she doesn't know what she's saying.

*Ding-dong, ding-dong, ding-dong…*

Xena's body stiffens when I stop stalling, and my tongue slips across her knot. I watch her eyes expand, and her sexy mouth opens as she sucks air. The elevator bell keeps ringing, and Xena looks toward it until her eyes close tightly when I finally make her feel the first blossoms of orgasm. I work that same spot to make her come faster. I can tell she's faintly distracted because her fingers which felt good rubbing my scalp, have stopped.

"Umm…" she moans. "Ah, Lynx!"

My cock drips from excitement. We both know it's Penelope.

An "Um" escapes me as Xena shrieks my name. I press her quaking thighs against my face to feel her shiver.

"Lynx," she says as if she's out of breath. "Who's that?"

"Ignore her," I say, sliding my pants down.

Penelope bangs on the elevator door like she's gone mad.

"Shit!" Come first thing in the morning, I'm barring her from free access to my place.

But damn it. Xena sits on the sofa, glaring toward the elevator. I can tell she's done and isn't going to see what's happening between us to the end.

*Fuck.*

I scramble, collecting my pajama bottoms and gathering the opening of my shirt to cover my yearning breasts. I lost all reason during an elevated state of sexual attraction for Lynx. My body and heart kept saying yes, do it because no guy spends that much money for a date unless he likes you a lot. And so, when Lynx asked for my hand, I gave it to him. Then, without hesitation, he engaged me in the most sensual, toe-curling kiss of my life. My head felt as if it were floating in a cloud of hearts and unicorns. I thought I would burst from an emotion that felt a lot like love. I wanted to kiss him until infinity. Then, the doorbell rang. I knew immediately that it was Penelope. And that woke me up. I don't want to get involved with a man who hasn't broken it off with a woman who is that desperate to be with him.

"Xena, just give me a sec." Lynx's long legs stride toward the foyer. His extended cock makes the crotch of his pants look like a tent. He clearly still wants this, and my body does too, but my mind doesn't.

I shake my head, taking steps toward my side of the apartment. I don't want to flee the scene without explaining my reasons for bringing what was shaping up to be an epic night to an abrupt end. But I'm too vulnerable. If he says the right things, I'll end up on my back with him inside me.

"Lynx, let's talk about it tomorrow, okay?" I plead.

"Xena, come on, stay."

He opens a control panel I never noticed and pushes a series of buttons that starts the elevator. My guess is that he sent Penelope back to the lobby.

"Hell, Mr. Grove?" I recognize the voice. It's Laurel, who usually works the graveyard shit.

"Please kindly see Penelope Chastain out, and revoke all privileged access to my apartment."

"Yes, Mr. Grove," Laurel dutifully replies. "Is there anything else we can do for you?"

"No. Goodnight."

I stopped walking away from him. I've stood up to my mother. I quit a job that felt more like a prison. I've finally moved out of my shabby apartment; frankly, he's been the stimulant for each decision. I respect Lynx too much to walk away from the tough conversation.

He's coming toward me, and when he stands before me, I close my eyes to release the breath I've been holding. My sex sizzles when I open my eyes in time to see Lynx inhale my air.

"Xena." His arms are around me.

I knew this would happen.

Our lips meld, and tongues push deeper into each other's mouths with unbridled passion. My heart is overflowing, and with my fingers clinging to his scalp, I feel we are a moment away from becoming one.

*But we can't...*

So I pull away first. I drop my head and let his lips press against my forehead.

"You have to deal with your Penelope problem, Lynx," I whisper.

Neither of us says anything or moves a muscle. And I am battling the urge to become lost in Lynx's eyes as our gazes connect.

"So what happened?" he asks.

"What do you mean?"

"I thought you liked me."

"I do. But…"

"But?"

"There's Penelope, for one. But then you told me that you don't want to be in a relationship and don't spoon."

"Xena…" He draws me closer, and his hardness pressing against the bottom of my belly says he's lost none of his desire for me. "We're a long way from the first night we met. Because I've been here for you in every way. Why do you think I've done that? Why do you think I want to be close to you?" I'm lost for words as he puts his mouth next to my ear and whispers, "But, I'll respect your wishes. Goodnight."

I'm paralyzed by my thoughts and something unidentifiable as I watch Lynx disappear into his side of our apartment.

---

Tuesday Morning

I wake up to soothing instrumental music and the sight of subdued daylight billowing in through the large windows. Greeting the morning this way will never get old. But after last night, I wonder how long can Lynx and I go on pretending that we don't have active sexual chemistry that never ceases its attempt to lure us into making love.

I sit up in bed. It's time to work with my new boss. I should be tense about seeing him again, but I'm not. Also, I didn't spend the night tossing, turning, and beating myself up for letting my lust get the best of me. Not long after my head sank into my comfortable pillow, I went straight to sleep. I blame it on the best wine I have ever tasted. If it weren't for the wine, I probably would've spent most of the night rehashing what happened between Lynx and me.

Speaking of Lynx, I wonder if he will wait to walk me to the office. To cool off from last night, he probably wants to spend less time in my presence as possible. I'm on my feet and in my closet searching for something to wear. I saw what Penelope had on yesterday. There's no besting her when it comes to dressing classy, sexy, and stylish. I was wrong to set myself in competition with her for Lynx's attention. Competing with other women for a man's attention isn't like me at all. So today, I opt to be myself, and that means a comfortable black pantsuit with stretchy black skinny pants and my one-inch heel ankle boots that are made for wearing all day long. I luxuriate in the cotton fabric of my black and red checkerboard graphic-designed T-shirt worn under my jacket. I wrap my hair in a bun and pin it close to the top of my head. No heavy makeup. Instead, I wash, moisturize, and brush on mascara, shape my eyebrows and glide on a light coat of lip gloss.

I step back and admire myself in the mirror.

"There's the Xena I recognize," I whisper.

It's a relief to settle on just being me. One last smile at myself, and now I'm ready to head out.

---

I'M SHOCKED to find Lynx standing in the living room, admiring the view from our apartment. The man has the best physique on the planet. He's lean and muscular, and his proportions are perfect. For a second, my memory betrays me by flashing back to my hands on his toned shoulders and rubbing his hilly chest. He's like fucking a manly version of Michelangelo's David, and gosh does he look yummy in a suit.

"Good morning," he says as he turns to get a look at me. His smile brightens my day.

I can't stop myself from naturally beaming at him. "Good morning."

"Are you ready?"

I see we're not discussing what happened before we went to bed, and I'm okay with that, at least for now.

"I am," I sing.

Lynx and I head out. In the elevator, he informs me that I'll be working with Max at Grove Industrial Tech today. I immediately realize that he has indeed chosen to put distance between us. Meanwhile, he'll be at the stadium because he has Rambler's business to attend to. As he speaks, I look into his eyes, resisting the urge to explain how much I like being around him despite what happened last night. I'm afraid he'll soon end my job, ask me to move out, and never see me again, all because I didn't want to go through with having sex with him after Penelope crashed our night. I know it's crazy thinking and far from the truth, but I can't keep those irrational thoughts from affecting me.

"Take good notes," he says. "I want you to tell me what a day in the life as a co-CEO of GIT will look like and the best way I can hit the ground running."

We make it to the lobby, and I'm still nodding.

"Two cars are waiting out front. The first will drive you to GIT, and the second will take me to the stadium."

He comes to a halt before we walk into the gray morning. Instinctively, we face each other.

It's time to address the pink polka-dot elephant in the room. "About last night," I start, but what do I want to say?

"Listen," Lynx says, and I'm so happy he's taken the floor. "Yesterday you asked if we were friends, and the answer is yes. I'm your friend, Xena." His slow sideways smile always sends my heart racing. "I'm your new boss…."

I'm cheesing, caught in his allure. "And my knight in shining armor."

Lynx nods once in agreement. "I like that."

I drop my head, unable to focus on the floor.

"Xena," Lynx calls.

I quickly look up, eyes wide with curiosity.

"How about we have dinner tonight at the stadium?"

"At the stadium?"

"Yeah. Your driver will bring you at the end of the day. We'll eat, and I'll give you the tour."

My insides feel like they're being tickled pink as I nod happily. "Yes. I'd like that."

After a few moments of beaming at me, Lynx kisses me on the cheek and says he'll see me later. As I greet my driver, who holds the back door open so that I may enter, I buckle up and look down at the note attached to the top of a paper cup of coffee with my name on it that reads, "I'm not going anywhere unless you tell me. Enjoy this first cup of the day." I smile from ear to ear as I touch my cheek, still feeling Lynx's lips on my face.

---

THE MORNING GUSTS like a strong wind as soon as I arrive at the GIT building in the Flatiron District. Leticia, one of six of Max's executive assistants, met me in the lobby. When I asked why he would need six assistants, she replied that he has one for each major department and uses each efficiently and effectively. She actually used the words efficiently and effectively. Leticia is all business and hyper-focused on what needs to be done. As we grab a quick breakfast, I take out my pen and notebook and take notes as she explains daily interactions with the Finance department. After eating, she takes me to their offices, where all my note-taking feels like it sets my fingers on fire.

Eight hours later, I was shown four out of eight departments and sat in six meetings. In one meeting, I was served Mediterranean food for lunch. In the other meetings, I ate so many muffins, donuts, danishes, and bagels that now I'm carb-crashing while in the back seat of the car on my way to GIT Stadium. I also have to return to GIT tomorrow to finish touring the remaining departments. I liked every bit of today. GIT is a dream company with all its perks, forward-thinking, and happy employees. I didn't see Max today, but I heard he was around. His employees had nothing but great things to say about him. Our paths will cross tomorrow. I'll see him at his debriefing with all his assistants, which he holds every Wednesday after lunch.

"Miss St. James?"

My eyes flutter open, and I focus on Carl, the driver's face.

"We've arrived," he says.

I fell asleep, but we've made it to Connecticut. I turn toward the stadium's entrance to finally see it in real life, but Lynx's perfect physique blocks my view as he opens my door, dips his head inside the car, and says, grinning like he's thrilled to see me, "Welcome to my domain."

I EAT a light chef's salad for dinner in the Executive Dining Club. It's an authentic restaurant that opens Tuesday through Thursday during the off-season and Monday through Saturday during the season.

So this is a work dinner because Lynx listens attentively as I download him on everything I learned today. Intermittently, he'll ask questions to which I didn't even think I knew the answer.

Lynx folds his arms and eyes me carefully. There is something super sexy about his firm, all-business expression. "Then tomorrow you'll get the gist of marketing and promotions, product research and design?"

"Yes," I confirm with a brisk nod.

Here we go again, beaming at each other without shame until the waitress steps to our table to ask if there's anything else she can get us.

"No, thank you," he says, glancing at her briefly before focusing back on me. Lynx inclines his body across the table. "So, Xena St. James, Have you ever hit baseballs before?"

Intrigued, my eyebrows shoot up.

## 5 Hours Later

What do I do when this man has made my day so perfect? It was so fun swinging my bat at balls being lobbed over home plate. I missed every pitch until Lynx stood behind me, his hard body against my backside, breath against my temple as he helped me swing and make my first ball-to-bat contact. In celebration, I jumped on him, and he turned me around. We almost kissed again. Hell, I could've gone further as I imagined him stripping me naked and plunging his stiff cock deep into my dripping wetness.

But we didn't have sex. Lynx set me on my feet, and we climbed into a golf cart. The sexual tension between us couldn't be chainsawed as he showed me players' locker rooms, the training facility, large spaces where game and practice videos are reviewed, and players gather for learning sessions. At one point, we walked into his large office, and we came close to fucking again.

On the ride home, Lynx revealed that he had a sit-down talk with Penelope. He told her what they had in the past was over. She made a veiled threat about him crossing lines by screwing around with his employees.

I wasn't shocked, but when I asked what he planned to do about Penelope, he said, rubbing his jaw. "I'd prefer to keep it to myself if you don't mind."

He waited for my answer, and I said I didn't mind because I understood why he would need to keep his plans to himself. However, when I said he was not behaving like a man who was selling his team, Lynx winked and said he had a plan in the works and that tidbit was to stay in the car with us.

"Then Max doesn't know about this plan?" I asked.

"No."

"And you don't want him to know about it."

"I don't."

"Why not?"

"Because Max has his own agenda, and that's all that matters to him."

I nodded, pondering his excuse for not being forthright with his cousin. Today, I could see that Max is very much the head honcho of GIT, and he likes things to operate by his command and probably doesn't play well with co-leaders.

"Okay then," I said, nodding. If there will eventually be a Grove family duel, I don't want any parts of it.

Lynx and I never run out of conversation. We talked about my music and the song I sang the night of Anything Goes. I told him how easy songwriting is for me, but I don't like all the other shit that comes with it—working with artists, record companies, etc. I prefer the pragmatic and exciting world of corporate business.

Lynx hummed thoughtfully as he nodded, then mentioned his sister, who found her passion by becoming a chef. It almost appeared that he wanted to say something else about his sister and her cooking, but instead, Lynx changed the subject, and we compared our mothers. Jojo O'Leary and Londyn Grove have a lot in common regarding work ethic but not much beyond that. For instance, Londyn stays out of Lynx's personal affairs for one.

Then, we made it home. The hormone oxytocin had my head spinning as we walked side-by-side through the lobby. I felt as if I was moving in a dizzying mist of lust, noticing all the curious eyes on us. I even saw someone snap a picture of us with their cellphone. Then, I remembered that Lynx is no ordinary man, he's a Grove, and that is a big deal. We kept glancing at each other in the elevator, smiling, and like two teenagers, asking, "What?"

We both knew "what."

And now, we're gazing into each other's eyes. It's awfully late, and we have an entire day of work to get through tomorrow. But, my body is drawn to him like the opposite charge of a magnet. We should just do it and get it out of our systems already.

"Well, goodnight," I say past my tight throat.

"Goodnight, Xena." Lynx walks away first.

---

MY FEET FEEL like cinderblocks as I walk to my room. My brain keeps repeating Lynx's name as I strip out of my clothes, wrap up in my robe, and stand at the entrance of my shower.

I should do it…

I should stop fighting this feeling and give in.

I probably should've made the water cold because my cock is like an aluminum baseball bat. But it's been a damn long day. I'm worried about Penelope doing something stupid. I thought she realized what we had didn't have legs to stand on. I know for sure she fucked Archer once or twice, maybe more. And that's cool because we were never committed to each other.

"Hey," I hear and swipe the extra water off my face, snapping my attention to the shower's entrance. Xena drops her robe, displaying her body, and I don't know what to focus on first. Her succulent tits, velvety thighs, and pretty face compete for my attention.

I stand up straight because here she comes.

"I thought I'd get clean with you," she claims.

Adrenaline spreads through my chest as I work overtime to contain myself. "You sure you want to do this?"

She's in front of me, and water from the shower sprays her back as she wraps her soft hand around my cock tight enough to make me tilt my head back and grunt. One jerk and I'm already battling the urge to come.

"What do you think?" she asks, shifting me.

That's all I needed to hear. I take her by her waist and lift her feet off the floor. I'm tasting her mouth. Her pillow-soft lips send a thrill to my cock. I could grab myself, hold her against the shower wall and fuck her hard, but that's not how I want her. Xena wraps her legs around my waist, and I grip her ass, making out with her as I carry her to bed.

Her skin is wet, but I still spread her across my bed and then stand at the foot of the bed to take in her sexiness. I heave breaths as I plan what to do next.

"Good girl, Xena, baby. Just lay there and wait for me." However, she's not a girl. She's all woman. I lick my lips, tasting her on my mouth as I glare at her perfectly puffy pussy. She's not shaven, and her soft hair lies gently against her hood. It's a mouth-watering sight, but that's not where I want to start.

"Are you on the pill?" I'm asking because I want to feel every bit of her warmth, wetness, and tightness. And I want to come inside her when it hits me because I will come. Xena does it for me.

"No," she whispers.

"Fuck."

"But I'm not ovulating."

My eyebrows raise as I gaze deep into her eyes. She wants me skin on skin too, which turns me on more. It takes all my strength not to rush it. My impatient cock is patting my shoulder, yelling in my ear, trying to force me inside her already.

But not yet.

Xena's squirming. Look at her hips, her stomach, her thighs. It's time. I kneel between her legs, kissing, licking, and sucking the succulent skin of her inner thighs into my mouth and then sliding my tongue around her flesh. She tastes so damn good. I kiss higher, and when I see how she grabs fist fulls of my bedding, I inhale to calm my dick. It wants to feel her too. *But slow down Buddy; we have more to explore.*

I arrive at her pussy and brush my face against her hair. Shit, that feels good. Xena's fingers rub my scalp as she lets out a high-pitched moan. Her sound is too subdued, so I slide my tongue across her clit, and when she stiffens, I stick to that spot, pressing, rubbing, pressing, rubbing… I clamp her hips against the mattress to stop her from writhing against my mouth.

"Oh Lynx," she cries and then coos.

I'm enjoying the sound of her whimpering, grunting, and then gasping as her pussy shudders against my mouth.

I'm not done yet, though.

I kiss her sternum and sink my tongue into her belly button. I kiss, lick, and bite to excite and not hurt her. I can never hurt the beautiful woman that she is. Xena's body is alive as she gasps as though she's trying to catch her breath.

"Oh please," she begs.

Yes. I want her to beg.

Plunging two fingers into her pussy, I slide my tongue around her hard nipple. She's ripe, ready, and soon she will feel me. But not yet, I tell my cock because if I keep this up, I will come without being inside her. That's how much she turns me on. I run my fingers along the side of her hip.

"See how wet you are?" I say before my tongue plunges into her mouth. I'm all in with kissing her.

Shit.

I take her by her hips and put her on her hands and knees. Xena is in position, and her neck is twisted as her yearning eyes watch me. She's dripping with anticipation, and her pretty profile makes me drip too. I inhale deeply, closing my eyes, forcing my come back down.

Not yet.

First, I kiss, suck, and nibble her plump, round ass. But I want her overripe for my cock. I reach around, locate her pleasure spot, and stroke her.

Xena is full of sounds as her body trembles.

It's time.

I slide my tongue up the middle of her ass, tasting her sweat and the perfume of her sex. I take my cock in my hand, find her entrance, and watch my fingers dip into her flesh as I push inside her, inch by inch, nice and slow.

I suck in air through my teeth because sensation already grips my cock, "Shit." She feels too good. "Do you feel me, baby?"

"I feel you," she whimpers.

I know she does because her pussy grips me like a vice. I'm large, and I'm broad; my cock is a lot to take. I don't want to hurt her. I have a good grip on Xena as I ride in and out of her delicious pussy.

Each thrust brings me closer to the end. But I need to last for her and me.

But damn…

She's so… "Uh," I grunt. "Shit."

I take us to the bed, stretching her in front of me with my cock still inside her. Her skin against my chest is making it hard to last. If I come, then she must come. That's why I find her clit and rub it as I pump in and out of her.

Shit.

"Ah…" she cries, her breaths trembling.

She's like putty in my hands. "Come, baby," I whisper.

"I'm coming," she replies tightly.

"Tell me when." Shit, please say something. Because I don't know how long I can stand it.

"I'm…" Xena croons the sexiest song of enjoyment savored by all men who get the privilege of fucking a pussy as divine as hers.

*Fuck.* My cock is seized by the most incredible pleasure on the planet as I let loose inside her. This feels so damn magnificent that I white out.

# THIRTY-TWO

## XENA ST. JAMES

### Wednesday Morning

The tranquil sound of music makes me open my eyes. Last night after we made love, Lynx and I kissed our way over to another bed with a dry mattress, and we slipped under the covers. Lynx so easily guided me against him. I faintly remember thinking, "So he does spoon," as we said good night and that we enjoyed making love, and then soon after, we fell asleep. Coming down from heightened desire had worn us out. I feel his hard body against my backside before soft lips kiss my shoulder.

"Good morning, sexy," Lynx whispers, his voice hoarse from just waking up.

I smile and retreat deeper into his body. He feels

so good, and he's still spooning me. I can live in this position against him for the rest of my life. He pushes his cock against my bottom. He's hard, and I rub my ass against him because I need to feel him.

"Ha!" I gasp as he soars inside me.

I can hardly believe I'm having morning sex with Lynx Grove.

---

AN HOUR LATER, Lynx and I are forced to disentangle. It would've been nice to stay home and make love all day, but Max is expecting me for my second day at GIT, and Lynx has meetings scheduled. And so we part ways to prepare for the office. I miss him already as I shower and put on a black suit similar to the one I wore yesterday. My hair is wild and curly because I didn't blow-dry it before going to bed. In college, my guy friends teased me by saying I showed up for early morning classes with "fuck-hair." I hated it when my hair looked fluffy, messy, and dewy like this. But now I find it sexy, and if I were lying around with Lynx all day, I wouldn't do anything about combing it. My gosh, he was so horny yesterday. The way he relished my body was one for the history books. And when he came, he came hard, long, and loudly. I grow feverish just thinking about it.

I break away from the mirror, deciding to keep the fuck hair. Lynx and I will be away from each other today. He said he'll be working with Penelope. My fuck hair will be a reminder that he's to come home tonight and do me again. Pressed for time, I quickly put on my booties and long coat.

"Xena. Let's go!" Lynx calls from the foyer.

I hurry down the hallway, and when Lynx sees me, fire and desire coat his eyes.

"Are you fucking kidding?" he asks.

I touch my hair, playing as if I'm unaware I mean to seduce him. "What?"

"Xena, come on," he says, grinning.

"What?"

Lynx steps up to me and extends his arms through the inside of my coat, and embracing me, he draws me against him. "You feel that?"

He's hard.

"Mm-hmm." I swallow the moisture that pours into my mouth.

"I have important meetings today, and I can't think about you out in the city looking like this and functioning."

My head lulls back, and Lynx's lips are on mine.

Then we push our tongues into each other's mouths, kissing tenderly but fervently. I think I love him. God help me because I'm sure I do. I whimper because I'm unable to get inside his skin.

"We should leave while we can," he whispers against my lips.

My head feels buoyant as I nod. "I agree."

Lynx and I make out in the elevator. Our hands are all over each other, and we kiss so deep I see stars. We are like two hormonal teenagers who can't keep their hands off each other. This is so unlike me, but I've decided to go with the flow.

When we reach our private hallway, we chuckle as we make sure the other looks presentable and not as if we almost tore each other's clothes off and fucked in the elevator.

Lynx squeezes a handful of my hair and carefully tips my head back, pointing my mouth at his.

"You're too sexy today, Xena," he whispers.

A series of knocks echo through the space, and we both turn to see Penelope grinning and waving at us through a square piece of glass in the door.

She can't be that happy to view Lynx and me gazing into each other's eyes. Her expression is fake, which tells me that she's still in the game of seducing Lynx and ultimately claiming him as her prize.

"What is she doing here?" I ask.

Lynx narrows his eyes at her. "We have meetings today." His eyebrows are raised, and his intense focus is set on me. "Don't be threatened by Penelope, Xena. I choose you." He pinches my chin affectionately. "Understand?"

My nodding is automatic because I'm under his spell. However, I'm not so dazed by gazing into his eyes that I don't make my own power play. His lips hovering over mine, I go in for the kiss.

*Knock, knock, knock, knock.*

That's Penelope, but she doesn't stop us from tonguing. Our mouths break apart when desire forces us to stop or else.

Lynx takes my hand as we make our way down the hallway. He opens the door, and I exit first. Penelope pushes a sheet of paper against his chest. She's all sweet perfume, slender heels, tight pencil skirt with a form-fitting blazer. Basically, she's sex on a stick.

"I'm here because you're late, and we have meetings in Connecticut," she says to Lynx without acknowledging my presence.

She strides like she's the boss toward the glass doors. Lynx is on her heels, and I'm nearly running to keep up. She knows exactly what to say and do to get him under control. I recall Lynx explaining the power games he and Penelope have played for the duration of their relationship, and I'm worried that he will eventually reject what loving me has to offer. Penelope might feed his weakness derived from a wound that has not yet been resolved. Ultimately, he might be unable to resist whatever being with her gives him.

———

I'M RIDING to work alone while Penelope is with Lynx. I would've walked to work for more time to discuss what I feel with Lilly, but then I would be late. Lynx and I sucked away any extra minutes I might've had to walk to work by flirting around with this morning's sex session. I can never suspect that the orgasms Lynx gifted me on the first night we had sex were flukes. He did it again this morning, twice before he exploded with his own powerful orgasm.

The weight of time bearing down on me, I locate the button that raises a privacy window between the driver and me.

"Sorry, Carl," I say to him. "I need a moment."

"No problem, Xena," he replies.

When the window is completely up, I call Lilly, who answers on the first ring.

"I'll talk fast," I say after hearing her hello. "Then we can pick up where I'm leaving off later because GIT is less than ten minutes away, and that's where I'll be working today."

"I'm listening," Lilly replies in a serious voice.

I tell her the truth about the night she left Lynx and me alone in her apartment.

"I knew it!" she says so loud that I pull my cell-phone away from my ear. "Why did you feel the need to lie to me?"

I'm still speaking as fast as I can, explaining the no kissing, no spooning, and no relationship rules he smacked me with on that night, and I banged him anyway.

"Wait—you mentioned the kissing but not the spooning or no relationship. Oh, my God, Zeen, why didn't you tell me?"

"Because I was embarrassed."

"Embarrassed about what?"

"You know my issues, so why do you think?" I impatiently snap. I drop my head as I sigh. "I didn't call for my psychoanalyzing session. Lynx and I did it, well, we're doing it again, and um, I think it's going to be a steady thing."

"So the two of you have been having sex since last week?"

I know why Lilly asked that question. She wants to see if we were screwing on Sunday, and I was hiding it from her while we were at the café. "No, since last night."

"Oh," she says, sounding relieved. "And it's taken you this long to start up again?"

Her questions sound like extreme exclamations, and it's starting to annoy me.

"Lilly," I chastise. "Please hear me out. I can see my destination, and I really want to know your opinion about something."

"What is it?" she snaps.

I sigh, knowing she has every right to be snippy with me. If I were in her shoes, I'd be sour too.

"I'm sorry for holding back for so long, but Lynx has been in this weird relationship with Penelope. It's all about power or something. Why would a guy do something like that?"

"Zeen, I don't know what you're asking. What do you mean by a relationship about power?"

I try to recall everything Lynx said about what he does with Penelope. "Penelope and Lynx try to turn each other on, I think, until neither can stand it anymore. It's like a power struggle between them, and I'm not certain if he's ready to change whatever made him agree to that kind of relationship. I mean, am I just roadkill to him?"

"You want to know if you're trapped in the middle of something unhealthy?"

"Yes," I say with a sigh of relief. I can always count on Lilly to make sense of my confusion.

Lilly grunts thoughtfully as the car stops in front of the GIT tower. "Yeah. I'll think about it and get back to you."

And we leave it there just as Carl's voice fills the cab, letting me know we've arrived.

I've noticed Penelope has added action items to my schedule that weren't on it yesterday. If I go by this thing, Xena will be asleep when I make it home, and that's clearly the goal.

So far, Penelope's been on her best behavior. She's updating me about my first meeting with an outreach group. The team has pledged to donate a certain amount of money and resources to the group's foundation each year. She's running down a list of possible donations, and I nod as I listen.

"A brand new neighborhood kids' gym," she says.

"I like that one."

"And why were you kissing Xena St. James?" she asks out of the blue.

I whip my head back and forth. Her question took me by surprise. However, my response must be measured for the time being.

"Why do you care?" She's seen me with other women.

"You know why I care, Lynx."

I groan as I sigh. Every fiber of myself rejects the conversation she wants to have.

I lower my chin to glare at her. "Penelope. Come on."

"You come on," she retorts.

Her face is screwed. She's as mad as a nest of disturbed hornets. I engage the privacy window even though there is nothing that can be said that Luke, my driver, doesn't already know.

"We have what we have," I say calmly.

"Do we?" Her eyes narrow to slits. "Then show me." Penelope grabs my belt to undo it.

I put my hand over hers to stop her, but then her hand shifts to my cock.

"You can't get hard for me anymore, Lynx. And I get it. You have a new plaything. And go ahead and play with her, but I've been here for four years," she says as if she's entitled to something from me.

I put her hand back on her lap and then rub my

face. I don't know what to say to her. She's not ready to hear the truth, and I need her on my string until my plan is securely in motion. I'm still waiting to hear back from my brother-in-law.

"You know you're my boss, and you've been fucking me. What is that? Sexual harassment?" she adds.

I stop whatever I'm thinking to glare at her. "Wow, Penelope. I knew you had it in you, but damn."

She shrugs as if daring me to do something about her threat. Here's the thing about people like Penelope and her father, they don't know who to fuck with and who to say yes to. I'm not the man to fuck with.

"What's next on the list?" I ask, cool, calm, and collected.

Her eyes grow wide like she wants to explode.

"What's next on the list is that you take me seriously, Lynx. That's what's next on the list."

I keep my face expressionless. "What do you want from me, Penelope? Because it took two people to fuck around as we had. And I remember you saying you're not interested in a committed relationship."

"But Lynx, that was so long ago," she whines. "My heart got involved."

I am baffled about how and when that happened. But I need to end this conversation sooner rather than later. I'll give her a taste of what she wants because I can't have Penelope running back to her daddy crying. I can't have Rich, figuring out I'm not interested in incurring favor with him. The way he's handled himself since hearing about me possibly selling the team has put a bitter taste in my mouth. I don't want to be in business with someone like him.

"Mine too," I said, referring to Xena. I never expected to feel the way I do about her. Or maybe I had. The night we fiddled around in Delilah's kitchen, I knew I wanted to get to know her better. When I met Penelope, it was different.

"Okay, then, let's start getting serious about each other," she says.

"Sure."

She tips her head hard to one side. "Really?" She sounds as if she doesn't believe me.

"Yes, I'm ready to get serious."

Penelope nods as she studies my face.

"Now, can you continue with the list so we can get through this fucking day already?" I say.

Finally, she smiles, nodding. "Yes, and I have a proposition for tomorrow."

I smile tightly. Shit, I don't know how long I'll be able to manage Penelope. "What is it?"

And then she tells me.

---

6 Hours Later

Penelope has kept her eyes on me all day, and I find it interesting how territorial she's being. I texted Xena twice, and in each instance, she responded that she was impressed but busy. I informed her that I'll be home late but assured her it had nothing to do with getting cozy with Penelope. Although it was Penelope who added extra items to my schedule and made sure her attendance was required. It's going on 7:00 p.m., and I have one more meeting regarding a future player and management engagement event to boost morale.

However, a few minutes ago, I received a text from Achilles Lord. My brother-in-law was not my first option to solve my problem of accepting my father's seat, but he is my most favorable solution. And I understand that Max will not be a happy camper when he learns of the steps I'm taking to have my cake and eat it too. But he knows me, so he won't be surprised.

That's why I'm on the way to my sister's town-home on the Upper Eastside. So, I'm ditching my final, late meeting of the day to dine with them, and Achilles has agreed to hear me out.

# THIRTY-FOUR
# XENA ST. JAMES

Thursday Morning

The morning alarm plays its soothing music. I faintly remember Lynx returning home late last night and joining me in bed. I was naked, and he slid his hand up and down my hip.

"This is an unfair advantage you have over me, Xena," he said, kissing, licking, and nibbling my shoulder.

I was tired but not dead, nor was I angry that he came home so late. Before relaxing in a long, hot bath and then going to bed, Lilly called.

"So, I've spent all day thinking about what you asked," she had said. "And there is no easy answer, Zeen. Maybe he didn't kiss, cuddle, or want a relationship the night you met. But fuck, he gave you a job and a new place to live, and did any kissing occur last night."

I admitted that a lot of toe-curling sucking-face occurred between Lynx and me.

"There you go! And…" She sighed forcefully as she does before digging deeper into my psyche. "We know Hollis has made it hard for you to trust a good thing, and you're more comfortable settling with a bad thing like Greg. I mean, we've discussed that repeatedly. But Lynx is a good thing, so trust someone like him for once, okay?"

"But what about the games he played with Penelope? Isn't that concerning?"

"Well," she sighed. "It's tricky, isn't it? You'll have to have a conversation with him about it. We both know generalizing never leads to the truth.

"You'll have to find out if the gameplay is a relationship he's solely had with her or if it's how he does relationships in general. If it's the first, then you may be able to get past it and be something healthier in his life. If it's the latter, then there's a larger issue at play, and maybe you should take a step back."

We sat in silence for several seconds as gloom lingered.

I squeezed my eyes shut to bear the dread that rippled through me. "What if the worst is true?"

"Then, be proud of yourself for accepting something different from a man for once. Greg is a prick, and he's your norm."

"But am I Lynx's norm?"

"Are you?" she asked.

I remembered what he said about believing I was into power games because I became annoyed by his arrogance on the first night we had sex, and I tightened my pussy-walls around his cock to show him that I had power too. However, he followed up by saying that he had me all wrong, and instead of putting space between us because of it, he brought me closer. But was all of this about him breaking down my barriers? Had he hired me and moved me into his plush apartment to ultimately win?

"He's not home," I said. "He left with her, and he's not home," I whispered as a new strain of pain spread through my heart.

"Well, you don't have to worry about that because I heard he's at his sister's house tonight. Oh, I forgot!" she exclaimed as if a better topic of discussion came to mind. "Treasure's not hosting Sunday dinner this week. So she invited us to her place tomorrow for

Friendsgiving since Thanksgiving is two weeks away. The twins will be there, and I want you to meet them finally."

Of course, I accepted her invitation. I'm due for a fun dinner with the girls. I also felt relieved that Lynx wasn't out late with Penelope, so when he slipped into bed with me and started getting frisky, I let him enter my pussy from behind. We had delicious sex, and he remained inside me as we silently drifted to sleep.

"Xena," Lynx says, sitting up fast and rubbing his eyes. "Shit, we're late."

"No way." I roll over to swipe my cellphone off the nightstand. It says 9:30 a.m. "I was supposed to be at GIT for my final walk-through with Max thirty minutes ago!"

I hop out of bed. The only reason I become aware of my full-frontal nudity is because of how Lynx's gaze roams my body.

"Don't worry. I'll call him," Lynx says, jumping into his pajamas. "I'm flying to D.C. today for a meeting with my lawyers. I'll be home late. And um…" He's walking backward, crossing the threshold into the hallway. "Please be naked in bed when I get home."

It's too late to talk to him about his relationship

with Penelope, so I smile at him and say, "Okay." Then I blow him a kiss.

Lynx pretends to catch my kiss and presses it against his chest, over his heart, as he fakes the impact of my air kiss made him stumble backward. I giggle, and he raises his eyebrows at me twice and says, "I'm coming back to kiss you before I leave."

I tilt my head curiously. "So you like kissing now, huh?"

He winks. "It's because of you. You made me a kisser."

As we laugh, I feel like questioning him quickly about the power games he played with Penelope. But I'm running too late. Plus, I don't want him to spend all day worrying about whether I have a foot out of the door in our new relationship. We'll, talk tonight—definitely tonight. I race the clock to make it to Max Grove as fast as possible.

---

WHEN I ARRIVE AT GIT, Max's chief executive assistant, Margaret, meets me in the lobby. Margaret is a very conservatively dressed, put-together woman who can easily pass for VP of any department. She also thinks about everything because she hands me a chocolate chip muffin and a small Americano with a splash of oat milk, the on-the-go breakfast I ate yesterday.

"Is he upset that I'm late?" I ask her as we walk briskly to the executive elevator.

"No. Max reserves his anger for more pressing matters," she says with a straight face.

I think she's joking, but she doesn't build on her last comment with a humorous punchline. As we enter the elevator, I give Margaret a second glance. This is day three, and I have yet to notice a crack in her professional demeanor. And every single one of Max's assistants is similar to her: Leticia, Ashley, Mike, Chase, and Karen are all the same.

"Today, you'll be touring Operations with Max. Your interaction will be separate from your information collecting for Lynx Grove. Feel free to ask questions. He's expecting a frank and vigorous exchange of ideas during your time together."

Her eyes blink as she waits for my response. Is she a robot? I ask myself this as I finish the gulp of coffee I swallow.

"I understand," I say, wondering if Max hired his assistants that way or conditioned them to present in his image.

I recall yesterday's debriefing. Every assistant

rapidly answered Max's questions about each department. They articulated information about new projects, money spent, budgets, personnel usage, man-hours for each task, and more. It was impressive, and I eagerly wanted to be part of the team. I really do hope Lynx decides to take a seat as CEO of GIT. I'm sure he'll offer me a role in the company, and I will certainly take any job they give me. Just as long as it's commensurate with my qualifications and experience.

I tell Margaret that I want to finish off my muffin before I meet up with Max. She stops talking, giving me time and space to chow down like I haven't eaten in decades.

When I finally see Max waiting outside his office, I swallow my last bite and then down the rest of my Americano. I am so full of carbs and caffeine I could burst.

"Are you ready to get started?" Max asks without a hint of a smile.

"Yes," I reply loud and clear.

And then we're off.

WE SPEND most of the day in the corporate operations department. Max lets me review the spending numbers for various departments and asked how I would stay within budget while securing maximum output. I had answers for him, and he listened attentively. Staying on budget had been critical while working in TV production, and he knew it. He had more and more questions, and like his hired team, I had all the answers. I was proud of myself.

"You're good at this," Max said six hours later. "If I were interviewing you, I'd hire you on the spot, which is why the Corporate Operations Manager position is yours come January 15th of next year if you want it."

I stopped my jaw from dropping but not because I had been rendered speechless. I had to keep myself from jubilantly yelling, "Yes, Max Grove. I would love to be a piston in your well-oiled machine." Not to mention the big job title. Corporate Operations Manager? I loved it.

However, I wasn't sure what Max was playing at. First of all, I work for Lynx. Also, I was aware that Max had no idea what Lynx planned to do as far as taking over Leo Grove's seat. I had a sneaky suspicion that Max was reading my reaction to determine where Lynx was in his decision to become co-CEO of GIT. I already know that Lynx is doing something that will not make Max happy, and I'm bummed about it because I like Max Grove.

"Thanks for the offer," I finally said. "Is there a deadline for when I have to decide?"

"No," he replied coolly. "I want you onboard, especially when Lynx joins us. My team was impressed by you too, and that's a good sign, Miss St. James. They're difficult to impress."

I waited for him to smile just a teensy-weensy bit since it's required when paying someone a compliment. But he didn't smile. However, I believed his job offer was credible.

But now we're in his office, and it's the first time Max has allowed me into this space. I'm surprised by the warm decor since he's so austere. I admire his Shinto-style chestnut wood desk. I'm so surprised someone like him would own such a whimsical piece of furniture and work on it. And his sitting area is comprised of four mustard-colored leather Barcelona chairs congregating with a fluffy white rug. There are so many other design details to admire, but what's currently holding my attention as I sit in a chair is one of two large abstract paintings.

"Are those Lake Clarks?" My attention moves from the art to Max, but I stay with Max when his body tightens, and he appears jolted by my question. That's a reaction I've never seen from him.

"Or LC?" I barely say. For some reason, I feel as if I have to clarify further. Maybe it's because he looks a bit confused.

"Everybody knows her. If you are part of a certain party scene." He looks like he's waiting to hear more or needs me to elaborate on what I just said. "Those parties she used to have…." That's not a complete sentence. *When speaking to Max Grove, I should always speak in complete sentences, right?* So I try again. "For the longest, she used to throw galleries and drummed up mystery surrounding her identity as an artist. She made everybody wonder who's LC and what they looked like. And the remarkable part was that she attended every single event, and nobody put one and one together." I beam nostalgically, remembering those fun nights. I should shut up now, but I finally remember the point I want to make. "But Lake often hung with my girlfriends and me, so we were pretty good friends. Then she married a guy she met at work, and then he died way too young. And no one I know hardly sees or hears from her anymore. So…"

And still, his expression has not changed. Oh my God, this man is a machine. But I'm not uncomfortable. Since yesterday, Max Grove has made me feel extremely important without even trying. He takes me seriously, and he listens attentively. In that way, he's very much like Lynx, making me feel as if I matter. So I know he's not being a prick. This is just the way he is.

"I guess you know her well, too," I say to get him to say something.

Max's nod is almost imperceptible. "Lake is my sister's best friend." He abruptly crosses his legs. "You should meet Paisley, my sister." Max Grove narrows his gorgeous eyes to peer past the opened door of his office and into the hallway. "She's not in today, though. I don't think."

"Oh," I say, raising my hand like a student seeking to recapture her teacher's attention. "I'll meet her tonight at Lynx's sister's Friendsgiving."

"He's taking you?" he sounded stunned.

"No, he's out of town. I'm going with Lilly, and she wants me to meet the twins."

"Mina and Lina," he whispers, rubbing his chin

thoughtfully. "Where did he go?" he asks in a louder voice.

Cold air spreads through my eyes as I tense up. I hope I haven't revealed something Lynx wants to keep secret. However, I don't want to lie to him. Maybe I'm being paranoid. "He said he's flying to DC for business."

Max grunts thoughtfully and then quickly rises to his feet. I follow his lead.

"Xena, it has been a pleasure getting to know you, and I'm sure we've given you enough information to impart to Lynx. I'm also certain we'll get to know each other better in the future. It's not every day Lynx takes to a person as he's taken to you."

"Same," I faintly say, processing the actions that have transpired between us within the last minute. I'm happy that Max assured me I'm special to Lynx. However, I'm afraid I might have exposed a secret Lynx meant to keep quiet.

***

LILLY and I are in the backseat of her hired car that's burgundy, shiny, and ostentatiously expensive. The leather smells brand new, and the soft white leather seats make me feel like I'm sitting on a squishy marshmallow.

I shimmy my back against the material. "Look how far we've come from the subway."

Lilly laughs as she situates herself, mirroring me. "I guess that happens when you fall in love with billionaires. Believe me, this is all Orion's doing. You know me, I live for the smell of funky subway stations and trains in the morning."

"True indeed," I say as I hold my hand out, and she places her palm on mine.

Lilly and I always play with each other's fingers when we haven't seen each other in a long time. I miss her so much that I want to cry from joy now that we're spending a long overdue evening together.

"So how did it go with Lynx and you?" she asks and then says, "Ooh," watching me simper. "That good, huh?"

"It's good between us, but we didn't talk about Penelope. I'll make sure we discuss the full scope of their relationship tonight. But I like him, Lill. I like him a lot."

She raises an eyebrow. "Is it because he's tall, gorgeous, and gives you multiple orgasms?"

I giggle, knowing I'm blushing.

Lilly raises a finger. "And to add icing to the cake, he's a billionaire, who owns a professional baseball team, and hires a car to drive you around."

My eyes roll around our immediate surroundings. "Well, it's not as over the top as this one, but...."

"Make no mistake, Zeen. This is the pregnant wife's car."

I grimace because I thought she said... "What did you say?"

Lilly's hand is on her belly as she beams at me like a noon sun. "You're going to be aunt, cousin, sister, godmother, and everything to our baby because Orion and I are pregnant!"

My cheering is stuck in my throat as I unbuckle my seatbelt to hug her tightly.

"A baby?" I finally say. "You're going to have a big round belly and push a whole human out of your lady parts?"

"That's the plan," she says with a laugh.

The world beyond the window turns fuzzy as tears cover my eyes, and we continue hugging each other. She feels different in my arms. Her body is warmer and softer, and she even smells different. I'm sure the changes I feel with her are all in my head.

Then, Lilly and I reminisce about the old days when we were two gals let loose in New York City. Oh, the hours and days we spent dancing, drinking, and theorizing about the opposite sex with our girl-friends. We never sought out a prince charming to rescue us, yet she ended up with a man with enough money to save a small country.

"And you're screwing a guy who can save an entire continent!" she exclaims.

"True. The Groves have way too much money. But I've been talking to Lynx about his grandfather and what drives him in business and life. I don't think their success is about the money per se. It's about the love of invention and discovery."

Lilly nods contemplatively. "That makes sense." She leans her face closer to me and whispers. "Have you heard about TRANSPOT?"

I incline closer to her. "Heard about it? I've seen it in action."

"No way?"

"Yes, way."

We stare at each other as if we've just seen an extraterrestrial being. But there will be no more discussion of TRANSPOT. First, I've signed an NDA not to say anything about it, which means I've already said too much. Secondly, we arrived at our destination. And finally…

"Wait," Lilly says, scooting to the edge of her seat as her nose almost pushes against the glass. "Isn't that Lynx?"

Now my face is next to hers. "Yes. And that's…."

"That woman, Penelope."

My heart sinks to my toes.

## THIRTY-FIVE
## LYNX GROVE

"Good evening, Lynx," Lilly says boldly as she enters the foyer with Xena.

I'm caught. And I hadn't done anything wrong other than not informing Xena about where I'll be this evening. I've never seen that subtly ravenous look on Lilly's face. She appears to want to scratch my eyes out on her cousin's behalf.

Penelope clings tighter to my arm, making us present as an actual couple. She lays it on thicker by gazing up at me, flapping her eyelashes. "Thanks for bringing me, Hon."

*Hon?* I'm dumbfounded until Shanique, one of Treasure's friends, calls my name, entering the foyer from the hallway that leads to the garden dining room.

Shanique looks the same. Her outfits are often out there. Tonight she's wearing gold Jeannie pants, a tight, thin T-shirt that leaves nothing to the imagination, and strappy shoes with spaghetti-sized leather crisscrossing her calves. She's a pop star who never fails to dress like one.

Shanique's arms are open wide. I happily hug her because it gives me an excuse to detach from Penelope.

"I'm shocked you came," Shanique says, stepping back to get an eyeful of me. "You never show up to these dinners."

I nod because it's true. I have way better ways to spend my time than sitting through an elaborate dinner and engaging in stupid games like asking personal questions that are nobody's business.

"You look good, Lynx Grove," she says as her gaze lands on Penelope.

Right. She's looking for an explanation of the girl on my arm. "She wanted to come," I point my thumb at Penelope.

"Oh." Shanique sounds highly curious. "Your girlfriend?"

"Work colleague," I immediately correct.

"For now," Penelope says, wrapping herself

around my arm again as she reaches out to shake Shanique's hand.

"I'm Penelope Chastain."

I slip out of Penelope's grasp. "And this is Xena St. James, who's my roommate. And this is Delilah O'Shay."

"Hi…" Shanique's voice trails off as she grimaces like what I told her is still working through her brain. I meant to trip her up. She shakes Xena's hand. "Your roommate?"

"For now," Xena replies without looking at me.

Shanique shakes Lilly's hand. "And your Orion Lord's wife?"

"Yes. Nice to meet you," Lilly says.

Xena's arms are folded across her chest as she rubs her flushed cheek. "By the way, is there a bathroom nearby?"

"Um, sure…" Shanique says and instructs Xena to go down the hallway to our right and to make the first right.

"I'll come with you," Lilly says, throwing me one last nasty look. Her arm is around Xena as they walk away together.

"Is everything okay, Lynx?" Shanique asks, checking out the negative energy in the air.

"Yeah. Are Lord brothers here already?" I ask Shanique.

"Not yet. But you get to meet my boyfriend. He wants to meet the guy I had a crush on for most of the decade. Oh," she says as if suddenly remembering something. "Oh, ladies!"

Xena and Lilly stop, but only Lilly turns. Xena looks fragile, her shoulders curved forward as if she's keeping herself from breaking down.

"We're in the garden dining room, and it's down this way." She points down the corridor to our left.

"Thank you," Lilly says. She's angry. I can hear it in her voice.

I watch Xena and Lilly until they enter the bathroom.

Shanique snaps her fingers to claim my attention. "This way."

I go, choosing to leave Xena in the dark for now.

## An Hour Later

Cocktails have been served, and people have gotten to know each other. I've been asked questions and my answers have been short. The only person who has my attention is Xena. I get I'm staring at her intently, wishfully wanting my thoughts to be transmitted to her. I want her to know that yesterday, Penelope insisted that she be my date for Treasure's Friendsgiving. Her friend, Jason Matthews is dating Claire, one of Treasure's closest friends. This Jason person mentioned he was having dinner at my sister's house on Thursday evening and thought it strange that I wouldn't take her.

Fulfilling Penelope's wish seemed like a low-risk move on the way to having my cake and eating it too. Last night, during dinner with Achilles, I had to make him aware of Leo's plan to hand over his seat as co-CEO of GIT to me before the launch of TRANSPOT. I promised to be fair and put business before egos or family strife.

"But Max and you are like brothers?"

"You and Orion are actual brothers, and he's promised Max a vote in his favor no matter what. How's that been working for you?"

Achilles answered by narrowing his eyes to slits.

I know all about Achilles and Max's battle of egos. I think it's terrible for the company, especially if someone like Richard Chastain could get a foot in the door. I didn't mention Rich wanting five percent of my shares because I needed Achilles to focus solely on what I was offering and not figure out how to maneuver around me. I have the best offer. I've thought through every avenue he can race down. There's nothing better for his or my family than what I'm offering. Then, I made the pitch to hand the Lord Family Trust an opportunity to own half of my sports team, but they would have to act fast. I explained how each owner who allowed me to form my team agreed to accept the terms of our new ownership.

"What about Richard Chastain?" he asked.

I knew he would ask. "He has no say-so if I change ownership. He was to stay with me for five years, after which I could buy him out for no more or less than one billion dollars."

Achilles grunted, smirking as if he admired my answer.

"Why would they only let you start an expansion team if you hooked up with Chastain?" he asked.

There he went, regardless, searching for an advantage.

I told him how Rich makes money as a pirate in the sports field. He gets written into contracts, assuming the risk for a short period and then making a mint on buyouts. I keep it there, not adding that Rich never saw TRANSPORT coming. If he had, he wouldn't have allowed me to drop him for one billion dollars after five years.

Scratching at the side of his face, Achilles asked, "And you want to sell quickly because you don't want resistance from Chastain on absolving him of his fifteen percent?"

"That's correct," I said with a straight face.

Then I watched Achilles closely. I saw he was highly interested. Why wouldn't he be? I've done all the hard work. I made the fucking cake, and I was sitting at this same table, offering him half. But then something suddenly occurred to me, and it had to do with Max.

*Fuck him. I know exactly what he did and why.*

My last words to Achilles were that I would have my lawyer send over the paperwork, and we'll have to move fast before Max discovers this deal I'm making behind his back, which would definitely end it.

"How soon?" Achilles had asked.

"We should have it wrapped up by tomorrow midnight," I replied.

I didn't reveal I had a team of ten people working on completing the deal as we spoke. They're all still working, brick by brick, pushing the deal to the finish line.

Before heading home and to bed with Xena, I asked Treasure to make space at her table for Penelope and me and why. I also told her to warn Claire about any guy affiliated with Penelope. She has no female friends, and all her male friends will die for a chance to fuck her.

"Then why are you with her, Lynx?" my sister asked.

"I'm not with her."

"That's not what she's been telling our mother."

That made me feel a sting between my eyes, and I rubbed at it to soothe it. "We had a sexual type relationship, but I'm done with that."

"Ha, says you," she exclaimed. "Claire will be fine because Penelope doesn't bang to bang. She bangs for the buy."

"What?" I snapped, agitated by the shit situation I got myself into by getting involved with Penelope. I knew I should've left her the fuck alone.

"Penelope doesn't want Claire's boyfriend. He's not a billionaire and looks nothing like you, dear brother."

And that's how we left it. But I wish Treasure would've told me that Xena and Lilly were invited to dinner. That was pertinent information, especially since she knew Xena is my roommate and employee. Maybe she believed me when I said Xena and I were not involved. Of course, Treasure believed me. Penelope has my whole family thinking I want to "buy her."

The dinner table is long but not wide. It's crafted to bring many people together so we can hear and see each other. If I let myself, I could reach out and touch Xena. She's still avoiding eye contact, and I still want her to look at me. If she stares deep enough into my eyes, she will see that Penelope is business; this whole dinner is business.

Suddenly, Orion enters the dining room and joins the table of guests, which includes Shanique and her boyfriend, Hector, the twin cousins related to the Lords Mina and Lina, Summer, who's also one of Treasure's closest friends, and her fiancé Benny. And then, there's Claire and Jason.

"So how does this happen?" Mina asks as Orion settles in his chair.

"How does what happen?" he asks, taking the bait before kissing Lilly. "Hey babe, missed you."

Lilly's smile is faint and heavy as she kisses him back and then closes her eyes to press her forehead against his chest.

Orion frowns at Lilly, wondering why she's upset. I would raise my hand and take the blame, but all this will be resolved before the night ends. Either the Lord brothers take my deal. Or, I'll have to give Rich five percent, effectively letting the fox into the Lord's henhouse.

"O used to be balls deep in love with Treas, and now?" Mina's eyebrows raise curiously. She's unable to read a room to realize Orion and Lilly are not in the mindset to answer her question.

"It's called growing the hell up," Treasure answers.

Mina laughs. "Our boy has grown up."

I'm staring at Orion, watching for any sign that his family has accepted my offer. The clock is ticking. But he's all wrapped up in Lilly, who says she's okay. They kiss again, and he tells her she looks beautiful. He apologizes for being late, but still, he doesn't give me any sign that he and his brothers have accepted my offer.

"How was your day?" Lilly asks him.

I follow every word they speak to each other.

"It's going," he says as he glances at me.

I got his message, and I'm trying to breathe evenly. I'm too anxious, and I know everybody can tell because finally Xena is watching me, and the skin between her eyebrows is puckered.

## THIRTY-SIX
## XENA ST. JAMES

Lynx doesn't look good at all, but Penelope looks like she's the winner. And she has won. Lynx lied to me. He proved that he was playing with me all along. But I'm fine. I got all my crying out in the bathroom. I cried, hiding my face between my arms as I stood against the wall. I cried while on the toilet, peeing. I cried as I washed my hands. And finally, I hugged Lilly tightly while crying some more. Then we cleaned my face. She gave me eye-whitening drops. She powdered my skin, ensuring I looked as fresh as a summer daisy.

"Are you ready to show him he can go to hell?" she asked.

I nodded, beating back an urge to sully my face with tears all over again.

Lilly took me gently by the shoulders. "I'm sorry this happened tonight, Zeen. I can have my driver take you home and…."

"No," I said, shaking my head adamantly. "I'll stay."

"You sure?"

I said yes. I did not want Penelope to think she had obliterated me. I could tell Lynx was uncomfortable though. He probably wanted to fuck me a few more times before casting me aside. As far as he's concerned, I'm wearing a chastity belt. His cock will never ever mate with my pussy.

So we walked into the dining room, smiling and greeting the twins and Treasure's other friends and their partners. I wasn't surprised they had tons of questions for Lynx. He had gruff, short answers. They also had questions for me about my parents.

"I ran into your mother while jogging in the park. I jumped in her face and said, 'Oh my God, you're Jojo O'Leary,' to which she pulled a price tag from under her sleeve and attempted to sell me her tracksuit," Mina said. "To which I told her she was hot and asked if I could take her out sometime. And she said, 'half off until Monday midnight' while jogging away."

"You went home empty-handed?" Claire asked.

"I guess I'm not her type," Mina replied.

Everybody laughed, including me. But that broke the ice, and now I'm feeling better as long as I keep pretending Lynx is not at the table. However, I couldn't help but notice his reaction to Orion's entrance. I've never seen Lynx so anxious.

"By the way, where's Achilles, Paisley, and Herc?" Treasure asks Orion.

"They'll be here soon." Orion throws his hands up and asks, "Did I get here late enough to miss the first topic?"

"Nope," Treasure shoots to her feet even though she appears slightly annoyed by her husband's tardiness. "We're going to get dinner rolling, and our first course will be grilled radicchio salad with smoked bacon, butter pears with a creamy white truffle dressing."

Now that she's seated, several servers carrying plates serve each guest. Treasure drums lightly on the table when everyone starts eating and says, "Okay, our first-course conversation prompt is to tell us about your worst date ever."

"No, no, no, no, no," Mina says, whipping her head with each 'no.' "We have too much drama at the table to start with a prompt."

"Drama?" Claire asks.

"For instance, I heard Lynx Grove lives with her."

I'm staring in horror at the tip of Mina's finger.

"Then, why is he here with her," Lina, the other twin says while pointing at Penelope.

"Now I remember you," Hector, Shanique's boyfriend, says out of the blue. His eyes are narrowed at me. "You sang that song at Anything Goes last Friday."

Heat rises up my neck even though I'm glad he ended the silly conversation the twins wanted to have. "Which song?" I ask.

He starts singing, "Greg, you fucking troll, you should know, you took everything from me. Greg you fucking ass, I should've passed, but you played mind games with me…

"And then the hook. One day I'll see you on fire and wouldn't piss on you. One day you'll expire and I wouldn't bury you."

"Oh no," I groan, massaging my temples. "I had forgotten the lyrics but knew they were mean as hell." I sniff an embarrassed chuckle.

"Nah, that song was hella good. We felt your agony."

"I was there too," Shanique says and then turns

to Hector. Together they re-sing the verse of a song I free-styled while drunk.

I'm so embarrassed I cover my face with my hands.

"Xena," Lynx calls.

I remove my hands, and now Lynx and I gaze into each other's eyes. I feel as if I'm tumbling deep into him. It's like he's a vista made just for my eyes, and I can't look away.

"Oh my God," Lina's voice erupts. "He's off the market. Lynx is off the fucking market."

Treasure claps loudly, reclaiming the attention of the table. "Okay, enough embarrassing our first-time guests. They'll never come back if we keep this up. I finally have my brother at the fucking table, so lay off you two." She stares daggers at Mina and Lina.

"I have one more thing to say," Hector says with a finger raised. "Xena, if you ever want to record that song or any song, I'm a producer, and it'll be an honor to make your first record."

I shake my head adamantly. "No thanks."

"It's a good idea," Lilly says simultaneously.

"I don't like singing. I was mad at my ex-boyfriend."

"Clearly," Mina blurts.

I scowl at the twin who wants to fuck my mom. Truthfully, I don't like Mina or Lina. They have no boundaries. I'm surprised Lilly would think I could be friends with them.

"That's too bad," Hector says. "But if you get interested, Treas has my number."

"Everybody, just back off," Lynx erupts. "Give Xena a break."

Everybody's attention floats to him until two very handsome men, who are definitely related, and a woman who resembles Treasure file into the dining room.

Treasure is out of her chair. She kisses the man, who I assume is Achilles Lord, and then she hugs the woman, who I presume is Max's sister Paisley.

## THIRTY-SEVEN
## LYNX GROVE

I'm holding my breath, laser-focused on Achilles, waiting for any sign that the deal is in motion. Orion hasn't given anything away as of yet, and Hercules might, but I keep my attention on Achilles since he's the one in charge.

Achilles appears casual. The top buttons of his shirt have been loosened, and his arm is stretched across the back of my sister's chair as her head rests on his shoulder. I take the display of affection as a good sign. Surely, he can't turn down my offer of a lifetime while canoodling with my sister.

But I'm impatient, so I eagerly turn to my cousin, Paisley. I forgot about her. And how can I forget about Paisley? She's the sole reason we have

TRANSPOT. Her genius cultivated by our grandfather has paid off in a big way.

Paisley, who realizes I have both eyes on her, smiles and nods.

Bingo!

"Done for the day?" Treasure asks Achilles as Paisley carps about missing the radicchio salad.

"The day's done, babe," Achilles replies, finally looking me in the eye.

That's the second guarantee I received that the Lords and I are co-owners of The Ramblers. I'm waiting for one more sign of proof that as of tonight my life will forever be changed.

Suddenly, my cellphone vibrates in my pocket, and I slide it out. I have one text message from Tobey, the point man pushing the deal along. It reads: Signed, sealed, and delivered. Congratulations. The Lord brothers are your new partners in Ramblers ownership.

"Are you texting?" Penelope whispers in my ear as Treasure tells Paisley she'll be served her salad with the second course. I turn my body, keeping the screen of my phone from Penelope's eyes. I type: All signatures acquired?

He replies: Achilles Lord administrator of the Lord Family Trust. Signed. Funds have been transferred. Payment to Rich. League approved. It's done.

*Yes!*

I type: Good. Submit my co-CEO acceptance for processing.

Toby replies with a thumbs up.

Woo-hoo, I want to yell, grab my girl, and dance with her victoriously. Instead, I slouch deeper into my chair, releasing the tension I've been holding since running into Xena at the door. She thinks I'm an asshole who doesn't deserve her love. But I'm not an asshole, and I worked my ass off proving I deserve her love.

"You're really in the thick of it, Lynx," Mina remarks. Her eyebrows are held high like she's asking for an explanation of what I've been doing on my cell phone.

"Lynx, no cell phones at the table," Treasure scolds.

I can't sit here any longer. If Xena was my dinner date, then maybe. But I'm done with Penelope and want to do something else tonight. I want my second date with my girlfriend. Plus, at this juncture, there's nothing Rich can do to stop the flight from landing. I'm suddenly energized by a bolt of energy, and I'm on my feet. Xena is the only person I care about now, and she's all I see.

"We should go. We have a lot to talk about," I say, speaking to her as if she's the only person that matters.

"What?" Penelope exclaims, pulling on my arm.

I clap my hands together and rub my damp palms. "Treas, sorry about dinner. It's no longer in our plans for the night. Xena and I are leaving."

"You're not leaving," Penelope grouses.

Xena's eyes are glossy, and she hasn't moved a muscle. I think she's shocked or too angry to take me seriously.

"Please, Xena," I plead. "Please."

She turns to Lilly, appearing to ask for help.

I rake my fingers across my scalp. "You were right, Lina. I'm off the market." I point to Xena. "Because I'm in love with this woman."

"Lynx, what the fuck!" Penelope shrieks and then claims, "I'm pregnant. By you."

There's a chorus of surprised gasps as I glare at Penelope. I don't want to say that she can't be pregnant by me because I never came for her and no matter what, I wore a condom. Xena already knows that and so I don't have to embarrass Penelope.

I hold my hand out to Xena, who narrows her eyes.

"I said I'm pregnant," Penelope yells. "And I have a positive test to prove it."

I shake my head. "Then you should square things away with Archer. Haven't you been fucking him? I never came with you Penelope, and I never fucked you bare. So you're not pregnant by me." Shit. I hate she made me say it.

I turn away from Penelope whose mouth is caught open as if she's trying to scream but can't.

"Xena, I wouldn't hesitate if I were you," Lina chimes in. "This guy is fucking primo."

"Lynx, sit," Penelope orders like she's talking to her pet. "Or else I'll call my father."

I would tell her that her father has received a payment of one billion dollars and a delivery that includes a sale and a summary of the new purchase documents. I would tell her that he's no longer my partner and thank her for working rigorously for the Ramblers, but given her recent threats, she has to go. But I don't want to fire Penelope in front of all these people who are strangers to her and me. Evie's already revoking her access to any facilities associated with the Ramblers or LGI. I'm probably jumping the gun a second too soon by waltzing out of here before dinner's over, but I no longer have anything to lose but the woman I'm looking at.

Finally, Xena nods stiffly and rises to her feet.

"Okay," she whispers as she takes my hand. "I'll go with you."

"Fuck you, Lynx," Penelope cries.

It doesn't compute that she's hitting me until her palm connects with my jaw and the strike is hard enough to make me feel the sting.

Penelope's friend Jason pulls her away and encourages her to calm down as she shouts derogatory names at me as she goes. She's telling everyone that I crossed a line with her. She was my employee, and I fucked her. I'll be hearing from her lawyer, and her father will make me pay. Soon they're gone, and Penelope can't be heard. Jason must've gotten her to shut the hell up.

But my heart expands as I focus on Xena by my side, cloth napkin in hand, patting my face.

"You're bleeding," she says.

All I can do is nod and then kiss her lips.

Lynx and I are in the back seat of his car. We're sitting closely, but there's still so much distance between us. I momentarily lost my resolve during our kiss at the table, but my barrier rose again. Lynx has a lot to answer for. I could tell that Treasure thinks highly of her brother, but she doesn't know what I know.

I turn, and his eyes are already up on me as he studies me thoroughly.

"It's done with Penelope," he says, thinking that's why I can hardly look at him.

I release a deep breath, and again, he inhales my wind. It's sexy when he does it. But I can't become distracted by Lynx's sensuality.

"What about the power struggle games you

played with her? It's an indication of a larger issue with you." I feel anguish, and it must show on my face.

Lynx grunts bitterly as he nods. It's like he's insulted by my question.

"I mean, put yourself in my shoes," I add.

"I have," he sighs. "Honestly, I don't know why I participated in that shit with Penelope. I've never been in a relationship like that. I think she saw a weakness in me and exploited it."

I frown because I don't like his answer at all. "You're going to blame it on her, are you?"

"No," he says ardently. "I'm not blaming my choices on her. I'm saying I've never played around like that before her." Lynx lets go of my hands to rub his ears. But then he suddenly stops and stares at me. "But that's Penelope's thing. Make you hard and walk away thinking about her."

I take a moment to absorb what he revealed about Penelope. Was their relationship that much different than mine and Greg's? He would make me feel like shit then I would jump through his hoops, trying to get back in his good graces. It was a power game in its own way, and I was driven to play the underdog just like Lynx. But suddenly, it ended. I turn to face the person who inspired the change.

"That night we first had sex," I began. My throat is tight, and the waiting come-hither look in Lynx's eyes makes my heart tumble in my chest. I'm excited because an incredible illumination has struck me, and I must calm myself to get my words out coherently.

"There was so much happening beneath the surface for us. It's like you said you didn't kiss or spoon and didn't want a relationship. But you weren't a dick about it. You were actually charming. You gave me a choice to take you as you are or leave you."

Lynx grunts thoughtfully. "And you didn't put me out."

In the darkened cab of the SUV, I feel a loose string on the thigh of my pants and pick at it. "I didn't. I think because I was able to absorb your rejection without being in crisis mode. You kissed me before you left; it was the best kiss ever. It made me take a step back and think, fuck, this is my life. I guess I'm trying to say that I understand how we can be lured into power games without even real-izing it. It's said that humans exit the womb seeking to be empowered, and empowering ourselves can easily turn into a drive, an addiction.

"But it makes sense how our one night stand

woke me up, and maybe, it woke you up too."

Lynx's Adam's apple lifts and lowers as he swallows. "It did. You woke me up. And…" Lynx shifts abruptly to face forward. Elbows out like the wings of an eagle, he presses his hands against the back of his head. "I made my team and worked my ass off. I almost won the World Series twice, but that co-CEO of GIT seat, it's where I knew I belonged. And my father kept it from me." His arms drop as he sighs, then he looks intensely at me. "Then you came along when my father handed me the grand prize. Truth be told, Xena, I don't know why I did what I did with Penelope. But I know it doesn't turn me on anymore. But what you said makes sense. I don't want to reject you. And I sure as hell don't want you rejecting me." He retakes my hands. "Give this a chance. Give us a chance. I'm not going to fuck it up."

"Okay," I whisper, the word escaping my heart. "Yes, okay." That time it came from my head.

"Okay?" He sounds surprised.

"Yeah. I will choose your kind of imperfection because you've already chosen mine."

Lynx shifts suddenly, and his lips hover over mine. Our breaths press and spread. Desire is causing this pause. I sip the warm air that protects us from the cold night as I grab his collar and squeeze. Our staring deepens some more. Then, his naughty boy smirk sends a thrill through my body, and I yank his mouth to mine. Our tongues lap and dive deeper into our mouths. My mouth wants to merge with his.

"Umm," I moan because he tastes so good. But he also tastes delicious, like... "What are we going to do for dinner?" I whisper against his greedy lips.

"Hmm?" Lynx frowns as if dazed and confused.

"That radicchio salad. It was so good." That's what I taste on his tongue.

The lustful haze disappears from Lynx's eyes as he stares into my eyes. Then, as if the director yelled, "action," Lynx and I laugh our heads off.

We're rolling across the seat, and I'm laughing so hard that I clutch my belly.

"That salad was fucking perfect!" he exclaims.

"Oh, my God. I was dying for the second course. That's why it took me so long to stand up."

Lynx laughs harder until he says he'll call Treasure and asks if Penelope's still there.

I've wrapped myself around Lynx's arm as Penelope did in the foyer. This time I'm claiming him. "But she scolded you for using your phone at the table. Will she answer if you call?"

"She always answers my calls," he replies.

And he's right. Treasure says, "Lynx?" after the first ring.

Her call is on speaker, so I hear her say, "Penelope is gone, and you were right about Jason. He went with her, leaving my girl at the table without a date, asshole."

"Then we can come back because my girlfriend"—Lynx gives me a quick kiss on the lips—"She can't stop thinking about your radicchio."

"Ooh… Girlfriend? You haven't had one of those since… Arguably never. But I love your girlfriend already. So please you two, come back, and let's celebrate my husband being part owner of your team!"

My jaw drops as I gasp. That's news to me.

———

ON THE RETURN to Treasure and Achilles's townhome, Lynx explained his nerve-racking day.

"Then you're the official new co-CEO of GIT?" I asked.

"Yes," he said, grinning like the epitome of happiness.

"And you're keeping your team?"

"Yep."

He said he'd deal with Max soon. Their conversation will be difficult, but they'll eventually reach the sunnier side. Tonight, we celebrate.

"But I want to ask you something," he says, chin up and eyes narrowed.

My eyes expand. I'm worried. "What is it?"

Lynx tilts his head slightly. "You wouldn't piss on your ex or bury him if he's dead?"

That's all? I laugh with relief. "I'll spit on him," I say with a shrug. Then, I straddle Lynx's lap, cradling the back of his head. "But I'll jump into the fire with you because I wouldn't want to live without you."

His erection pushes into me, grinding my clit.

"Um," I moan at the sparks of sensations.

"This is going to be fast," he whispers lustfully.

My eyes widen with intrigue. And then, striking with the speed of a lion charging its prey, Lynx lays me on the seat to unbutton my pants, unzip them and pull them down my legs.

My heavy breaths threaten to choke me as he frees his robust cock. We keep our gazes fastened on each other as he sits on the seat and guides me onto his lap, lowering my pussy onto his erection inch by inch.

"Um." I whimper as he fills me up and shifts me up and down his length.

We don't look away from each other until this feels so good that all I can do is let my head lull back as I release a hot and deep breath against the vehicle's ceiling.

---

SEX in the car was fun, and Lynx finished with an astounding release. We cleaned ourselves, but not too much since we plan to continue fucking when we get home, but now we're at the table, and dinner is fun. Lynx and I are served the second and third courses together: Meyer Lemon and Sweet Potato swirl soup with roasted Brussels sprouts crumb and herb-encrusted lamb-chop pops. My tastebuds have lived and gone to Heaven. It's incredible sitting beside Lynx as his girlfriend. This feels right, natural. I'm safe, and it's like I've known him forever.

"Okay, next question," Treasure says. "The last time you cried, and you two"—she shifts her pointed finger between Lynx and me—"It can't be today when you made up on the way home."

Everyone laughs. If only they knew how we

"made up." The only crying involved was the orgasmic kind.

"I still can't believe he's off the market," Lina says and blows an exaggerated sigh. "I don't know who to obsess over anymore."

"Don't worry you'll find a new victim," Orion jokes.

"And it's not like you really want to find someone anyway, right?" Lilly says, one eye narrowed.

"Ugh," Lina groans as she flops her head from side to side. "Can we leave the shrink out of this, Lil?"

"For now, but we should have lunch and discuss, yeah?"

Lina rolls her eyes. "No. Maybe. We'll see."

Lilly scrunches up her nose, grinning victoriously. "I'll be in touch."

"Now, to the question. Lynx, you go first," Treasure says.

Lynx sets his fork and knife down and takes a sweeping view of those seated at the table. "It was the night Leo offered me co-CEO of GIT." He sounds choked up as everybody looks at him, waiting to hear more.

But Lynx presses his lips. There's nothing more

for him to say, and I understand that about him now. He'll express his deep feelings to me but not to others.

"Nice," Hercules chimes in. "I can't wait to work with you, man. I've been a fan of your business acumen for a long time."

Lynx nods graciously. "Thank you, and same."

"Who would've ever believed that the Groves and Lords would share a dinner table like friends and family?" Paisley says, beaming.

Achilles nods toward Paisley and Hercules. "It started with you two finding out about our grand-parents."

"Yeah, that was wild," Hercules says, then turns to his wife, watching her adoringly. "But I've always loved this beautiful lady, from the day she saved my ass from an F in high school computer programming."

Chuckles erupt.

"But I didn't know Paisley and Hercules attended the same high school," Claire says. If she's missing Jason, then it doesn't show.

"What about you?" Treasure asks, looking at me.

I slap myself on the chest. "Me?"

"When was the last time you cried, and not when you made up with Lynx."

"Oh." I nod, thinking. "Well, I cried in the bathroom when we arrived for dinner." Lynx wraps his arm around me and draws me against him to kiss my forehead. "But, before then?" My tone rings highly curious as I try to recall the last time I cried.

"You're not a crier, Zeen," Lilly chimes in.

"I guess not. No wonder all that crying I did felt so cathartic." I laugh a little while realizing that I only achieved that level of crying when I saw Lynx and Penelope together. I thought I had lost him or he wasn't everything I hoped he'd be. But he is what I hoped he'd be. I throw my finger up, ready to announce something. "I have a song."

"You do?" Hector exclaims.

"We have a guitar," Treasure says. "I heard you're great with a guitar."

I wave my hands. "No guitar is necessary."

"A cappella, then?" Shanique's tone rings highly inquisitive.

Lilly shakes her head resolutely. "No, you have to have a guitar."

Treasure has already sent Achilles to wherever to retrieve the guitar, and he's back fast, so it must not have been that far away.

Now that the instrument is in my hand, I test it for sound quality.

I raise my eyebrows at Treasure and Achilles. "Nice." It's finely tuned.

Achilles nods as if to say, "you're welcome."

In my chair, I face Lynx. "This is for you." I can feel myself blush as he moves his chair so that he faces me too. And yes, I'm embarrassed, but it will kill me if I don't get this song off my heart.

Lynx grins at me with his arms crossed. As I start strumming the melody, it feels like we're the only two people in the room. And then I sing:

---

You say, open your heart and give me everything.

And I take, you at your word because you show me that I can.

In one night by the Highline, you floated into my universe. We made love by the question mark even as you marked my heart.

And now...

You're a brand new emotion I'm putting in motion. I was heartbreak unlucky at this until you.

I'm trusting your actions, and what you
show me is... Devotion.

---

I stare deep into Lynx's watery eyes as I strum
the melody and then mouth, "I love you."

He says, "I love you too."

My chest is about to burst as I sing:

---

You say, give me your trust, your hope,
heart and all I can hold.

I take, the bravest leap but I'm the most
frightened girl that you met and you'll ever
know.

And I'm the last girl you'll ever know.

But...

---

I take a long pause as lovely warm tears trickle
from my eyes. I feel this love so profoundly. This
trust so earnestly.

"We'll take it day by day," I whisper. "Okay?"

Lynx nods gently and then leans in for a kiss
that makes me see fireworks, stars, and red hearts as
our onlookers applaud.

## EPILOGUE
### MAX GROVE

It's Thanksgiving and today my family, including the Lords, are gathering at our Lake Como, Italy, estate. Riddle me how a traditional American holiday is celebrated in Italy. I mean, I can make the links between the Romans and their religion that they used to fucking dominate. But regardless, it's the largest assembly of family and friends to date. Lynx is there with his girlfriend, Xena, and her mother, who's Orion's wife's sister. And the fucking ties that bind us to the Lords grow stronger. However, despite how I despise the way Lynx went about, as he said, "getting his cake and eating it too," I still offered Xena the position of Corporate Operations Manager, and she accepted.

It's been a torturous two weeks. *Who the fuck do I*

*have left in my corner?* My grandfather, that's who. But he's dead, and I swear the Lords killed him. There are many ways to lay a man to eternal rest—stress, heartbreak, and maybe they used poison.

Regardless, Lynx stabbed me in the back, and the front left side of my chest with that deal he made with fucking Achilles of all people. I can still feel the blade and pain. He could've given up that goddam team.

Yes, I struck a deal with Richard Chastain. I'm not surprised Lynx sniffed it out. As a five percent holder in Lynx's shares, he would've received one of Lynx's three votes. Chastain agreed to sign over that vote to me. He only cared about our record-breaking profits, which will multiply more than our wildest dreams when TRANSPOT technology rolls out.

I've admitted to Lynx that he made a good deal for himself. I also admitted that he beat me, and it didn't feel great.

So another one of my family members entangling themselves with the Lords isn't why I'm at my desk, drinking scotch from the bottle and itching to get the fuck away from everybody for a hefty amount of days.

I narrow my eyes at the postcard-sized piece of

paper on my desk. It's been sitting in the spot since I dropped it after reading it for the millionth time. It arrived yesterday.

I glare at the handwriting which lures me into rereading the words.

---

Max Grove,

I know you're in love with me. But I have been in love with a man named Mason.

And Mason was not only good, but he was also my second chance, my true, real, healthy pick.

You are what I left behind. Look at you. You're emotionally void. You have never been in love because you don't know how to be in love. You can't love.

I can.

I will.

But you're not good enough to replace Mason. Sorry.

You're my best friend's older brother, so I wanted to be nice. But you are not nice, so fuck it.

Point your affection elsewhere.

Lake

---

I close my eyes tight in an attempt to banish whatever the hell this is I'm feeling. Who is she anyway? I can get any woman I want. *But not her.*

I tap my fingers impatiently on my desk as that craving hits me again. I bound to my feet. I walk. Fast. My strides are long, and steps deliberate. I'm gone. I'm leaving. And who knows when I'll be back.

---

If you haven't already, read the standalone books featuring the Lord Brothers:

### Crossing the Line

They've shared a cosmic attraction since high school. But their families are bitter rivals. Neither was willing to cross the line—until now.

### A Fake Love Deal

He's a miserable grump and she's the life of the party. But they've agreed to marry each other for their own benefit. But what happens when their fake love deal gets real?

## Boss On Notice

Her terrible boss accidentally read her two-week notice. He had no clue she despised him so. And now he'll do whatever it takes to turn her hate into something closer to love.

.

Made in the USA
Middletown, DE
30 July 2023